The Third Week of October

Introducing
DCI Bob Templeman

S J Goodfellow

First published 2023

ISBN 9798857923702
Copyright © S J Goodfellow

For Lisa and Margaret

MONDAY

ONE

As Alice Chandler walked out of her office on to the London pavement, she felt the hot rays of the sun on her cheeks. It occurred to her that climate change might be responsible for the unseasonably warm October weather, although the forecast was for cooler and windy weather midweek. Alice removed her suit jacket and balanced it across her forearm whilst briefly closing her eyes and turning her head directly towards the descending Western sun. It felt good to be alive. 'It's been a productive day,' she thought to herself as she took in the buzz of Wanstead High Street with its usual mix of minors, majors and misfits. However, Alice reckoned that no one was really a misfit in the capital. It was such a melting pot of people with different cultures and attitudes that no one batted an eyelid at the unusual. The first rule of the city was 'be tolerant'. And she appreciated that her unusual ways needed to be tolerated as much as anyone else's. And now she was going home to spend the evening with her best friend and husband, Dave. She entered the tube station, descended the escalator and took the journey home.

Alice knew, of course, that life has a habit of kicking you where it hurts. She knew not to take happiness and stability for granted and did not feel any sense of entitlement to have a charmed life. However, these were not her thoughts on that particularly Monday in October 2017, whilst journeying the short distance home. As she entered her house, before she surveyed the grim scene inside, she was, in fact, contemplating what she might prepare for dinner.

When Alice spotted her five-foot-seven-inch husband hanging dead from the metal curtain pole in the sitting room, she did not scream as you might expect. Nor did she attempt to cut the tow rope to release his lifeless body. Dave's eyes were still open, rolled back revealing the whites. His neck was distended from the weight of his lower body and his arms hung loose like those of a rag doll. Just beneath his body lay a kitchen stool on its side which Dave had seemingly kicked away at the moment of hanging. It was obvious to Alice that Dave was long dead, and that nothing she could do would bring him back, so she quietly picked up the phone and called emergency services:

"My husband has killed himself," she stated matter-of-factly to the call handler, and after being prompted to attempt CPR, she replied simply, "You must be fucking joking – he's been dead for hours!"

She was consequently asked calmly but kindly to give his name and the address. The Police arrived first, followed five minutes later by an ambulance. Alice was in shock.

*****

After making her a cup of tea, Detective Constable Sanna Malik from Newham CID sat down next to Alice at the dining room table. DC Malik guessed that Alice had just walked in from work by observing the navy-blue suit skirt that Alice wore, with the accompanying jacket folded across the back of a dining room chair. Sanna found out quickly that Alice worked for Harvey and Blackman Solicitors. She was struck by Alice's good looks; her five-foot-five slim, but well-proportioned frame, her shoulder-length blonde hair and large piercing blue eyes. Alice told Sanna that she was in her late twenties and four years into her career, that her main specialism was property law which meant she was used to dealing with difficult and seemingly intractable problems. But she added that nothing she had experienced could have prepared her for this particular tragedy.

"He told me that he had a stomach bug and couldn't go to work," said Alice, staring aimlessly at the print of Gustav Klimt's 'The Kiss' hanging on her dining room wall. She explained how Dave had worked as Director of Business Services for Barnaby Lewis, a corporate law firm in Canary Wharf.

"It never occurred to me that he was going to do something like this," she continued robotically. Alice had not yet grasped the enormity of what was happening, uttering platitudes that seemed to come from somewhere outside of herself.

DC Malik said nothing – Alice would need to be interviewed, but that could wait. For the moment it was enough just to let her talk and gauge from her words the circumstances of what looked to be a routine suicide. Sanna was the same age as Alice though physically broader set with shorter dark brown hair and from a middle eastern ethnic background. Her immediate thought was that they did not have a lot in common – she wrongly assumed that Alice came from a privileged and protected middle-class upbringing that gave her confidence. 'Probably privately educated,' Sanna thought to herself. The Victorian terrace Alice lived in was immaculately decorated and dressed, suggesting a monied background. 'I bet the bank of Mum and Dad stumped up the deposit' she speculated. DC Malik's assumptions were wrong, for Alice's backstory was a lot more complex than Sanna could have imagined. The detective jumped to false conclusions because her family had struggled in their early years in the United Kingdom and her instinct was to contrast this striving with the seeming ease and privileges enjoyed by the English white middle classes.

"I guess I need to tell Sophie," said Alice.

"Who's that?"

"Dave's mum."

*****

Alice contemplated the emotional reaction which would be forthcoming from Dave's seventy-year-old mother. David had been ten years older than his wife and the relationship between Sophie and

7

Alice was strained. It had started to go wrong immediately after they met, when the zealously religious Mrs Chandler had asked Alice whether she believed in God.

"Not really," replied Alice. "If God existed, I think he would have created a much more compassionate and meaningful universe than is evidently the case. What's more, I think you've asked me the wrong question. The question should not be 'Do I believe in God?' but rather 'Do I believe that God exists?' The whole premise of your question is wrong for it assumes that God exists and that non-belief in something that exists is delusional. Whereas I would argue that believing in the existence of something that we cannot empirically verify, is in fact the real delusion."

This went down like a lead balloon with David's mother who, whilst respecting Alice's obvious intelligence and capabilities as a lawyer, wanted her son to marry a good Christian girl. Sophie also had trouble dealing with Alice's Asperger's syndrome which meant that she often appeared to others as rude and aloof. It was not that Alice lacked empathy or emotions, but it did mean that she had trouble reading other people's body language and reactions. Yet, typically of people with Aperger's, Alice had a very logical, practical brain; her reaction to emergencies was instinctively to be sensible and follow the most pragmatic course of action.

In order to function at a high level, Alice had developed a mask to hide her Asperger's, so as to appear at least superficially normal. And in her work environment she achieved this to a certain extent because most of her work was the practical problem solving at which Alice excelled. But at times of stress, her mask would invariably slip, and she could become difficult to the point of hostility. When not at work, she had a tendency to withdraw from other human company to her 'safe place'. This involved mainly staying at home with a good book or doing online quizzes. She also enjoyed travelling and learning about the geography and culture of other countries, but that was only with Dave.

Faced with the overwhelming tragedy of her husband's death, the last thing Alice was feeling at this moment in time was 'safe'. David had been her rock. His patience, understanding and unconditional love gave her confidence to navigate the non-Asperger's world without too much difficulty. Now, she would be out on her own. This feeling of vulnerability was only brief as Alice made a conscious effort to suppress it. She knew that in order to cope, she would have to go into 'practical' mode, and deal with this situation without showing too much emotion. For if she let herself go, the tears would become a torrent and she could end up having a complete mental breakdown.

"We can talk to close family for you," suggested Sanna gently.

"Yes, I'm sure," replied Alice, "but there's only Dave's mother and I need to make an effort with her – she can be awkward."

"We'll need to see his mother in person, and I don't recommend you drive after what you have experienced today."

"I won't be driving anyway, because I have neither a car nor a licence."

"I'm afraid you may have to wait a little while for the funeral, but we'll be here to help you in any way we can," said DC Malik.

"Of course – they'll have to be a post mortem and the coroner will do an inquest – I get all that – I am a solicitor, remember!"

"It's alright," continued Alice, "I'm happy to answer any questions you might have now."

*****

Sanna was taken aback by Alice's seeming composure. Here was a woman who was able to keep her emotions in check whilst in the next room her husband's dead body was hanging from a metal curtain pole. She guessed this might be just a front to cope in extreme circumstances, but on the other hand, perhaps her coolness indicated an involvement in Dave Chandler's death. DC Malik was keeping an open mind; 'Let's not get ahead of ourselves here,' she thought to herself. Of course, she was pleased that Alice wanted to talk, so decided to take her up on her offer and ask a few non-threatening questions:

"So you said that David stayed off work today because of a stomach bug. Had he been suffering with any health problems recently?"

"No, not at all. He was in excellent health. He ran four times a week, went to the gym regularly, ate healthily and was rarely absent from work. I guess the only thing that might have indicated there was a problem was his drinking. We used to share two or three bottles of wine at the weekend, but recently Dave had taken to drinking during the week, often downing a bottle on his own. I had commented on it, but he just said the drink helped him to relax in the evening."

"And did he work long hours?"

"Increasingly, yes. He used to get home by 5pm, but recently he has been working until half-six. And in the run-up to Christmas, there are a lot of events he has to manage, which sometimes keeps him at work even longer."

Sanna noticed that Alice was talking about her dead husband in the present tense which made her think that perhaps Alice was in a state of disbelief and had nothing at all to do with her husband's death after all.

"This must be a terrible shock for you Mrs Chandler. I'm guessing there was no indication that he might do something like this."

"No, he's pretty laid back and doesn't seem to get depressed. I'm genuinely surprised that he has done this. It's a mystery, and I want to know why this has happened even more than you do."

"That's understandable," commented Sanna, although in her experience a complete explanation of why someone had committed suicide was an impossible thing to achieve. Yet, based on Alice's responses thus far, she strongly suspected that David Chandler was keeping something from his wife. Her best guess was that he was having an affair.

"We're going to have do a forensic examination of your house I'm afraid," explained DC Malik, "and as part of that we're going to have to take some of your husband's possessions. We've already found his phone but did he have a tablet or laptop that he used regularly?"

"Only a laptop that we shared. I think it's in our bedroom."

"And you're going to have to sleep elsewhere for a short while."

"I wouldn't want to stay here anyway," stated Alice matter-of-factly.

TWO

Alice's mother-in-law, Sophie Chandler, lived in Wanstead, East London, just a couple of miles from Alice. Her house was an immaculately presented Victorian semi which maintained some original features including elaborate coving in the sitting room and master bedroom, together with cast iron fireplaces and decorative tiles. The property had been improved with a rear extension, a downstairs lavatory and central heating. Sophie had recently added plantation blinds to enhance its appearance, something that had become 'de rigueur' in her road, with over half the other houses adopting the trend.

Although Sophie took care of her house - aided by the twice-weekly visit of a cleaner - she spent less time looking after her own appearance. When Alice arrived unexpectedly, Sophie was dressed in a pair of old slacks, a plain pink top and an oversized cardigan. Her grey hair had not been brushed or washed that day, and looked a little sad and thin. She had not slept particularly well the previous night, so her eyes appeared sunken and her crow's feet more prominent. The bags under eyes extended in two droops almost as far as her cheeks.

Sophie was surprised when Alice turned up on her doorstep with DC Sanna Malik. She didn't recognize the woman with her daughter-in-law and wondered who she was – Alice did not have many friends. Sophie's surprise turned to deep concern when Alice introduced Sanna as a police officer.

"It's David, isn't it!" she exclaimed.

"Yes," replied Alice, whilst Sanna suggested they all sit down.

Sophie stumbled into the sitting room and placed herself in her Chesterfield armchair, knowing that what was to come was not going to be good. She found herself shaking and consciously trying to fight against the sickness she felt in the pit of her stomach.

"He's had an accident, hasn't he! Is he dead?"

Sanna was glad she wasn't doing this on her own. She would have preferred to have been accompanied by a family liaison officer but none was immediately available and Alice had been insistent. Although she did not get on particularly well with Sophie, Alice felt it would be better if a member of the family broke the news rather than a stranger. In any case, she wanted to stay busy and was relieved to be out of her house. Alice's Asperger's meant she could not wrap up the news in a sensitive way, so before Sanna could stop her, she blurted out:

"No, it's not an accident - he's hanged himself and yes, he is dead."

Sophie's reaction to the news was the very anthesis of Alice's. Whereas Alice was making a determined effort to keep herself together, Sophie let her emotions out immediately. From deep within her, came a primaeval scream that filled not just the sitting room, but the whole house. Accompanying the scream was a voice which uttered the words:

"NO, NO, NO! That can't be!" Sanna thought her reaction far more normal than Alice's and a good deal healthier. Sanna's parents came from Palestine and on the couple of occasions she had attended funerals there, she had witnessed the traditional howling of women mourners. It seemed to her that these emotional outbursts helped to speed up the mourning process.

Alice's reaction to her mother-in-law's grief involved a greater denial; a denial of her own inner trauma as she deliberately and overtly suppressed her emotions in order to keep calm.

"I'll make a cup of tea!" she announced.

"For fuck's sake," shouted Sophie, who rarely swore, "this is your husband who has just died – can't you show some emotion for once in your life."

"Don't presume to know my emotions or lack thereof," replied Alice, who promptly decided to leave the house, already regretting her visit to her mother-in-law's.

Once outside, she marched down the road to the corner shop and bought 30 grams of Golden Virginia Bright Yellow, a packet of liquorice Rizla, some extra slim filters and a lighter. Alice had not smoked for eight months, but at that moment in time she needed a distraction and a fix. Making the self-rolled cigarettes would provide the distraction and smoking them would give her the nicotine that she still craved. The first one tasted disgusting, but by the third, she remembered why she enjoyed smoking so much – it was comforting and helped create her 'safe place'. She embraced the phenomenon of smokers being treated like lepers and cast out of social gatherings. They invariably ended up lurking outside in doorways. It gave Alice an excuse to break from formal interactions so that she could be either on her own or create camaraderie with a fellow smoker. Although Alice found other human beings difficult, she got on quite well with people who smoked, judging them to be more tolerant and genuine than non-smokers.

Alice knew she had to go back and make peace with her mother-in-law, but she was also aware that she could not go home and spend the night in the house where Dave had taken his own life. For her, it would be in any case forever tainted and she already knew that she would be moving out of it as soon as possible. She needed somewhere else to spend some time, and fortunately there was an option that provided at least, a temporary solution – staying with her brother in the rural Essex town of Chipping Ongar, just fifteen miles away. She stamped out a half-smoked rollie and made the mobile call.

"Hi Simon, it's Alice. Dave's killed himself."

"Fuck me - that's awful! I don't know what to say!"

"It's alright, I'm okay - but I can't go back home – he hanged himself in the sitting room!"

"What the fu…. Bloody hell Ali… I'll come straight over…"

"I'm at Sophie's - she's taking it badly."

"I'm not surprised. I'll come and pick you up and you can stay at ours. I'll be over in half-an-hour."

"Thanks Simon."

For the first time since David's death, Alice felt some semblance of normality. She had support from family. She knew that Sophie would be too wrapped up in her own grief to be of any use, but at least her brother could help her pick up the pieces of her shattered life.

However, she also felt a responsibility to make sure that her mother-in-law was looked after. So, she knocked on the door of Sophie's next door neighbour and best friend, Poppy, to explain what had happened. Poppy was a warm, rotund woman who had placed a cup of tea in Alice's hand before she had even managed to sit down. 'Does she have a Star Trek Replicator in her kitchen?' wondered Alice.

"I think Sophie is going to need your support over the next few days," explained Alice, "Her son has committed suicide and she's taking it badly."

"Oh that's terrible, my dear," said Poppy with genuine concern in her voice, "But, can I just check – when you said 'her son', you did mean, David, your husband, didn't you?"

"Yes, of course we're talking about Dave – as I said, Sophie is pretty grief-stricken and is going to need your support."

"Oh, my dear - I'm so very sorry," said Poppy as she came over to Alice, sat next to her on the sofa and cupped her hands gently. "This must be terrible for you. Of course, I'll look after Sophie, my love, but what about you – who's looking after you?"

Alice appreciated Poppy's compassion but felt very awkward when she touched her, something that was very much part of her autism. She could just about cope with a firm hug or even a strong handshake, but a gentle touch from anyone else besides a lover, made her feel nauseous. Alice's instincts were to pull her hands away but she made a very strong mental effort for a few seconds to accept Poppy's well-intentioned physical contact.

"I'll manage Poppy – I'm going to spend some time with my brother in Chipping Ongar," said Alice as she stood up and withdrew from Poppy's hands as naturally as she could manage.

As Alice left her house, she was pleased that Poppy was going to look after Sophie; relieved that she would not have to spend much time with her mother-in-law in the coming hours and days.

Alice went back into Sophie's house, told her how sorry she was that 'this has happened' and then explained to Sanna Malik that her brother would be coming over shortly. It was a relief when Simon finally arrived. She felt no guilt at that moment about abandoning the widowed Sophie, even though David had been her one and only child.

THREE

When Detective Constable Sanna Malik got back to Newham CID's base at Stratford Police Station, she reflected on what had happened and something bothered her. To all intents and purposes, David Chandler's death seemed to be a routine suicide, yet his wife's reaction did not seem normal. She was too calm about it, showed less emotion than you would have expected, and had wanted to take control, which proved disastrous when it came to her mother-in-law Sophie Chandler. Even when Alice had tried to be kind, Sanna felt there was an awkwardness about it. DC Malik decided to have a word with her boss. She popped her head round his office door, which at that moment happened to be open.

"There's something not quite right about this one, Sir" she said to Detective Chief Inspector Bob Templeman. Her boss was an exceptionally tall, brown-haired man in his mid-forties. Well-built, but not obese, Templeman was a physically imposing individual who had an equally forceful personality.

"Take a seat Malik," replied DCI Templeman as he shut a filing cabinet drawer and spread his six-foot-seven-inch frame into an armed desk chair adjusted to its highest setting.

"So what d'you think?" he enquired.

"The wife was far too cool. She showed remarkably little emotion when faced with the death of her husband."

"May be in a state of shocked denial? Couldn't compute the enormity of what was happening? Keeping it all together as a survival instinct?"

Sanna found it annoying that DCI Templeman rarely used pronouns when referring to people – it was almost as if his brain worked so fast that he had to get his ideas out as succinctly as possible. Pronouns and sometimes verbs were redundant to the task.

17

"Yes Sir, she seemed a little shocked, but not as shocked as I would have expected. And I guess it's possible she was in denial about her emotions, but she was not in denial about what had happened."

"Really?"

"Yes, when she told her husband's mother about his death, she just came straight out with it – not, 'I've got some dreadful news' or 'I'm really sorry to tell you about this…' Just came straight out with it – 'he's hanged himself and is dead.'"

"Interesting," commented DCI Templeman, pausing in thought, "Maybe Asperger's? On the spectrum?"

"Perhaps, yes. Come to think of it, she did seem a bit on the spectrum. Her mother-in-law challenged her about her lack of emotion and she came out with an odd phrase about not presuming to know her emotions or lack thereof. I mean, who ends sentences with 'thereof'? She was a bit odd."

"Anyway, forensics will be through soon, and the PM will give us more info, so let's wait and see," concluded Bob.

*****

It was late when Sanna got home – eleven o'clock. Laura, her wife, was still up.

"Why are you still up Lozzie?" asked Sanna, giving her a hug.

"Oh, I don't know – just can't sleep."

Sanna suddenly remembered that Laura had been to the maternity clinic that day. Normally they would go together, but it was just a check-up, so Laura had insisted on going on her own.

"How was the check-up? I should have rung but it's been manic at work."

"Yeh, I'm sure you didn't have five minutes spare to call your other half," commented Laura sarcastically.

"Now don't start getting passive-aggressive on me - I've had a stressful day doing pointless paperwork and then dealing witha a suicide."

Laura and Sanna looked at each other intensely. Sanna's large, deep brown eyes had been one of main attractions to the grey-eyed Laura when she had first met the young police officer. She had been brooding over the lack of communication from Sanna, but she knew how stressful the job of a detective police officer was. As an accountant, she had the opportunity to work from home much of the time, but Sanna's job meant they were apart a lot more than Laura would have wished. She instantly regretted her sarcasm and decided to row back from an argument.

"It went well – everything normal for four months apparently," commented Laura grinning.

"Great!" said Sanna smiling, whilst putting her right hand around the now visible pregnancy bump of which Laura was proud. They kissed each other affectionately.

"It's a wonderful thing Amin did for us," commented Laura.

Sanna's brother, Amin, had been their sperm donor, something they had not planned, but which he had offered to do for them when he found out that they were intending to have a family. They had discussed it long and hard, for they wondered whether it was right that an uncle could also be the biological father of a child. On the other hand, it meant that their baby would contain the genes of both families, something that definitely appealed. Amin was very relaxed about the whole thing, so in the end, they went for it. On the third try, after two years of consultations, stress and heartache, an intrauterine insemination had finally worked. At last, their journey towards parenthood was looking as if it would reach its destination, something they were eagerly anticipating. They would have loved any child, but by being the result of a tortuous road, this baby would be especially cherished.

*****

At 10.55pm the same evening, DCI Bob Templeman was sitting in The King's Arms in Wanstead catching last orders with his colleague, Detective Sergeant Felicity (Flick) Featherstone. Their 'quiet ones' - as they referred to their late evening, stress-relieving pints - had become increasingly frequent. Bob did not normally fraternise with junior colleagues, but he made an exception with Flick who he had always found to be unstintingly loyal to him. Besides, Flick, like him, drank real ale - something that created a good camaraderie between them in his mind. They were confident that the two pints they each consumed before going home, would neither be harmful for their health nor tip them over the drink-driving limit.

Bob had just finished recounting his earlier conversation with Sanna regarding David Chandler's death.

"What d'you think, Flick?"

"Sounds like suicide to me," Flick replied. "He was obviously depressed which suggests that there was some problem connected with sex or money. They had no children, he could have been playing away, or may be she is, or may be both. Perhaps a secret gambling habit? There's usually something odd going on in these situations."

"Yep, reading too much into it," pondered Bob.

"You mean Sanna! – Yes, she's ambitious, that one – and an imagination to match. The most obvious explanation is more often than not correct, but our less experienced colleagues do like to come up with their fancy theories."

Bob resisted the temptation to join in Flick's criticism of Sanna. He rated her and wondered whether DS Featherstone felt a little threatened by an up-and-coming female detective.

"Well, best be making a move," said Bob as he downed the final third of his 'Old Baggins' pint of ale thinking that the imagination that went into naming these craft beers was not altogether a bad thing. He valued imagination as an essential tool for a detective, albeit imagination based on evidence.

"You can always come back to my place for a drink," Flick proffered as casually as she could.

Bob was taken aback. He and Felicity had shared these quiet drinks on several occasions in the last few weeks, but not once had either of them made any advances towards each other. He had become aware of a growing sexual attraction towards his colleague, but he had no idea that this was reciprocated on her part. And his long-term partner, Sue, would be mightily upset if he strayed. In addition, as the more senior of the two, it would be reckless to respond to Flick's invitation. On the other hand, she was an extremely attractive thirty-something woman with shoulder-length brunette hair, high cheek bones, large brown eyes, plump lips and a voluptuous figure to match. He briefly undressed her in his mind, imagining what it would be like to massage her large breasts, before replying equally casually,

"Nice idea, but got a long day tomorrow, so will have to take a rain check on that one."

Disaster averted, Bob was equally relieved when at that moment his mobile phone rang. 'I bet it's Sue - she's telepathic,' he thought to himself, but the call was work-related.

"Oh right," he said and then paused as he listened to his colleague. Eventually, he concluded the conversation with "Okay. Thanks. Let me know what the tests show up."

21

*****

Flick was pleased by the phone call and the distraction that it had created from a potentially awkward moment with her senior colleague. She had been in love with him for over a year and it had been a huge moment for her to casually suggest taking the relationship further. Unbeknownst to Bob, Flick had separated from her previous boyfriend because of her obsession with DCI Templeman. She had only told one other person about how she felt about him. The previous few weeks had been her happiest for some time, as she lapped up the precious moments that she had spent sharing quiet pints with Bob. She did not like real ale, but had forced herself to drink it because she hoped that it would create the closeness between her and Templeman, that would help take their relationship to the next level.

She didn't feel rejected by Bob's response to her offer, for she knew he had a partner. Flick was prepared to play the long game if needs be. In any case, he had said that he would take a 'rain check' on her offer, suggesting that there would be other opportunities in the future. When Bob finally got off the phone, she said,

"Is everything okay?"

"Yes, and the plot just thickened."

"In what way?"

"That was Forensics. Found a syringe by the sofa, near to where Chandler hanged himself."

"So perhaps someone injected him, and hanged him," proposed DS Featherstone.

"Or may be he injected himself with something before he killed himself," replied Bob.

"Was there a suicide note?" asked Flick.

"Not that we know of."

22

"Well there you go – knocked out with an injected sedative and then hanged. It would explain the lack of a suicide note," proposed DS Featherstone.

"And you're criticising others for coming up with 'fancy theories!" said Bob grinning.

"Fair comment," replied Flick grinning back. "Are you going to take charge of this one Bob?"

"You bet - I'll be on to the coroner first thing tomorrow." replied DCI Templeman.

"I'll see you tomorrow," said DS Featherstone, flicking her hair and giving Bob a broad smile.

"Yeh, see you tomorrow," replied Bob with an equally friendly and knowing smile. They went back to their respective cars and drove home.

*****

Bob Templeman was the son of a primary school headteacher, who had not been surprised when the young Robert had declared his intention to enter the 'Police Force' as it was then known, before the more benign sounding 'Police Service', became the popular nomenclature. With two academic older sisters, both of which studied at Oxford University, Bob was viewed as the least intelligent of his clan. In fact, this was very far from being the case. He was a late developer, possessing a fine brain, which rarely exhibited itself at school. Templeman had little interest in academic study except to the extent that it helped him in his obsession with 1930s crime novels. As a boy, he voraciously consumed the writings of Agatha Christie, G K Chesterton, Dorothy L Sayers and Margary Allingham to name but a few. His penchant for 'Golden Age' whodunnits made him appreciate old-fashioned detective techniques and made his future career an inevitability rather than a choice.

Bob's nostalgia for the past made him a little out of place in the modern world despite his determination to use all the latest technology in his detective work. His parents had also inculcated in him an old-fashioned sense of service to the community, something he took on board as his body grew to dimensions that defied all the school uniform sizes available to him. So, despite unexpectedly passing three A Levels with decent grades, he eschewed the opportunity of a modern university education and instead decided to realise his ambition of becoming a 'Peeler' in the Metropolitan Police.

When he started Police training in 1989, there was a still a minimum height requirement, something that caused much amusement to the official who carried out his medical. The six-foot-seven Bob bashed his head on the top of the door frame as he entered the room: "Well, that's the height test passed," declared the medic, chortling.

DCI Templeman was now a divorcee. He had married in his mid-twenties to an administrator who had a 9am to 5pm job. Their relationship had been built on a joint interest in water sports, running and travelling. Emily was passionate, determined, and as Bob came to realise, possessive. Ultimately, she could not cope with his shift work, the unpredictable hours and his commitment to his job. As he rose up the ranks, he became more and more married to the job and less and less married to Emily. It took seven years, but he was relieved when he had finally broken free of a woman who resented what he did and demanded more attention than he was prepared to give. Yes, he had undermined her at times, had not been totally faithful and said things which he now regretted, but in his mind her possessive and irrational behaviour had made their relationship untenable. He was sad rather than angry about the end of his marriage even though she made the split as difficult as she could.

Bob met Sue Morrison two years after his divorce. They had hit it off immediately. Patient, understanding, and far more relaxed and independent than Emily, Sue proved to be a breath of fresh air after the suffocation of his first marriage. Sue was a life coach and although she was aware that Bob's work-life balance was skewed far too heavily towards work, she knew that the personal rewards he felt from serving the community and solving crimes made him a happy person – much happier than if he had a normal job. So she accepted his frequent absences and got on with her own projects. They had been together for six years and not once in that time had they discussed the idea of marriage or starting a family. Neither of them particularly wanted children and having both had failed marriages, they were not keen on entering into that institution again. In many ways they were very similar.

Recently, Bob had become distracted, distracted by Flick Featherstone, and although he did not dare admit it to himself, the narcissist within him felt flattered by her attention and friendship. Although he still valued his relationship with Sue, he was beginning to think he had more in common with Flick. And as his sexual attraction to Sue waned, his desire for Flick increased. Sue knew instinctively that he fancied someone else, so was making a greater effort in their sex life. She assumed, wrongly, that regular love-making would deter him from fantasising about anyone else. Unfortunately for her, it had exactly the opposite effect.

When Bob got back to his house from the pub, he brushed his teeth and then slipped into bed next to Sue. Bob rubbed her back and she responded by turning over and kissing him on the mouth,

"Missed you today," she said.

"Missed you too," he lied.

Sue put her hand down Bob's pajama bottoms to discover that he was more than ready for love-making. Their intercourse was brief but passionate. Bob closed his eyes and imagined himself inside the woman he had shared a couple of quiet pints with that evening. As he came, his eye balls rolled back whilst he experienced a moment of intense physical release and emotional pleasure. Within a couple of minutes, he was fast asleep.

TUESDAY

FOUR

The following morning Alice Chandler woke up at 6am distraught. Not only was she in tears, but she was howling. It wasn't just grief; it was anger, confusion and guilt as well. How could David have done this? How could he have abandoned her like this? How had she not picked up on the extent of his depression? How had she made him so unhappy?

Simon came into the spare room where Alice had slept barely three hours, and sat next to her while she wept. Simon was taller than Alice but average in both height and body type for a male. There was a family resemblance, but Simon's hair was a dark brown compared to Alice's blonde-dyed light brown mane. Their eyes were a similar shape and size though Simon's were a greeny grey, not the bright blue that Alice possessed.

"I'm not sure I can cope Simon," wept Alice as she cried in her hands.

Simon was at a loss to know what to say. There was no belittling this situation or trying to pretend that everything was normal. It was a nightmare for her, and saying otherwise would only make things worse. All he could come up with was:

"We're always here for you Alice – we will support you whatever."

Simon's wife came into the room with a mug of freshly brewed filtered coffee. Karen Bennett was a down-to-earth, calm woman who seemingly had an inexhaustible level of patience when it came to adversity.

"Here you are, lovely," said Karen as she handed Alice the mug.

"Thanks," sniffled Alice as she took a sip. The strong, black coffee had an immediate effect on her. It was fuel for the day – a necessary pick-me-up so that she could face the horrors that awaited her.

The first thing she had to do was ring work, and then pick up some clothes from the house which was now eternally tainted by her husband's death. And she hoped that the coroner's office would be in contact with her. Perhaps, she could get some idea of when she would get a death certificate and be able to bury her husband. She knew it could take a few weeks, but it was important to keep the pressure up so that the coroner released the body as soon as possible.

Simon made no comment when he saw his sister smoking outside with her mug of coffee. As far as he was concerned, anything that helped her cope with the death of her husband was good, although, as a recent convert to teetotalism, he did not feel comfortable watching her down a bottle of wine the previous night.

He had felt protective towards her ever since their parents had been killed in a car crash twenty years previously. He had been eleven, Alice eight. The drunk driver who caused the accident served two years in prison, but Simon wondered whether this was sufficient punishment for someone who had not only robbed him of his parents, but also his childhood. Their grandparents had stepped in to look after Simon and Alice, but things were never the same again, and both grandparents were now deceased too. Simon suspected that their early deaths in their late sixties from a heart attack and breast cancer were due to the stress that had been caused by his parents' tragic demise.

Simon had become a secondary school teacher partly because he wanted children of that age to have a better time of it than he had experienced. He was more interested in the pastoral side of the job than the academic, although his career trajectory had taken him up an academic path. He had a reputation for being an excellent head of department and outstanding form tutor. Today, however, he was not going to school. Supporting his sister was much more important.

Alice made the phone call to Harvey and Blackman Solicitors, forced herself to eat a small breakfast even though she was not hungry, and continued to ply herself with coffee and rolled up cigarettes, half-smoked, and then discarded in a plant pot outside.

When the phone call from the Coroner's office did come, it went pretty much as Alice had expected. No, they could not release David's body yet. In addition, a certificate of the fact of death would not be issued until the post mortem established the cause of death, and the Police investigation was complete. The reason for his death was blindingly obvious to Alice, but as a lawyer she knew how these procedures worked.

No sooner had she finished speaking to the Coroner, than the doorbell rang. Simon answered it to discover DCI Bob Templeman and DC Sanna Malik on the threshold.

Alice was somewhat alarmed that the police had made the trip out to Chipping Ongar in order to interview her, especially as one of them was an excessively tall detective chief inspector. But she was determined not to show any weakness or panic. As a lawyer, she was far from intimidated by the Police.

*****

"We're very sorry for your loss Mrs Chandler and I know this must be terrible for you, but we've just got a few questions – it shouldn't take long," commenced Bob Templeman on stooping into the house and being led into a beamed dining room with a low ceiling.

"Isn't it a bit overkill for you two to come over to Ongar when I would have quite happily given a statement at Stratford," replied Alice, gesturing to the Police Officers to sit down opposite her. She was not at all taken in by Bob's superficial politeness.

Bob Templeman was a bit taken aback by Alice's directness and apparent composure. However, he knew she was a lawyer, so there was no point trying to be anything other than straight with her.

"Well, in cases of suicide, we need to find out all the circumstances surrounding the death of that individual – and to that end, without hopefully being too invasive, we're just asking you a few questions, so that we can establish the facts," stated Bob.

Sanna noted how when talking to his colleagues about a case, DCI Templeman was abrupt in the way he talked, but when he was interviewing a member of the public, he inserted all the necessary pronouns and verbs, and even went so far as to use subordinate clauses. It occurred to her that he might be a bit of a chameleon although she reasoned that this was in any case a necessary characteristic to rise up the ranks. Sanna was a little in awe of the cerebral Bob Chandler. Yet she got on with him professionally largely because she detected a kindness within him and felt that he could be a very effective mentor to her.

"Okay, fire away!" said Alice.

"Can you tell us how you and your husband met?" enquired Sanna. She and Templeman had already agreed that she would start with some easy personal questions and he would do the more difficult ones.

"We met at Oxford – Worcester College. He was ten years older than me, but we matriculated at the same time. Dave studied History and I read Jurisprudence."

Unlike Bob, Sanna had never heard of 'Jurisprudence', but she guessed correctly that it was another name for 'Law'. She had also never heard of the word 'matriculated' but assumed from the context that it meant Alice and David were in the same year at Worcester.

"So David was a mature student – what led him to Oxford?"

"Dave dropped out of school at sixteen, went into catering and became a sous-chef at the Barchester. However, it didn't satisfy his intellectual curiosity, so he got a day job, did A Levels at night school, and gained a place at Worcester."

"How long had you been married?"

"Four years. I've had two miscarriages."

31

Sanna was getting used to Alice's directness, but even she was surprised by this revelation.

"That must have been very difficult for both of you."

"Yes. Dave was even more upset by it than I was. Maybe it had something to do with it...." speculated Alice.

A natural pause ensued which was broken by Bob Templeman:

"You told my colleague that your husband liked to drink wine. Did he take any other drugs?"

"Not to my knowledge, and I think I would have known."

"Did he have any health problems that required him to take medication?"

"No, he was in perfect health."

"And what about yourself. Do you take any medication?"

"No, none, apart from the occasional paracetamol and codeine tablet."

"What about David's mother?"

"She's diabetic and injects herself with insulin. I think she also takes tablets for high blood pressure. But frankly, I don't see the relevance of asking me about her."

Bob knew exactly the relevance of his question, but did not want to reveal his hand yet to Alice.

"Just doing our job Mrs Chandler," Bob found himself saying, slightly riled by Alice's directness.

"Mmmm... are you?" commented Alice, "From my point of view, I think there are things you're not telling me Detective Chief Inspector Templeman. It seems to me that your presence today means you suspect that my husband's death is more than just an ordinary suicide. Do you think I had anything to do with it?"

Both Bob and Sanna were stunned by how Alice had turned the tables on them. In order to regain control, Bob said simply:

"Did you have anything to do with it?"

"Of course not, and I find that question offensive. I think we should end this conversation."

Alice got up, left the room, and went outside for a cigarette. Sanna and Bob sat in the room, alone together, in silence for a while before DC Malik said:

"That could have gone better."

"Yes, but informative nevertheless," replied DCI Templeman.

"And I've met the brother and his wife before, Sir."

"Have you?"

"Yes, they attended my church about three years ago, around the time Laura and I got married. They even came to a Bible study group at my house once."

"D'you think they recognised you?"

"Don't think so… they weren't at the church long…"

FIVE

Bob Templeman enjoyed post-mortems. He was fascinated by the science behind them and was able to suppress any empathy he might feel for the dead person or their family. He was a detective after all, and as such problem-solving was his art. An art that he enjoyed. For DCI Templeman, the journey was the enjoyable bit. Collecting evidence, interviewing witnesses and suspects, examining theories and motives. It was all about putting the pieces of the jigsaw together in order to build up the picture – a game that he relished.

Sanna Malik, on the other hand, hated post mortems. As a junior officer, she usually managed to avoid them, but Bob had been insistent. He was beginning to form the view that David Chandler's death could be an important stepping stone for Sanna's career, and if she were going to progress, she would need to get used to the less pleasant elements of the job.

Patricia Newton, the pathologist, was an experienced doctor in her mid-fifties. She had seen it all, so David Chandler's autopsy represented a routine job that she would carry out in her normal meticulous, professional manner.

Sanna swallowed hard as she and Bob Templeman watched Dr Newton weigh David's internal organs and examine every inch of his body. She spent an especially long time inspecting David's neck and right arm. At the end of it, Bob asked simply:

"What do you think?"

"Judging by the temperature of the body taken at the scene, it seems Mr Chandler died between 12.30pm and 1.30pm yesterday. Primary cause of death was asphyxiation due to a ligature round his neck," replied Patricia Newton. "No signs of any abnormalities in his internal organs and BMI in normal range."

"So he was in perfect health?"

"It looks like that, but there are a couple of other things."

"And what are they?" enquired Bob, his interest piqued.

"Have a look at the inside of his right elbow," said Dr Newton as she held David's arm, "Do you see this patch of blood here and the small puncture wound?"

"Yes," replied Sanna who had suddenly got over her post-mortem phobia as her detective training clicked in.

"It suggests that prior to death he had injected himself with something. We'll have to do further blood tests to determine what he injected himself with."

"Further blood tests?" said Bob.

"Yes, I've done an initial cholesterol check and blood sugar level test. And here's the thing:"

Bob raised his eyebrows.

"Cholesterol was normal but his blood sugar level was abnormally low," continued Dr Newton.

"So you think he injected himself with insulin?" proposed DI Templeman.

"That would seem logical," replied Patricia, "But as I said, we'll need to do further tests to establish exactly what he injected and how much.

"Is it possible he was injected after he had died?" asked Sanna.

"No, it looks as if it got into his whole blood system, which wouldn't have happened if the injection had happened after death."

"Very useful Pat – thank you," said Bob. "Oh yes, and could you run some tests to see whether he had a stomach bug, please."

"No problem – that shouldn't take long."

*****

"Why the fuck would they ask me about Dave's Mum?!" uttered Alice in frustration, as she stood in the kitchen letting off steam at her brother.

"I don't know Ali. Perhaps they're wondering if Dave had some sort of inherited condition from his mother," replied Simon

"That's impossible – Dave was adopted!"

"They don't know that!" retorted Simon

"If they were thinking along those lines, perhaps they would have asked me about his childhood, but they didn't. No, there's something else going on here and I'm getting a bad feeling about it."

"Look Ali, there's no point worrying about what the police might or might not think. Concentrate on yourself and how you're going to get through this. There's no point fretting over things beyond your control."

"Simon – I think I am right to worry. I'm convinced they suspect I had a hand in Dave's death, and are building a case against me."

"Oh, that's just paranoia. They haven't arrested you, so even if they think you killed him, they've got no evidence to back up that suspicion."

"Yeh, maybe I am being a bit OTT about this and you're right, I need to concentrate on things I can do, such as replying to some of these messages and emails that are mounting up. It seems bad news travels fast."

"Always," stated Simon simply.

Alice gathered her thoughts. She was sorely tempted just to lie down in bed and sob, but her nature was to make a plan of action in times of stress, so that she could achieve something constructive and fill up the time that would otherwise be spent on introspection.

"Right, I know what we're going to do," she announced. "I'll catch up on those emails and messages, and then we'll pop in to see Sophie. We'll find out if she, too, has been asked any odd questions by the Police. And I guess I need to do my family duty however difficult I might find her."

"Okay Ali, we'll go over to Wanstead, but be sensitive with Sophie – she's in a fragile state."

"Her and me both."

*****

At Stratford Police station, Detective Chief Inspector Templeman and Detective Constable Malik were reviewing the evidence of the case thus far.

"Pat Newton just got back to me and no sign that Chandler had a stomach bug," stated Bob Templeman.

"So, we need a motive for him staying away from work on Monday."

"Correct."

"What about the syringe?" enquired Sanna

"Forensics have confirmed a trace of insulin in the syringe found at Hitchen Road,"

"So it looks like Chandler was injected with insulin in his right arm before he was hanged," replied DC Malik.

"Or injected himself with insulin before hanging himself," suggested Bob.

"Either way, whether it was murder or suicide, it's very unusual. A lot of people who hang themselves do take pills or alcohol first, but injecting yourself isn't normal. Which is why I suspect foul play, Sir."

"See your point Malik, but forensics also confirmed that there was only David Chandler's fingerprints on the syringe."

"Left hand or right, Sir?"

"Very good question DC Malik. Left hand thumb, index finger and middle finger."

"So if it was suicide, he would have had to stand on the stool, tie the rope to the curtain pole, put the noose round his neck and then inject his right elbow using a syringe held in his left hand," summed up Sanna.

"Indeed! Which raises an important question!" said Templeman.

"What's that Sir?"

"Was he left-handed?"

"Maybe, we should pay a visit to David Chandler's mother, Sir. She'll be able to answer that question."

"Good idea Malik. I'd like to meet her anyway, to get her take on the state of Alice and David Chandler's marriage."

*****

It was late afternoon when Alice and Simon arrived at Sophie Chandler's house. On their drive over, the two siblings had discussed how they were going to approach Sophie without upsetting her too much. In the end, Alice had agreed that it would probably be better if Simon did most of the talking as his relationship with David's mother was less fraught.

"I guess I'll just have to bite my tongue and swallow my pride," Alice had said, mixing her metaphors.

Alice was sorely tempted to stay in the car and let Simon check up on her mother-in-law. Yes, she could hold her tongue if needs be, but she knew that just a look or a huff could be enough to wind up Sophie. But although their shared grief could create tension, she reasoned that avoiding Sophie's emotional needs altogether, would be a worse option.

They rang the bell and waited. There was no answer.

"She's probably on the loo," opined Alice.

They rang again but still there was no sign of Sophie at the door.

"We could always go next door and chat to Poppy – she'll have a key," suggested Simon.

"No need. I've got one - we can let ourselves in," said Alice opening her hand bag.

Alice called Sophie's name while they were entering the house, but once again there was no response. It was only when they went into the sitting room that they saw her; slumped in her leather Chesterfield armchair with her head bent to the right, her eyes in a fixed and lifeless gaze, and her mouth askew. Her arms were flopped over the sidearms of the chair, whilst her legs were bent at a right-angle in a natural sitting pose, her slipper-laden feet flat on the floor. Her skin was a pale blue colour.

"Oh, fuck!" exclaimed Alice whilst Simon went over to Sophie and placed the back of his left hand on her forehead. At the same time, he held her wrist with his right hand in a futile attempt to feel for a pulse.

"She's still warm," he said, "Not been dead very long – we could try CPR?"

"No, it wouldn't work, Simon – she's gone."

Alice walked slowly towards her mother-in-law and gently closed her eyes. She and Simon stood over Sophie, shocked, and in total silence. At that moment, they heard the sound of a loud, deep male voice saying loudly:

"Hello, Mrs Chandler. You've left the door open."

Alice's heart missed a beat as she recognised the voice:

"Oh shit, it's that bloody Templeman fellow again," she whispered.

"We can always leg it out the back door," replied Simon quietly.

"Don't be stupid – we've done nothing wrong. We'll have to allow him in."

"Are you there, Mrs Chandler?" called out Templeman again.

Alice's mind was made up. There was no other option but to invite Bob in.

"It's alright, you can come in DCI Templeman – we're in the sitting room," she called back.

Alice and Simon turned round to see Bob Templeman dip his head under the door frame and enter the room, closely followed by Sanna Malik.

"This isn't what you think," said Alice not really knowing what was going through the mind of the tall detective.

In just a few seconds, Bob took in the scene and issued an instruction:

"Don't touch anything and move outside."

They did as they were told, following Bob through the front door that Simon had left ajar. Sanna left the house too, shaking her head in disbelief.

"We need to talk," said an unsmiling Detective Chief Inspector Templeman.

SIX

"So you asked Bob Templeman to go back to your place! That's laugh-out-loud funny Flick!" exclaimed Detective Sergeant Lucy Bebbington sniggering.

"Oh come on Luce – it was worth a try – if you don't ask, you don't get," replied Flick Featherstone smiling.

"I don't know Flick – you're playing a dangerous game here and God knows how it's going to end. He is virtually married!"

"Virtually married is not the same as actually married! Why d'you think he's never gone that extra step and sealed the deal?"

"Maybe it's her that doesn't want to tie the knot!"

"Whatever! I know it's complicated, but there's something there, and I can't let it go."

"Good luck to you Flick, but please tread carefully – you know what a rumour mill the nick is – I wouldn't want you to be at the wrong end of it."

"Don't worry Luce – I'll cover my arse."

"Yes, with Bob Templeman..."

Both detective sergeants laughed heartily as they looked through the windscreen of the Ford Focus car they were staked out in. Flick felt a fairly strong breeze through her partially open window that helped cool her from the unseasonably warm sun. She spotted a mother pushing a pram. A few minutes later, an old man shuffled past wearing a flat cap with a tabloid newspaper under his arm. Halfway down the street, she could see a skip, and could occasionally hear the laughter of the men working on a loft extension. If DS Featherstone had been on her own, she would have been bored, but the task at hand was many times more bearable with her colleague by her side.

*****

Lucy Bebbington was Flick's best friend. Flick was not someone who trusted others easily, but she had total confidence in Lucy. So much so, that she could tell her things that she dare not share with anyone else, especially things that could harm her professionally. The two thirty-six-year-olds had joined the Police at the same time, meeting as young constables in their teens. They soon struck up a close friendship based on a shared sense of humour and a determination to hold their own in a male-dominated profession. It was not long before they became known as the 'Chuckle Sisters' as they constantly fed off each other's eyes for the absurd and comical. They knew that together they could tackle any hints of sexism or condescension from the less progressive colleagues amongst their ranks, but at the same time earned respect for their hard work, results, and their ability to laugh at themselves. So, it was not surprising that their careers followed an identical trajectory, passing their sergeant's examinations at the same time, and joining CID within three months of each other.

Their personal lives had, however, taken different paths. Lucy had married in her mid-twenties and since had two children, both boys. Her husband, John, worked part-time as an IT Consultant from home and looked after their offspring, which allowed Lucy to pursue her career working odd shift patterns.

Flick had married in the same year as Lucy to the man she considered her soul mate. Martin had been a fellow Detective Constable and their relationship was based on love and laughter. He was a brilliant impressionist. If a colleague annoyed them, Martin was able to mimic them in such an exaggerated, believable manner, that Flick would crease over in hysterics and would ask him to repeat the impression over and over again. Martin was also able to mimic her when she slipped into her tendency to be too controlling, which burst the bubble of her pomposity, and brought her back down to earth with a laugh.

Martin and Flick worked hard together, laughed long and loud, and made love intensely. It was, as it turned out, too good to last.

Within twelve months of tying the knot, Martin had been diagnosed with brain cancer, and two years after that she had watched him die over a three-week period. It was a traumatic experience watching Martin's body shut down with his brain only achieving a minimum level of functionality. He entered a vegetative state yet his body fought on.

The final few days of his life were horrific. Flick witnessed him coughing up blood and bile and then there was a night two days before he died, when his involuntary loud groaning cut through the dignified calm of the hospice, and even upset the nurses and doctors treating him. She saw that Martin's catheter was coloured red with blood as his organs gradually shut down. Together, it traumatised her far more than anything she had witnessed in her job. Seeing the dead bodies of brutally killed victims and witnessing body parts of railway suicides, were far less upsetting than having to watch the love of her life undergo a very primaeval demise.

Two years of counselling had helped Flick's mental state but she still had nightmares and suffered from what she considered to be a post-traumatic stress disorder. And she had not found anyone else that made her happy until she met Bob Templeman. Yes, he could be sarcastic, mischievous and cutting; and there was no denying that in his professional life he was a bit of a dinosaur (and a large one at that). However, Flick felt comfortable with him and knew that whatever superficial faults he had, underneath he was a very kind man.

*****

DS Featherstone and DS Bebbington were supposed to be watching a semi-detached house which they suspected was a drug den. Intelligence had led them to believe that a young dealer, Thomas Peats, who was also a murder suspect, was hiding several kilogrammes of cocaine in the semi-detached house two doors down from where the CID officers were parked. Lucy Bebbington was on camera duties, but as nothing seemed to be happening in the former council house, the Canon single-lens reflex camera lay unused on the centre console of the Focus.

"Still no sign of Peats," commented Lucy

"Or anyone else for that matter. I can't help thinking that this is a waste of our time," responded Flick.

At that moment a young man dressed in jeans and a bomber jacket fell out of the front door of the house next door to the one they were watching. He was followed by a young woman wearing a pink dressing gown. The black-haired begowned woman started shouting in his face, whilst the crying of a child could be detected in the background.

"You touch him again and I'll fucking kill you," screamed the young female.

DS Featherstone and DS Bebbington looked on half-concerned and half-bemused.

"Looks like we've got a domestic here," commented Lucy

"Yes – if he's got any sense he'll back off and Foxtrot Oscar," replied Flick.

"I'll fucking kill you first - you bitch," shouted the young man producing a flick knife from his jacket pocket.

"I'm going in," declared DS Featherstone jumping out of the car. Flick's personal tragedy had made her more cavalier than she had been as a young woman. Losing her soul-mate husband had stripped her of the fear of death, and made her proactive in the face of danger. The instinct to protect another human being drove her on regardless of the risk to her own safety

Lucy also saw herself as a woman of action, but she was momentarily startled that Flick had decided to tackle a dangerous man without her or a Taser. So it was, that two seconds after Flick left the car, Lucy sprang into action as well.

"Stop! Police!" screamed Flick as she approached the man. The brown-haired male turned round to see a determined looking DS Featherstone just a metre from him.

"Fuck off!" shouted the man as he moved forward and struck Flick hard on her right eye with his left fist. At the same time Lucy darted past her colleague and grabbed the assailant by the wrist of his right knife-bearing hand. Holding his right wrist firmly, she swiftly ducked under his arm and twisted it up behind his back. The sudden movement forced him to drop the knife and made him yell loudly. Whilst the man was distracted by his pain, Lucy placed a handcuff over his right wrist, and then twisted his other arm behind his back and placed the left wrist in the other handcuff.

"You've broken my arm, bitch!" shouted the young man.

"Wish I had. You're nicked, sunshine!" replied DS Bebbington.

*****

"Three weeks of work wasted!" declared Detective Superintendent Karen Michaels whilst Flick and Lucy sat in her office. DSU Michaels was an ambitious and capable senior officer. She had risen through the ranks by total dedication to the job and sheer willpower. And she was setting her sights even higher - she firmly believed that she could ascend all the way up to Commissioner. Fortunately for the two detectives that sat before her, she was also known for being demanding, but fair.

"We had no choice Ma'am," said Lucy. "He pulled a knife out and was threatening to kill the woman! We had to disarm him."

45

"Yes, I guess you're right Lucy and personally, I think you did well. But we're back to square one with the Peats case."

Both detectives stayed silent. With their cover blown, their colleagues advanced the plans to storm the drug den. There was no sign of Peats or his cocaine. They assumed he had fled out the back when he heard the commotion with his neighbours and saw the Police van arrive to take away Flick's assailant. There were a couple of officers checking local CCTV as they spoke.

"Well Flick, you've got a good shiner for your efforts – I'm sending you off for a medical check-up to make sure there's no serious damage."

"Oh, I'm fine Ma'am – no need to worry – there's no broken bones or concussion."

"We'll let the doctor decide that. Now off you go whilst I decide where we go next with the Peats case, and what I'm going to say to the Deputy Assistant Commissioner."

DS Featherstone and DS Bebbington walked out of Karen Michaels' office with a certain amount of trepidation. Flick's eye had swollen up, and now looked as if someone had placed a golf ball under her eyelid, and smudged her with dark blue and purple paint. It made her self-conscious and much more nervous than she had been when facing a knife-bearing recidivist. She knew exactly how her colleagues would react:

"Forgot to duck, did you!" commented Detective Constable Steve Cook, smirking, as she walked past. Flick smiled and shouted back,

"Not quite as bad as the time you drove your cop car into a ditch Cookie. I've still got the photo with the 'Police Accident' sign!

"That was a killer door that attacked you," remarked Detective Constable Mike Tyrrell.

"How's your groin Tyrrell," retorted Lucy, "Still hurting from that attack dog?"

46

"Dickheads!" shouted Flick as the two women laughed their way down the corridor.

Their joviality subsided as they bumped into Detective Inspector Aanya Patel.

"What happened?" asked Aanya as Lucy Bebbington excused herself from the conversation.

"Oh, just got caught by a fist as we were apprehending a knife-wielding idiot," replied DS Featherstone.

"Sounds like an eventful day!"

"Yes it was," replied Flick as she fantasised about Bob Templeman kissing her injury better.

SEVEN

Bob Templeman did not believe in coincidences and the fact that Alice Chandler had witnessed two dead relatives on two consecutive days sat uneasily with him. But being a professional, he was not going to jump to conclusions. The immediate priority was to separate the sister and brother to see whether their stories corroborated each other, yet Alice seemed in no mood to co-operate. What was he going to do with a recalcitrant recently widowed lawyer who had been found peering over the dead body of her mother-in-law?

As Bob ushered them towards two Police vehicles, Alice asked: "Are we under arrest?"

"Let's put it this way - either you're going to assist us with our enquiries, or you're going to be arrested. And either way, you're going to the station in separate cars. Which would you prefer?"

Bob had already clashed with Alice Chandler and had her measure. She was fiercely intelligent, hard to intimidate and possessed a good legal mind. He wanted to play this one by the book, but he was also in no mood to take any nonsense.

"Of course, we'll help you with your enquiries, but we'll go to the police station under our own steam – I'm not going to let you treat us like criminals. And if you arrest us when we've done nothing wrong, I will take great pleasure in suing you later."

"So, are you refusing to go in separate cars to the station?" asked Bob.

"Yes!"

Templeman was infuriated by Alice's hostility but also wary of her. Yet, in that moment he made a decision. A decision he came to because he wanted to shut up the argumentative Alice and get the job done:

"Alice Chandler, I'm arresting you on suspicion of attempting to pervert the course of justice. You do not have to say anything. But it may harm your defence if you mention something which you later rely on in court. Anything you do say may be given in evidence."

The first thing that went through Simon Bennett's mind at that moment was: 'Maybe she was right after all – they do suspect her of murdering David.' Simon, of course, knew that she was not capable of homicide, but he was also annoyed by his sister's in-your-face approach. Yet he wanted to be loyal to her, a loyalty that was sorely tested when DI Bob Templeman turned to him and said in front of Alice:

"So what about you Mr Bennett?"

Simon was torn as he was a teacher and any arrest would appear in his triennial enhanced Data Barring Service disclosure report. He knew that he could potentially lose his career and livelihood if this went against him. Yet, his loyalty towards, and love for his sister ultimately trumped all of that. He found himself saying:

"You're going to have to arrest me too."

Bob Templeman paused for a moment before saying:

"Simon Bennett, I'm arresting you on suspicion of attempting to pervert the course of justice. You do not have to say anything. But it may harm your defence if you mention something which you later rely on in court. Anything you do say may be given in evidence."

"Do not answer any questions until I've got you a solicitor," shouted Alice to Simon as the two of them were led away in separate cars.

*****

When Mr Blackman got the phone call from Alice, he rang his fellow partner, Mr Harvey, to tell him to drop what he was doing, so they could go to Stratford Police Station. The company Alice worked for - Harvey and Blackman - had established itself as a well-respected firm of solicitors in Wanstead. The two partners were cousins and constantly being confused for each other. Not because they looked like each other – Blackman was slightly below average height, overweight and had a penchant for cream cakes, whereas Harvey was marginally taller, thinner and a connoisseur of fine wines. No, the confusion came from one of them having Harvey as a first name and the other having it as a surname. Whenever anyone phoned the company or walked in asking for 'Harvey', the receptionist had become accustomed to asking:

"Would you like Mr Harvey Blackman or Mr Stuart Harvey?"

A conversation more often than not ensued, in which the name of the client had to be established and their previous dealings with the firm discussed, so that the appropriate Harvey could be contacted.

Both of them were practising criminal barristers, so they were not daunted by the prospect of representing clients at Stratford police station.

"Hop in Stuart," said Harvey Blackman, as his partner moved the seat back, so he could fit comfortably into the the Porsche 911 Carrera. Blackman enjoyed displaying his wealth as he believed that people would be impressed by his ostentation or at least make his well-healed clients feel at home. It worked to the extent that he attracted business from the millionaire golf-playing bourgeoisie that populated Wanstead. Their poorer clients generally went to the branch in East Ham where the hourly fees were lower, but not economical.

Stuart Harvey was a less pretentious individual, happy to play a low profile to his more extrovert cousin. It was him, however, who had the better business acumen. Blackman knew that the success of their company was more down to his Stuart, than himself.

"Alice has got herself arrested with her brother, Simon, for being mouthy, so it seems!" stated Blackman as he sped through an amber light turning red.

"Why doesn't that surprise me!?" commented Stuart, sniggering.

"Haha – it doesn't surprise me either. But apparently, the coppers think she and Simon killed David and his mother. Or so Alice reckons."

"So who are you going to represent? Alice or the brother?"

"I'll take Alice – it will be more fun! You can do Simon. But seriously, I know she can be rude, but do you really think she's capable of murder?"

"Of course not! Her husband committed suicide and the mother died of grief. It's not that uncommon for an elderly parent to drop dead after the death of a child. Look at what happened when Carrie Fisher died – her mother, Debbie Reynolds, passed away the day after."

"Yes, I don't think Alice did it either. Don't know about the brother – only met him once, but we'll see what the Police have. They've got to have something, or maybe they're just clutching at straws…as usual."

*****

"Where were you between 12:30 and 1:30pm on Monday 16th October?" enquired DCI Templeman whilst he was sat next to DC Malik. On the other side of the interview table sat Alice with Harvey Blackman, who was studiously taking notes.

"I worked at my desk until 12.32pm and then took a lunch break," replied Alice.

"So where did you go during your break?"

"I wandered down Wanstead High Street, popped into a couple of shops, had a drink, bought and ate a wrap at Patty's Delicatessen, and then went back to the office. I was back at my desk at 1.18pm."

"How can you be so accurate about the time?"

"Because that's my routine – I allot 50 minutes for lunch between 12.30pm and 1.20, however, I always work two minutes after my allotted time and ensure I'm back at my desk two minutes before resuming work."

It occurred to Templeman that Alice's obsession with following the same routine every day may well be another manifestation of her Asperger's syndrome or perhaps an associated obsessive-compulsive disorder.

"Can you tell me which shops you went into?"

"Yes, I went into Charles Deneuve and had a look at a handbag, some shoes and a headscarf, I went into Bric-à-Brac to get some Christmas present ideas, and I popped into The King's Arms and drank a blackcurrant and soda whilst I looked at the News on my iPhone. After that I went to Patty's"

Bob Templeman was amused that she had frequented the same pub on the same day as him, albeit much earlier.

"Now I know this is difficult for you Mrs Chandler," continued DCI Templeman, "but I now need to take you back to later on that afternoon when you discovered the body of your husband. Was there any item that you saw in the sitting room which you did not recognize?"

"Not that I'm aware of," replied Alice.

"Okay, what about the tow rope specifically. Had you seen that before?"

"Yes, I'd seen it in the shed."

"Are you sure that it was his tow rope or could it have belonged to someone else?"

"If it was someone else's, then it was a fucking carbon copy. Now what are you trying to infer here DCI Templeman – that someone brought their own tow rope over to murder my husband? Sounds pretty far-fetched to me. Do you not know how to do your job?"

Bob flinched inwardly, smarting at Alice's continued belligerence. The one thing he was sensitive about was the accusation that he might in some way not be good at his job. He was an outstanding detective and knew it. He wanted momentarily to tell Alice that she was arrogant, and not half as clever as she thought. But he was professional and practised at keeping a poker face. He also did not want to give Alice the pleasure of showing her that he was riled.

DCI Templeman remained expressionless, and did not reply. Instead, he turned to Sanna Malik and nodded at her. They had agreed that she would ask the more difficult questions this time, although it seemed to both Bob and Sanna, that Alice Chandler found any questioning difficult.

"Mrs Chandler, could you tell us whether your husband was left-handed or right-handed," commenced Sanna.

"I really don't see the point of that question," interrupted Harvey Blackman, "and would advise that Mrs Chandler not answer it until the relevance has been established."

"Of course, you are quite at liberty not to answer any question," interjected Bob Templeman, "so do you want to move on to something else?"

Before Harvey Blackman could come back at Templeman, Alice said, "It's alright – he was right-handed if you must know, but I, too, don't see the relevance."

Bob had at last scored against Alice; this pleased him. He knew that her curiosity would get the better of her. Her desire to know why the question was being asked, exceeded any caution that she might have. And so far she had shown herself to be confrontational rather than cautious. Bob turned to Sanna and said:

"Do you want to explain?"

"Our team found a syringe at your house. In it was detected a trace of insulin," commenced DC Malik.

Alice remained impassive.

"Your husband's post mortem revealed that he had been injected with insulin in his right arm just before his death."

Alice felt crushed. Inside she was screaming, but determined not to show weakness.

"So that's why you asked me whether he was right-handed or left-handed," commented Alice, "You're wondering how a right-handed person could inject himself in his right arm."

"Exactly," said Bob Templeman and Sanna Malik in unison.

"A lot of people are ambidextrous," pointed out Harvey Blackman, "I, for instance write with my right hand, but when I'm eating, I hold the knife in my left hand. I really think you are grasping at straws here. Do you have any firm evidence to link my client to the death of her husband?"

Bob Templeman did not, and had not wanted to arrest either Alice or Simon, but his hand had been forced. He had teams going through Alice and Simon's houses at that moment. The tech guys were examining the contents of David Chandler's mobile phone and laptop. He had very little apart from the fact that Alice had discovered two dead bodies in two days; Ignoring Harvey Blackman, DCI Templeman turned to Alice and said:

"Mrs Chandler, you have not been charged, but I'm sure you appreciate that we would like to get some sort of explanation as to why and how your husband died. Do you have any idea where the syringe and insulin may have come from?"

"The only syringes we had in the house were in the Red First Aid case in the bathroom cabinet. A couple of years ago we did a tour of Eritrea and were advised to take our own medical equipment with us. I can only imagine that the insulin came from Dave's Mum."

"Which brings us on to Sophie Chandler," commented Sanna Malik. "What was your relationship like with David's mother?"

"I really think it's very insensitive to ask that when the lady in question has so recently died," interrupted Blackman.

"I see your point Mr Blackman," replied Sanna. "We are of course extremely sorry for your loss Mrs Chandler, and if this is too painful for you, we can take a break."

"It's alright – I'd like to continue - I've got nothing to hide," commented Alice. "We clashed as you witnessed yourself DC Malik. We are very different people, but she was Dave's Mum so when he was around, she and I made an effort to get on."

"When was the last time you were at Sophie Chandler's house before David died?"

"We popped in the day before. Dave used to take her a Sunday newspaper and, on that occasion, we had a coffee with her as well."

"So today you went round to her house. What happened?"

"Simon and I wanted to check up on her, so we decided to pop in. When there was no answer at the door, I let us in with my key, and found her dead. Simon checked to see whether she was still alive and I closed her eyes. Then you two turned up."

"That was it?"

"Yes! And DC Malik, I'm assuming that as a detective you realise that a murderer is the last person to see someone alive! I was not that person – I just happened to be the first person to see Sophie dead!"

"A murderer is actually the last person to see someone alive *and* the first person to see them dead," retorted Sanna, "Were you *that* person?"

"No, don't be stupid!" replied Alice before Harvey Blackman could intervene.

"Why did you leave the front door open?"

"I didn't. I went in first and then Simon followed. He must have failed to close it."

"Did you not think of going next door to talk to her friend, Poppy Smith – may be to ask how she was doing?"

"No – it was Sophie we wanted to talk to."

"So you went round because you wanted to talk to Sophie, not check up on her. What did you want to talk to her about?"

"Can I just stop you there DC Malik," interjected Harvey Blackman, "You're assuming that checking up on someone does not involve talking to them. That's ridiculous."

"Fair point Mr Blackman, but it sounded to me as if you wanted to talk to Sophie Chandler about something specific Mrs Chandler. Am I right?"

Alice was an unusual lawyer in that she found it very difficult to lie. Yes, she could put forward a case that presented someone else in the best possible light – to do a role play. Yet, when it came to personal issues, her Asperger's caused her to be unfailingly direct and blunt on a personal level. Most people would have just said that they wanted to talk to Sophie about how she was and whether they could get her anything. But Alice was not like most people.

"Yes, we wanted to talk to her about why you and your colleague came round to interview us in Ongar and were asking us about her health. Of course, I now know why you were asking me those questions, so it's a pity you were not more transparent earlier."

It was clear that Alice was annoyed with both DCI Templeman and DC Malik, but they both remained impassive. A silence filled the room, broken after a few seconds by Harvey Blackman:

"It seems to me that you have no evidence of wrongdoing by Mrs Chandler, should not have arrested her, and have shown a callous disregard for her welfare when she has so recently been widowed. I would request that she be released from custody immediately."

Bob Templeman knew that he was on thin ice keeping Alice detained with so little evidence, yet she had not helped herself by her belligerent attitude. If she was determined to be so cavalier with the Police, was she not also capable of murdering her husband and mother-in-law? He had potentially up to four days to keep her in custody before charging her, but if he were to do that, he needed something in the next twenty-four hours. He had already made up his mind that he was going to detain both his suspects for the time being, even if it caused him problems later:

"We do of course realise that this is a very difficult situation for you Mrs Chandler, and we will look after you as best we can, including access to our counsellor and doctor, but I am afraid you will have to remain with us overnight," replied DCI Templeman.

*****

"So where were you yesterday between 12noon and 2pm?" asked Bob Templeman to Simon Bennett?

"I was at school DCI Templeman; teaching, form tutoring and lunching if you must know. Go and have a chat with the kids – they'd love a visit from a detective inspector. I'm sure you could regale them with lots of crime stories that they'd lap up. You might even get one or two recruits a few years down the line."

Templeman reflected on the old adage, 'once a teacher, always a teacher!' Even while facing the stress of a Police interview, Bennett was thinking how the situation could be turned into an educational experience for his pupils. He suspected that Simon was very good at his job. But Bob could think of nothing worse than being stuck in a room with twenty or thirty unformed human beings. It was bad enough having to deal with dysfunctional people one or two at a time in a police station. Templeman admired, but had no desire to emulate teachers.

"Okay, so tell me about your relationship with your sister."

This question made Simon pause for a moment.

"Well, we're close. We've had to be. Our parents were killed in a car crash twenty years ago. I was thirteen, Alice was eight. I had to look after her – she was vulnerable. Yes, we went to live with our grandparents but it wasn't the same…"

"And where do your grandparents live now?"

"Oh, they're both dead. I think it was partly to do with the stress of it all…"

Bob Templeman reflected on the tragedy that had befallen this family. He wondered whether it was partly this that made Alice so combative. She and Simon were obviously survivors who had needed to fight hard to succeed in life.

"So can you think of anyone who might have a motive to kill your brother-in-law Mr Bennett?" interjected DC Malik.

Templeman was taken aback that his colleague was getting straight to the point. It was almost as if she had broken a precious moment of raw emotion. He wondered whether she could have attempted a little more empathy. But then, he sometimes struggled with that too. He observed Simon Bennett eyes flicker with annoyance briefly, and then answer the question calmy:

"No, I can't. David did not have any enemies as far I know."

"So you knew him well and liked him?" continued Sanna.

"Yes, we were brother-in-laws. We had a joint interest in ensuring Alice's health and happiness."

"Let me ask you about the events of today," said Templeman, changing the subject. "What happened?"

58

"Well, Alice wanted to check up on her mother-in-law after you had visited us. She wondered whether you had talked to Sophie too."

"Couldn't you have just rung her?"

"Yes, but we didn't want to alarm her with a phone call when she was obviously in a fragile state. We felt it would have been much better to see her in person."

"Didn't she have a neighbour who could have popped in on her?"

"Yes, Poppy, her best friend. But she's also a bit of a gossip. The thing is DCI Templeman, going to see Sophie was not my idea, it was Alice's. Now, I know she can be difficult and doesn't bear fools gladly, but Alice is actually a very kind and dutiful person. She might not have got on particularly well with Sophie, but she did care about her."

Bob wondered whether Simon was telling him the truth. It sounded convincing, but then he had heard it all in the twenty-eight years since he started with the Metropolitan Police. He had come to the realisation that he would need to speed up the investigations into the two deaths. He was not sure where it would lead him, and whether he would be able to find any evidence that linked either Alice or Simon to the deaths of David and Sophie. But with the clock ticking, all he knew, was that he was now in a race against time.

EIGHT

A severe gale was blowing as Sanna Malik drove home that evening. At one point, she had to swerve round a tree branch in the road and then wondered whether she should have stopped to deal with it. But it was eleven o' clock, she was on her own, and did not have the physical strength to move it. In any case, it was safer to stay in her car than venture out in the storm.

'What would Jesus do?' she thought to herself.

Sanna was a committed Christian from a liberal Catholic tradition. She had been baptized and confirmed into the Church of England when she was twenty years old. She had been born a Muslim, and still maintained a respect for, and appreciation of the dignity of her birth culture. Amin, her brother, occasionally went to Friday prayers at the mosque, but religion for him was not a central feature of his existence. His lifestyle of drinking, womanising and occasionally gambling, was not something he talked about with the more socially conservative members of his community. Family was more important to him, and now that his father had passed away, he felt a keen responsibility towards his younger sister.

Sanna's faith had been nurtured by Laura Sullivan, who was brought up in the Anglican Church. They had met in their late teens when Sanna had just started her career as a police officer. The story of The Passion – Christ's death and resurrection – helped Sanna deal with the suffering that she had to encounter as a young officer. The burglaries, muggings and general social dysfunction that she was exposed to in her job, had the potential to depress and make her question the existence of a divine being. How could a loving God allow such evil to occur?

But Sanna's answer to this perennial conundrum, was not to question the existence of God, but to believe that suffering had been transformed by Christ. Sanna started to see the positive even in the direst situations, and found that her faith helped her deal with the constant exposure to the less well-integrated members of society.

As, she drove home on that Tuesday evening, her answer to the question 'what would Jesus do?' was to stop her car and report the incident to the fire brigade:

'Jesus wouldn't want anyone to have an accident because of that tree branch,' she thought to herself.

Eventually, Sanna arrived at her two-bedroomed maisonette in Vardy Road. She had no problem finding a space for her car as just a couple of months earlier, the Council had introduced residents' parking. The free parking that existed before, had sometimes forced her to leave her car hundreds of metres from her house, such was the competition for street footage. She was more than happy to pay the £40 annual permit fee, in order to guarantee proximity to her home.

When she slipped into bed next to Laura, Sanna assumed that her pregnant partner would be asleep. She wasn't.

"Thanks for the messages," whispered Laura as Sanna curled her body against her wife's. Sanna had ensured that she had regularly texted Laura throughout the door, knowing that her failure to do so previously, had upset her.

"Glad to be home – it's been quite a day." replied Sanna.

"How about a cup of tea and a chat?" suggested Laura.

"I'll put the kettle on!" said Sanna as she sauntered off to the kitchen.

Laura and Sanna would regularly drink tea in the middle of the night in order to help them work through worries and relax before sleeping. On lazy mornings, when Sanna was not working, they would stay in bed drinking coffee and putting the world to rights. They found these rituals deepened their relationship and provided mutual support.

"So what's up?" enquired Laura. Sanna proceeded to sum up the day's events including the interviews with Alice Chandler and Simon Bennett. At the end of it all, she commented:

"You know - it's him that I'm more suspicious of!"

"What, the brother? I thought you said that she was the aggressive one!"

"Yeh, but I think he's hiding something. His story matched hers as regards the death of Sophie Chandler, but he was cagier when it came to David. I wonder whether they got on that well despite Alice's assertion that her husband and brother were good friends. Simon Bennett seemed completely unaware that David was drinking more, and did not talk about his brother-in-law with particular warmth or sympathy. He just gave brief answers to our questions about David, but was gushing about his sister. He talked about her Asperger's, how he had looked out for her all her life, how fiercely intelligent she was and how her rudeness was just a mask for a deeper sensitive and kind nature."

"So he's a big brother that cares about his kid sister – I don't see how that is particularly suspicious."

"True, but when it came to David, you would have thought he would have been a bit more positive if they really had been good friends. It felt almost as if they had fallen out over something."

*****

Alice's accommodation at Stratford Police Station was far from salubrious. Her cell measured 3 and a half metres by four metres, and was fairly bear apart from a small bed, a mattress, a couple of blankets, a basic toilet, drinking water and a basin. There was an extractor fan that allowed air to be circulated, but no window. Alice had to request a towel and a pillow.

Alice asked to see a doctor whilst being held in her cell. She was feeling at a low ebb so knew she needed some sort of drug in order to survive what was becoming an increasingly stressful situation. The horrific image of finding David hanging from a curtain pole, was etched indelibly on her mind, however much she tried to forget about it. And that day, she had found her mother-in-law deceased as well. It was beyond her comprehension that two such traumatising events could have happened in two days.

She knew that Sophie would have found comfort in her faith but Alice had a tendency towards nihilism. How could there be any meaning in these events? What was life about when everyone ended up dead? Alice realised that like all animals, humans had an urge to reproduce and carry on the species, but beyond that, she could not find any metaphysical reason for her existence or anyone else's. Yes, she had wondered whether consciousness opened up some sort of universal meaning. If there was an essence in the universe that permeated throughout the physical, maybe that was the key to understanding our existence. But ultimately, Alice reckoned that she was an empiricist, only really trusting the physical world around her. And at that moment, the world seemed grim. She understood why people were tempted to end it all. 'No wonder suicide is the bigger killer of people in my age group,' she thought to herself, yet, she was not feeling suicidal herself. Despite, or maybe because of her desperate situation, Alice's instinct to fight was greater than any thoughts of self-annihilation.

In reality, she was in shock and consumed by grief. Alice also felt guilt at how she had dragged her brother into what was increasingly becoming a surreal situation. She knew that there was no way she was going to be able to sleep without medication. Alice was in survival mode.

"You've got to give me some sleeping pills!" she announced to the doctor. "Otherwise I won't be fit for anything tomorrow!"

"What do you normally take for that?" asked the female locum.

"Nothing! I don't normally have insomnia! But given that I've discovered my husband and mother-in-law dead in the last two days, and my brother and I find ourselves wrongly incarcerated in this shit-hole, my mind is in overdrive. It requires some medical intervention in order to prevent it from keeping me awake."

The doctor nodded and said simply, "I take your point – give me a few moments and I'll see what I can find."

Fifteen minutes later the locum returned.

"Are you pregnant?"

"No."

"Do you suffer from heart, liver or kidney disease?"

"No."

"Do you take any other medication?"

"No."

"In that case, here's a Zopliclone tablet. It should knock you out within an hour."

"Thanks, doctor," replied a relieved Alice. "I appreciate it."

"We are here to help, Mrs Chandler. I realise this must be an extremely stressful time for you."

"It is indeed," replied Alice, "and it's also going to be a stressful time for the Metropolitan Police when I sue them for wrongful arrest."

The doctor made no comment.

WEDNESDAY

NINE

At 8am, Bob Templeman had already gathered his colleagues to allot tasks for the day. Flick Featherstone was delighted to be on the team but her feeling of 'being special' soon evaporated when she saw that virtually every other free detective had been recruited for the investigation. Her fellow detective sergeant, Lucy Bebbington handed her a coffee as she, too, found herself perched on the edge of a table to get instructions from their Chief Inspector.

"Time's short folks!" announced DCI Templeman, "Got reason to believe that David Chandler death was foul play so we're treating this as a murder enquiry. Got 'til 1700 hours to find some evidence that links our suspects to his death and his mother's - Sophie Chandler. Tech guys will be reporting back to us about what they've found on the devices of Alice, David and Sophie Chandler as well as Simon and Karen Bennett. As I speak, DI Patel and DC Cook are at Harvey and Blackman's and will be looking at Alice Chandler's work computer and interviewing her colleagues. Already got data from David's workplace, Barnaby Lewis, but I need DCs Green and Holloway to go round there and interview the staff. Already got some guys working on Emails, internet searches and financial records bank/credit card records and personal notes/letters from the Chandler's house – will see if they pick up anything unusual. DCs Lake, Edney and Lofthouse – you're going to the neighbourhood of Sophie Chandler to do house-to-house investigations – find out from her neighbours if they've seen anything unusual going on - strangers, cars etc. DS Bebbington and DC Hussein – you're going to do the same in Hitchen Road. DS Featherstone, DCs Richards, Smith and Tyrrell, you're on the CCTV team. You need to get CCTV footage for the 16th October around Hitchen Road – look for any vehicles, bicycles or pedestrians that stayed for more than a few minutes. I've already got a team working on the CCTV round Harvey and Blackman's and Wanstead High Street. Want to see if

Alice's story holds out. DC Malik and I will be going to Simon Bennett's school to check out his alibi for 16th October. Any questions?"

There was a brief pause whilst Templeman's colleagues racked their brains to see if they could come up with any significant questions, but as usual Bob Templeman's cerebral processes were way ahead of most of his colleagues'.

"Right then, convene back here at 1500 hours to see what we've got!" he concluded.

*****

As DC Malik drove the ten miles to Simon Bennett's school accompanied by DCI Templeman, both officers were struck by how much devastation the previous night's storm had caused. The ten-mile journey turned into fifteen due to two diversions for 'fallen trees blocking roads'. As they listened to the car radio, they found out that the Metereological Office had declared the winds in the South of England as being almost hurricane force. They had reached levels only surpassed by the great storm of October 1987, exactly thirty years earlier. Bob had teenage memories of this event – a tree had blown down in his parents' garden and crushed their front wall. It had been the first time he had personally witnessed the extreme power of nature.

As this memory popped back into his consciousness, he reflected on how it was not natural evil that consumed him, but man-made evil. Was this current weather event a metaphor for a gathering storm at work and perhaps even in his private life?

They eventually arrived at Simon Bennett's school. Hailsdown College was a co-educational Independent School on the edge of Essex. It boasted 120 acres of grounds with a 400 metre drive, leading to an impressive neo-Gothic Victorian building. Dotted either side of the

67

drive were poplar trees that had been blown and battered like punch bags in the previous night's storm, though none had succumbed to the elements. Bob was impressed by their resilience, thinking that this was a quality he sought and generally achieved.

"It's Hogwarts," exclaimed Sanna Malik as she parked the Ford Mondeo, a comment that numerous others had made during the previous twenty years.

DCI Templeman ignored her as he observed a couple of anoraked individuals exiting the school, one of whom was holding a camera.

"Press!" he opined, pointing to the man and woman as they got back into their car.

"Do you think they've got wind of our investigation, Sir?"

"Don't believe in coincidences!"

The two detectives found Reception relatively easily despite the poor signage at Hailsdown College. The school had already been prewarned of their imminent arrival, so they were ushered into the headmaster's office straight away.

Doctor Marcus Ashdown was a grey-haired wiry man in his early sixties. He had worked at Hailsdown all his career and had been leading it for over twenty years. The school had been formed in his own image – academic, old-fashioned and eccentric.

His office also reflected these qualities – there was a large book case down one side with a range of History books and biographies of various politicians, generals and academics. On the opposite side were dozens of whole school annual photographs, all framed and going back the thirty-eight years that Dr Ashdown had been at the school. He was in all of them. Although Templeman did not have time to look at the photos, if he had, he would have seen a young, brown-haired begowned Ashdown in 1979, and then traced the annual aging process of the teacher/headmaster right up to 2017.

On the far side of Ashdown's office was a large oak desk above which was mounted a twelve-point stag's head which stared intensely at anyone who entered the room. Sanna was somewhat taken aback by it, thinking that no child would dare question the headmaster's authority with that creature eyeing them.

Dr Ashdown was accompanied by his much younger female deputy, Jess Stephens, who was quietly modernising Hailsdown College whilst providing unstinting support to her boss. What criticism she did have of Marcus Ashdown was shared only with her husband.

After introducing himself and DC Malik, Bob Templeman said:

"I'm sorry to have to visit your school like this Dr Ashdown, but we've just got a few questions for you."

"No worries DCI Templeman – we're always happy to answer questions from the Police, and I understand that those questions might be pertaining to my Head of Geography, Simon Bennett," replied Dr Ashdown.

"Indeed, but before I ask you about Mr Bennett, I'd like to ask you whether you've had any contact with journalists recently?"

"You obviously saw them leaving," commented Marcus wryly, "I sent them packing with a 'No comment'!"

"Good!" said DCI Templeman, relieved that the headmaster had not queered the pitch for him, but worried that he might have someone in his team leaking information to the Press without authorisation.

"Now, the first thing I need to make clear Dr Ashdown, is that Simon Bennett has not been charged with any crime. As far as we are concerned, he is at this current time an innocent man. However, we are carrying out an investigation and he is assisting us with our enquiries."

Sanna Malik looked on agog at the way Bob Templeman was talking – how could such an abrupt speaker be so elegant in his language when dealing with members of the public?

"So as part of these enquiries, we need to check Simon Bennett's movements on Monday between the hours of midday and two in the afternoon," continued Bob.

"As far as I'm aware, he was teaching until 12.30pm and then with his form until 1pm, and then on his lunch break after that,"

"Do you have proof of that?"

"Perhaps, the best thing would be for you to look at our CCTV. We'll get the Estates Manager to show you the footage around the Geography block at those times."

"That would be helpful," replied Bob Templeman. "I've also got a couple of other questions about Mr Bennett, which I would like to run past you."

"That's no problem at all DCI Templeman. I will answer any questions as best I can."

"Have you noticed any change in Simon Bennett's demeanour or mood in the recent past. For instance, has he seemed distracted or stressed by anything?"

"Not that I'm aware of, no. Of course, I don't have a lot of contact with staff on a daily basis, but have you noticed anything Ms Stephens?" enquired Marcus turning to his deputy.

"No I haven't, but I can make discreet enquiries with his colleagues in the Geography department if you like."

"That would be very helpful Ms Stephens," replied Templeman. "And has Mr Bennett kept up with his workload recently or are there any concerns about his performance in his job?"

"Not from my point of view, no." replied Dr Ashdown. "He is a very conscientious member of staff and involves himself in extra curricular activities, such as sport and music. He's even helped out with our multi-faith prayer room recently."

"So to all intense and purposes, he does a very good job?"

"I would say that he does an excellent job, yes, and the Geography results under his leadership of the department are just about the best in the school."

"I'm grateful to you both, and if you do have any further interest from the press, please continue to not comment and refer them to us at Stratford Police Station."

"Of course, DCI Templeman – we're always happy to cooperate with the local constabulary," replied Dr Ashdown as Sanna Malik laughed inwardly at the old-fashioned language of the headmaster.

An hour later, Bob and Sanna were on their way back to Stratford. The CCTV footage clearly showed that Simon Bennett had been in school during the whole of Monday 16th October. His alibi had checked out.

"So it looks like he didn't have anything to do with his brother-in-law's death after all," commented DC Malik

"Mmm, yes… certainly wasn't there, but may be too early to say he had nothing to do with it.

TEN

DS Flick Featherstone did not particularly like Detective Constable Bill Richards, who had been assigned with her to check CCTV footage. She found him a bit cold and stand-offish. Yet she did not want him to know this, as she prided herself on being professional. In some ways she preferred the company of Steve Cook and Mike Tyrrell who, although more laddish than DC Richards, were also more fun and communicative.

Bill was a tall, slim man of Afro-Caribbean heritage, just a couple of years younger than DS Featherstone. His reticence with Flick was more a defence mechanism than a reflection of his true personality. With close friends and family, he was funny, gregarious and a good raconteur. However, he was shy with Flick because he fancied her, and was determined not to show it. He knew instinctively that his sexual attraction to his superior officer would never be reciprocated, so there was no point in making himself vulnerable by revealing it.

It was fortunate that Hitchen Road, where David Chandler had lived, was a one-way street and all vehicles going into the road could be seen by a CCTV camera on the south side operated by the London Borough of Newham. A camera at the corner shop on the north side of Hitchen Road allowed one to monitor any vehicle leaving the street.

DS Featherstone had sent DCs Smith and Tyrrell to look at what the corner shop turned up while she and DC Richards went to the CCTV control room at Folkestone Road to view the Newham Borough footage.

"Right, Bill, we're looking for any vehicles going into Hitchen Road between 1200 hours and 1400 hours on Monday. Write down registration numbers, so we can cross check them later. I'd also like a count of any pedestrians and bicycles entering and leaving the road."

"Okay ma'am – I'm on it."

Within a few minutes, Bill Richards had realised that the CCTV camera was placed at an angle which prevented him from picking up registration numbers. He could see the sides of vehicles as they came round the corner to enter Hitchen Road, but for the life of him he could not see the front or rear plates.

"I can't make out any registration numbers, Ma'am," he announced to DS Featherstone looking at her black eye and thinking that she was still incredibly attractive with or without an injured face.

"Right then, in that case, we need to note down the time of every car that enters Hitchen Road on Monday lunchtime plus their make, model and colour. Steve, the control room manager, will give us a copy of the recording, so if you can't identify a car, we can work it out later. Just do as much as you can now. I'll give Smith and Tyrrell a ring to see how they're getting on with the other camera."

"Okay ma'am - will do my best."

A few minutes later, Flick Featherstone was almost banging her head against the wall as she had found out that her colleagues were having exactly the same problem at the corner shop on Hitchen Road. The only thing that stopped her headbutting the wall was a fear of either exacerbating her existing injury or creating a further shiner on the other eye. No number plates could be deciphered. Her frustration was not so much that the cars could not be identified, but that she would have to feed back to Bob Templeman that the CCTV footage for Hitchen Road was 'work in progress.' It would be a humiliation in front of her colleagues at 3 o'clock that afternoon and lower her esteem in the eyes of Bob Templeman. In her imagination, she had solved the case by identifying the name and address of David Chandler's murderer and was ready to soak up the praise and prestige that went with her outstanding investigatory work. It would be the final coup de grâce in her conquering of Bob Templeman! But, alas, this outcome was not now going to occur, and she would have to bury her fantasies in favour of good old-fashioned hard-graft detective work.

*****

DCI Templeman had briefly visited the scene of David Chandler's death the previous day, but now he wanted to have a closer look. Bob and Sanna put on protective gloves and disposable overshoes as they entered the Victorian terrace in Hitchen Road. They sensed the eerie silence of a house that had been the scene of a tragic event. Sanna wondered whether the walls remembered the event, as if some psychic imprint had been left.

"Okay, sitting room first," announced DCI Templeman strolling in and standing by the door to observe every detail. The metal curtain pole that had held the hanged body of David Chandler was heavy duty with three strong brackets holding it up. As Bob had requested, the tow rope had been left hanging on the curtain pole. The stool lay on its side beneath the curtain pole in exactly the same position as it had been found after David's death. Everything had been checked for finger prints, and indeed some had been found, mostly belonging to either David or Alice Chandler. DNA testing was still ongoing. The syringe found next to the sofa had been removed but a taped outline of it had been placed on the carpet, once again at the request of Bob Templeman.

"That tow rope – where did Alice Chandler say it had come from, Malik?"

"The shed, Sir."

DCI Templeman looked beyond the French doors below the curtain pole into the garden.

"Yes – the shed, Malik!" he announced as Bob viewed the contents of the Chandlers' backyard. "Let's have a butcher's!"

The key to the French door was in its lock, allowing the two detectives to go through into the fifty-foot garden and amble down to Alice and David's shed. There was a padlock on the door but it was not locked, so they were able to access the shed and its contents without any obstruction. DCI Templeman bent his head below the top of the door frame and stepped inside, followed closely by DC Malik. He was not at all surprised by what he saw – a various array of tools, paints, and garden implements lay before him. There was also a large box half-full of car-related paraphernalia. It contained a pair of jump leads, an emergency high-vis triangle, a couple of chamois leathers, car shampoo, and some polish.

"Tow rope was kept in here, I reckon," announced Templeman.

Also amongst the contents of the shed was another item that Bob hoped he would find – a step ladder.

"Bingo!" he exclaimed as he picked up the step ladder and headed towards the house. Sanna was somewhat nonplussed as she followed her ladder-laden boss through the French doors back into the Chandler's sitting room.

Templeman placed the step ladder underneath the curtain pole and climbed one rung up. With his six-foot-seven frame, he didn't need much extra height to perform the examination he was intent on. Sanna looked on quizzically and then laughed out loud as he produced a magnifying glass from his jacket pocket.

"Something funny, Malik?" asked Bob with a wry grin.

"I'm just admiring your Inspector Clouseau impression, Sir!"

"Old-fashioned ways are often the best!"

"But do you always carry a magnifying glass in your pocket, Sir?"

"Yep! Look and learn, Malik, look and learn!"

At that moment Sanna Malik realised just how fortunate she was to have Bob Templeman as a mentor. It certainly was not in the modern training manual to carry a magnifying glass on your person, but Templeman was not interested in that – his only aim was to get the job done as thoroughly and as effectively as possible. Yes, he carried a smart phone, and sometimes took photos with it. However, he also had a whistle, a notepad and a magnifying glass in his jacket at all times, along with half a dozen 'Bic' biros.

DCI Templeman spent a couple of minutes looking at the curtain pole and tow rope with his magnifying glass. Neither he nor DC Malik said anything. She resolved to do exactly as he had suggested – 'look and learn!' At the end of it, Bob said simply, "Now you have a look!"

Sanna climbed the step ladder purposefully. She was not a great fan of heights, but this was only four rungs up the ladder for her, and she certainly did not want to show weakness in front of her boss. Templeman handed her the magnifying glass:

"What am I looking for, Sir?"

"Move the rope to the right slightly as I did and look at the top of the curtain pole. What do you see?"

"Scratches, and discolouration, Sir."

"Exactly. Now look at the rope, not just where it was touching the pole, but along it's curled length."

Sanna's eyes opened wide as she realised what Bob was getting at. "Oh, I get it now, Sir. There's some fraying and smudges along a good metre and a half of this rope. You can only see the fraying close up, and the smudges match the copper colour of the curtain pole."

"Indeed! And what does that suggest?"

"Murder, Sir! Murder!" DC Malik could not contain her excitement.

Sanna got down from the ladder and Bob grinned at her.

"What d'you think happened, Malik?"

"If it had been suicide, Sir, he would have tied the rope to the curtain pole, stood on the stool and then kicked it away."

"Yep! Continue."

"But, that rope has moved against the top of the curtain pole as if someone had put the noose round his neck and then hauled him up. It must have required a lot of strength, so I'm guessing that rules out Alice Chandler as a suspect."

"Mmmm! Unless there was more than one murderer. Maybe two people hauled him up!"

Sanna was kicking herself. She had been doing so well.

Templeman folded the step ladder, picked it up, and went back out of the house to the shed where he placed it in the same position as he had found it. Sanna stood by the French doors watching Bob, thinking that one day she would love to be in the same position – leading a major murder investigation as a detective chief inspector. Whilst contemplating this, Bob turned to her and said:

"Tell me what you see in the garden?"

"I see some pot plants, a tree, some shrubs, the shed and high fences on all sides."

"At the back – what do you see?"

"A high fence backing on to the railway line."

"What does that mean?"

Sanna thought for a moment, and then she understood what Templeman was getting at.

"That means there's only one way in and out of the house – through the front door. So the murderers couldn't have slipped out the back after killing Chandler."

"Exactly! Neither could they have come in the back and gone out the front, Malik!"

Bob went back into the sitting room. He was enjoying this – seeing a relatively inexperienced colleague thinking like a proper sleuth under his guidance. So, he decided to continue with his masterclass.

"Where next?" he asked DC Malik.

Sanna racked her brain. 'What else is there?' she thought. The outline of the syringe taped on the carpet caught her eye.

"Bathroom, Sir!"

"Lead the way, Malik."

Sanna went upstairs closely followed by Bob. The bathroom was through the first door they came to, and the mirrored cabinet above the basin easily opened.

"Slowly does it Malik – may be dealing with vital evidence."

Sanna carefully unzipped the red First Aid case. The contents included some bandages, sterile wipes, plasters, a set of butterfly stitches, tweezers, scalpel, a mouth-to-mouth facemask, four syringes and hypodermic needles.

"All seems to be here, Sir," commented Sanna.

"Apart from a 10ml syringe and hypodermic needle, Malik."

"Really?"

Bob Templeman flicked through his mobile phone and found the photo he had asked Forensics to send through to him. He showed it to Sanna. The photo was of the syringe found at the scene of David Chandler's hanging. It had exactly the same design as the others in the First Aid case. Two of the syringes were 2ml and the other two were 5ml. The 10ml syringe in the photo was clearly missing from the case.

"How come Forensics didn't pick up all this?" asked Sanna

"They did," replied Bob grinning, "It's all been checked for prints, DNA, and photographed. As has the curtain pole and the tow rope."

"So you knew all along!" exclaimed Sanna.

"Knew some of it, yes, but wanted to keep everything in situ, so we could have a look. Just need to bag the First Aid case and tow rope now. Oh yes… another question Malik – Do you see now why it makes sense to think that there were two murderers?"

Sanna thought for a moment, and said, "Yes, one person to hold down David Chandler while another injected him with insulin. Once he was unconscious they were able to haul him up on the noose together with one person holding his body up while another pulled the rope. It does make sense. But then again, Sir, it could have been one person if they were very agile and strong,"

"Yes – possible too. Mustn't rule that possibility out."

"Anything else?" enquired Templeman.

"Mmmm, uhhh, the murderers knew where the syringe and tow rope were kept, suggesting they knew David Chandler – in fact, they were – or perhaps one of them was very familiar with the house. There's no sign of a forced entry or struggle suggesting that Chandler knew and trusted them. Either he let them in or they had their own key to let themselves in."

"Or they rang the door bell and pulled a gun on him," commented Bob, as he headed for the front door to get a couple of evidence bags from the unmarked Ford Mondeo Police car.

Sanna was grateful to DCI Templeman. He had used the crime scene as a training exercise for her. He was showing an interest in her career and obviously cared more than he let on. This confirmed in Sanna's mind that underneath the abrupt and patronising exterior of Bob Templeman, was a very good man.

ELEVEN

Harvey Blackman was not happy about the presence of Detective Inspector Aanya Patel and Detective Constable Steve Cook at his firm with a warrant to access Alice Chandler's computer and email account, especially as had already attended Stratford police station the previous day and failed to get Alice released. However, he was very calm about it, showing the Police detectives the respect, he did not at all believe they deserved. Blackman had a low opinion of police officers, regarding them as lacking his level of intelligence and expertise in the law.

Harvey Blackman was, however, wide of the mark in his intellectual snobbery towards the two detectives. He did not realise that the twenty-seven-year-old DI Aanya Patel had a first-class honours degree in Psychological and Behavioural Sciences from Cambridge University. She had been fast-tracked through the Police graduate training programme becoming a detective after just two years. Within three years she had risen to the rank of Detective Inspector, not by accident, but by being outstanding in all aspects of police work. Not only was she superfit in body, having competed in several Ironman triathlons, but she also possessed a formidable mind, utilising her academic background to further her expertise in psychological profiling.

Aanya was well aware that as a woman of Indian heritage, she would have to be smart to negotiate an organisation that was still inherently male dominated and contained racist individuals, but most of the prejudice that DI Patel had encountered so far during her short career, was not to do with her ethnic background or gender, but her age. Her dyed-in-the-wool colleagues would mutter behind her back that she was too young and inexperienced to be deserving of rapid promotion and these comments would invariably find their way back to her. Interestingly, the old-fashioned, magnifying-glass-using DCI

Templeman was not among those who cast doubt on the advancement of talented young officers. His mantra was typically: "If you're good enough, you're old enough!"

As her colleagues had got to know Aanya Patel, such prejudice subsided and her record of solving cases impressed them. So much so that she had gained the enviable nickname of "Cracker".

DC Steve Cook was no dummy either. He had a History degree from Oxford University and had joined the Police because he could not think of anything better to do. He had considered teaching but could not bear the thought of spending so much time with children. As for other graduate professions, none really appealed – just the thought of accountancy made him yawn as did any other financial and business-related work. Being a barrister or solicitor interested him, but he did not fancy further academic study, and knew it would involve a hard slog. Steve was not someone who wanted to set the world on fire and was not particularly ambitious. He was laid-back, down-to-earth and had a wicked sense of humour. He liked watching Rugby Union, drinking beer and kept himself fit by hill-walking. However, he had been brought up to believe that public service was worthwhile, so Police work seemed to him a useful thing to do.

When DC Cook joined the Police, he soon worked out that detective work would be the most interesting area to specialise in, and found himself motivated by the prospect of getting out of uniform. For a man of his intellectual abilities, it was a relatively straightforward move to make. Whilst hating the paperwork, he enjoyed the problem-solving and camaraderie that his job entailed.

"Here's Alice's office," said Harvey Blackman opening the door and inviting the two detectives to enter. Once inside, he started to shut the door saying, "I'll let you get on with your work in peace…"

"…just a moment Mr Blackman," interrupted DI Patel. "We also need some technical support from your IT Manager so that we can access Mrs Chandler's account and work email."

"Of course – silly me!" replied Harvey Blackman disingenuously. "We actually don't have an onsite computer guy, but I'll let you have the phone details for our IT support company, so they'll be able to help you remotely."

"That's very kind of you – thank you," responded DI Patel politely.

"Well… uhh…good luck…" uttered Blackman whilst turning round to go back to see his secretary.

"…oh, yes, and just one more thing, Mr Blackman," interrupted DI Patel again.

'Who the fuck does she think she is – Columbo!' thought Blackman to himself.

"Happy to help in anyway I can," replied Harvey as he turned round to face the two detectives whilst smiling through gritted teeth.

"Is there a private room – a conference room or spare office where I could interview your staff? DC Cook will be investigating Mrs Chandler's computer-related activities whilst I'll be conducting short interviews."

"Yes, of course - I hadn't thought of that!" uttered Harvey feeling both riled and outmaneuvered. "I'm afraid we're a bit short of space but I'll tell you what – you can use my office to interview staff as I've got some work to do alongside my secretary anyway, so it's no problem at all!"

"That's most helpful Mr Blackman!" replied DI Patel whilst Steve Cook suppressed a smirk at how his colleague had got the better of a man he found to be arrogant and false.

"Well, you'd better come with me then," announced Harvey Blackman in an attempt to wrest back control of the situation. "DC Cook – you can talk to my secretary who will give you the details for our IT Support. DI Patel – I'll show you my office."

Harvey Blackman's office was just as one might expect from someone who considered himself of high status. His desk was some six foot across, two and a half feet wide, and made of solid mahogany. There were no papers lying on the desk apart from some neatly stacked in a leather letter rack. A gold pen stand stood prominently on the desk holding a Montblanc 'Meisterstuck' gold-coated fountain pen. There were two other items on the desk, one of them being a L'Objet 24-carat gold-plated photo frame with a picture of Harvey and his wife dressed for a black-tie event. The other object was a standard black office telephone hidden discreetly behind the leather rack. Blackman's mahogany leather-bound 'Admiral' office chair provided the perfect accompaniment to the desk.

Above the desk was an oil painting depicting a scene which looked to Di Patel as if it were a victorious Duke of Wellington at the Battle of Waterloo, and below this was a couple of framed certificates and a photo of a young smiling Harvey Blackman at his graduation from St John's College, Durham. The names of the College and University were inscribed in ornate calligraphy above the photo.

DI Patel took all of this in within a few seconds and tried in her mind to form a psychological profile of Harvey Blackman. Here was someone with a grandiose sense of his own importance who had a glib and superficial charm. He seemed to be cunning and manipulative and what empathy he did have, appeared to be affected rather than genuine. The painting above the desk suggested an identification with people who were winners – 'perhaps an identification with predators,' she wondered. All this indicated to her the possibility that Harvey Blackman could be a psychopath.

However, DI Patel also wondered whether his superficial displays of superiority might be just a mask for someone who was underneath lacking in confidence and highly insecure. This suggested a domineering parent who put him down, more likely his father given Harvey's obvious wish to be the Alpha male. If not a psychopath, probably one of the youngest of three or more siblings who was considered less able than the older ones and consequently belittled as a child. DI Patel decided to play a little game with Harvey Blackman:

"What a coincidence," she announced pointing at the framed graduation photo! "I went to St John's College as well!"

"Oh, you were at Durham too," responded Harvey cheerfully, thinking that perhaps he had underestimated the intelligence of this young Police detective.

"Well, no, not that St John's College, the one in Cambridge actually," announced DI Patel, feeling a little ashamed that she had descended to Harvey Blackman's pomposity.

"Oh right, good for you," replied Harvey patronisingly and then adding: "My older brother and sister went to Cambridge too – Downing and Emmanuel. Best years of one's life of course – university!"

'Bullseye!' thought Aanya – 'perhaps not a psychopath after all, but a pompous lawyer with an inferiority complex from having clever older siblings. Yes, and probably suffered at the hands of an overbearing father.'

"Are there a lot of Cambridge graduates in the Police?" enquired Harvey Blackman revealing overtly his intellectual snobbery towards DI Patel's profession.

"Some, yes, but other officers went to lesser universities… …like DC Cook, for instance, who only read History at Oxford."

"Very funny DI Patel!" replied Harvey, chuckling. He was warming to the young detective. "And as someone who went to one of those lesser universities, I will now vacate my office, and leave it in your good hands. I'll get my secretary to give you the names of our small team, and you can interview them in whatever order you like."

*****

DS Flick Featherstone wanted something to present to DCI Bob Templeman, so she had hurriedly got her CCTV team together at Stratford Police Station. By 2pm, she was getting itchy:

"Okay, how far have we got in correlating the footage from the CCTV camera at the entrance of Hitchen Road with the footage showing vehicles leaving the street at Khan's corner shop?"

The incident room had been set up with two separate screens, each showing simultaneous footage from the two cameras between 1200 and 1400 hours on Monday. DC Bill Richards looked up from the screens as did DCs Sam Smith and Mike Tyrrell.

"There's still quite a lot of work to be done on this, Guv," declared Sam Smith who had ambitions of becoming a Detective Sergeant, "but we've done our best!" Smith was determined to lower expectations hoping that his superior officer would consequently be pleased with the progress they had made.

"I know that, Smith!" declared Flick, suppressing a desire to swear, "but we've only got til 3pm to find something that will help move this investigation forward! Now you start Bill – what have we got so far?"

"It's a quiet road but we've counted 63 vehicles, 13 bicycles and 21 pedestrians that went into Hitchen Road between 1200 and 1400 hours. Out of those, 19 vehicles stopped in the street as well as 4 cyclists and 7 pedestrians. Of the 19 vehicles that stopped, we think 14 are deliveries as they only stopped for a very short while. Two of them were clearly supermarket vans. Of the remaining five, four did not reappear and one stayed for eighteen minutes and then reappeared. We're assuming the four that didn't reappear are residents. Two cyclists went into the street from the South side between 12noon and 1pm and did not exit the street. We assume they're also residents of Hitchen Road. Two cyclists stopped for three and four minutes respectively and then reappeared. Out of the 21 pedestrians, 11 walked straight through the road, 5 went into the road and did not reappear (probably residents), 4 pedestrians went into the road and seemed to have stopped for two or three minutes each. One pedestrian reappeared twenty-one minutes later."

"That's good work guys!" commented Flick, impressed by the diligence of her officers and surprised they had made so much progress. "So, the car that stayed eighteen minutes in the street – what have you got on that? And that pedestrian that stayed twenty-one minutes – what do they look like?"

"We thought you might ask us that," interjected DC Tyrrell. "Here's a picture of the car that stayed eighteen minutes in the street," A side-angle image of a Range Rover came into view on the nearest screen to Flick Featherstone.

"Nice car," she commented.

"Yes, it's a brand new black Range Rover Evoque," continued Smith, "We know that because the new model has only recently come out. Here's a similar one from their brochure." Smith conjured up an image from the Land Rover website.

"Well done! And at what time did that vehicle enter and leave Hitchen Road?" enquired DS Featherstone.

"It entered the road at 1336 hours and left at 1354 hours."

"What about the pedestrian?"

"He walked into the road from the North side past the corner shop and into Hitchen Road. Twenty-one minutes later, he came out of the road the same way," stated DC Richards

"Here's an image of him, Guv" announced DC Smith. A reasonably good photo of a figure dressed in a black hoodie that hid his face, navy blue jogging bottoms, and black footwear came into view.

"He seems quite athletically built," commented Flick, "How tall would you say he is?"

"We estimate about six foot," replied Sam, "but we'll need to do some more work on that photo and the video to get a precise height."

"And when did he enter and exit Hitchen Road?"

"I've got him as entering the street at 1227 hours and leaving at 1248 hours," commented DC Tyrrell.

"Great, that's a good start guys – we've got a car and a man dressed in a hoodie! My guess is that one of those links to David Chandler's death."

TWELVE

Sanna Malik was buzzing when she and Bob returned to Stratford Police Station. DCI Templeman had brought her into the centre of a major murder enquiry and she was determined that her contribution was going to be an important one. Her ambition was not driven by a desire for self-aggrandisement, but an impulse to make a difference – to create a better world than the one into which she had been born. She knew from personal experience that service; helping others, created a more profound sense of self-fulfillment than qualifications, awards or commendations.

So when she offered to make Bob a mug of tea, she was pleased that he gratefully accepted the gesture. As she handed him the mug, his mobile phone rang. It was Dr Patricia Newton who had just completed her post mortem on Sophie Chandler.

"So what have you got, Pat?" asked DCI Templeman in his normal business-like brusque manner. He put the call on speakerphone so his colleague could hear the conversation.

"Sophie Chandler was not a well woman," commenced Patricia ignoring Bob's abrupt approach, to which she was very accustomed. "As well as diabetes she had advanced atherosclerosis in three of the four arteries around her heart. Initial indications show that her death was due to cardiac arrest caused by this."

"What about her diabetes?"

"Her diabetes would have been a significant contributory factor to her heart disease."

"Is there any evidence that she had been injected with an unusually large dose of insulin like her son?"

"No, her blood sugar level is within normal range. She was an insulin dependent diabetic who would have injected herself four times a day.

88

Stomach contents show that she'd had a sandwich for lunch and she'd obviously taken an appropriate dose of insulin at the same time."

"Any sign of recent injury?"

"No, there was some light bruising round her stomach but that was probably caused by injections. You get that sort of thing with insulin dependent diabetics."

"So, you think her death was natural?"

"The evidence strongly points that way, Bob."

"Okay, thanks a lot Pat – that's very helpful."

Templeman turned to Sanna Malik and said simply: "Got the gist?"

"Yes! Sophie Chandler dropped dead of natural causes in shock at the death of her son! She literally died of a broken heart!"

"Yep, seems that way, but doesn't help solve David Chandler's mur….!

At that moment Bob Templeman's musings were interrupted by the ringing of his desk phone. He recognised the extension number as coming from his immediate line manager - Superintendent Karen Michaels.

"Better take this Malik," announced Bob.

All Sanna could hear this time was DCI Templeman say "Yep….. I see…. Yeh, of course… right, I'll be straight down… no problem!"

"So what's happening?" she asked with bated breath.

"Got two camera crews and six reporters downstairs asking after Alice and Simon Chandler. This'll be good experience for you Malik – come with me…"

*****

"How did you get on in Hitchen Road, Lucy?" enquired Flick to her best friend and colleague who had been doing door-to-door enquiries with DC Hassan Hussein.

"Okay, I suppose" replied DS Bebbington with the enthusiasm of someone who had spent the day doing routine and uninspiring work.

The two detective sergeants were meeting in the same incident room that Flick Featherstone had used fifteen minutes earlier. The two laptops and screens were still set up with the CCTV coverage from the north and south ends of Hitchen Road.

"So what did you find out?" enquired Flick.

"Most of the residents of Hitchen Road were guarded and didn't give much away – they were certainly surprised by the amount of activity outside the Chandler's house and were shocked at David's death. 'Quiet, professional couple' was the typical response when we asked them what they knew about the Chandler's."

"You said they were guarded! Why was that? It doesn't seem the sort of street that would be wary of the Police."

"Well, it was Hassan who got to the bottom of that. One couple confided in him that Hitchen Road is a popular street with drug dealers. They said that there are two groups of dealers that trade either end of the street from out of their cars. The residents were clearly concerned to stay anonymous. The dealers don't seem to cause any problems and keep a low profile. The amusing thing was that this couple seemed more annoyed by the rubbish the dealers chucked out of their car windows than by the fact that they were peddling illegal drugs."

Flick chuckled and said, "I can imagine a local resident going up to one of those dealers and saying in a posh voice, 'Excuse me old bean, I know you've got important work here trading in narcotics, but please can you refrain from littering the street – it contravenes Part Four of the Environmental Protection Act 1990.'"

Lucy responded with a laugh and commented: "Yes, I know you've done your time on the beat, Flick!"

"Haven't we all! But, seriously, that would explain why the residents are wary of the police – they want a quiet life so don't grass on the dealers. And of course, these quiet streets are popular with drug pushers – you wouldn't want to catch the eye of your local copper by dealing in the High Street. Anyway, it sounds like Hassan did a good job. Did he get a description of the cars the dealers use as well?"

"Well - let's ask him…"

A few moments later DC Hassan Hussein was sat down with them. Blessed with good looks and a winning smile, Hassan was the perfect man for gaining the trust of witnesses. Although a young detective in his early twenties, he had a maturity beyond his years and an astute mind. He took his job very seriously and showed respect to his colleagues. And respect was very important to DC Hussein. Having witnessed the way young women in particular were mistrusted and disrespected by certain members of his community, Hassan was determined not to make the same error. Lucy commenced their conversation:

"Thanks for joining us Hassan. I was just telling DS Featherstone about that young couple who told you about drug dealers in Hitchen Road. Did you get descriptions of the cars the dealers used?"

"Oh yes, it will be in my report, ma'am. The couple said the dealers used different cars but the vehicles were invariably black in colour. The most common ones were a black BMW for the group at the north side of Hitchen Road and a black four-by-four for the dealers on the south side."

"What is it about dealers using black cars?" mused Flick.

"Smart, high status, but not too flashy, I would imagine," replied DC Hussein, "You certainly wouldn't want to draw too much attention to yourself if you were dealing but would want to have a car that commands respect."

"Good point, and good work Hassan! As it happens, we have identified a brand new black Range Rover that spent some time in Hitchen Road. Here's a photo of it." Flick handed Lucy and Hassan hard copy images that had been printed off.

"You can see there's someone in the passenger seat," commented Hassan, "So that would fit in with what the couple told me – the dealers work in pairs."

"So it could be that the Range Rover was dealing and had nothing to do with David Chandler," commented Flick.

"That's entirely possible, ma'am."

"So, I guess we're no further forward in identifying who might have been involved in David Chandler's murder," concluded Lucy.

"Not quite," responded Flick, "Can I ask both of you: Did any of the residents see anybody unusual or suspicious in Hitchen Road between 12 noon and 2pm on Monday?"

"Hassan and I have compared notes on this Flick, and, no, nobody in the street said they saw anybody acting suspiciously."

"Well, perhaps we need to jog their memory with this photo!"

Flick handed Lucy and Hassan hard copy images of a man with a black hoodie, navy blue jogging bottoms and black footwear.

"That doesn't look particularly suspicious," commented Lucy, "People walk through London streets wearing hoodies all the time."

"Yes, they do, but this man stayed twenty-one minutes in Hitchen Road."

*****

Bob Templeman was ambivalent about the press. He was instinctively untrusting towards them because he thought their main motivation was to get a scoop that would sell newspapers or get themselves noticed so that they could advance their careers. Bob saw himself as a truth seeker not a creator of stories, and although he had respect for investigative journalists that shared his passion for the truth, he was doubtful that the average hack subscribed to the same agenda. On the other hand, he knew the press was useful when it came to communicating to the general public. If he wanted to identify a suspect or a car, or a murder weapon, recruiting the press to help out could sometimes bear fruit. Templeman judged that the press could be an effective tool for the Police; one which he nevertheless used very carefully indeed.

Fortunately, security at Stratford Police Station was tight, so none of the camera crews or journalists had got beyond the main door that afternoon. As Bob left the building, he felt the same warmth from the sun that he had experienced two days previously. 'After the storm, the calm,' thought Templeman, but then it occurred to him that the stillness of that moment in the London microclimate contrasted markedly with the flurry of activity that surrounded his investigation into David Chandler's death.

Bob Templeman agreed to stand outside with the sign of Stratford Police Station visible behind him and DC Malik, who was positioned on a step by his side. He stood up straight knowing that his physically imposing six-foot-seven frame would command respect from the journalists before him. Bob already knew what he was going to say:

"We are investigating the death of a thirty-eight-year-old male from Forest Gate and at this point we are in the very early stages of our enquiry. That's all I can tell you at this point."

"That's David Chandler you're talking about Chief Inspector, and can you confirm that you have arrested his wife, Alice and brother-in-law, Simon Bennett?" enquired the lead journalist from ITN London News.

"No one has been charged in connection with any alleged crime, but we do have two people here at Stratford Police station helping us with our enquiries."

"Is this a double murder case after Chandler's mother Sophie was also found dead?" asked the journalist from The Newham Observer enthusiastically.

"No, that is not the case. The main focus of our enquiries at this stage is the thirty-eight-year-old male. Now, you'll have to excuse me, as we have a lot of work to do. We'll make another statement shortly."

As Bob and Sanna walked back inside the police station, Templeman found himself talking to his junior colleague about the footballer Eric Cantona:

"You might not have heard this story Malik: In 1995, the Manchester United striker Eric Cantona was suspended from football for doing a sort of 'kung fu' kick at an abusive spectator. He then had to attend a press conference to explain himself. He famously came out with this saying - 'When the seagulls follow the trawler, it's because they think sardines will be thrown into the sea.'"

"And what does that mean, Sir?"

"At the time, the press pretended they didn't understand, but the meaning was obvious to everyone else. Journalists are seagulls. You've gotta feed them titbits from the trawler to keep them satisfied. I gave them just enough without compromising our case. Game of cat and mouse, Malik, or may be seagulls and sardines."

THIRTEEN

By 1455 hours, Bob's team was gathered for their investigation meeting. They all knew that tardiness was not something that DCI Templeman appreciated although he himself was sometimes late because he had been diverted elsewhere. That had been the case today – he and Sanna's encounter with the press ensured the meeting did not commence until 1507 hours.

"Okay folks - looks like Sophie Chandler's death was natural causes," Templeman announced, "but got evidence to suggest one or more people were involved in David Chandler's murder. The tow rope he was hanged with is frayed suggesting he was hauled up unconscious. A grim crime, so need to find the culprits. Malik and I have been to Simon Bennett's school and his alibi checks out for Monday. Now what have you got?"

Bob went round each team asking for feedback. Nothing significant had been discovered from Sophie Chandler's neighbours, the searches on David and Alice Chandler's devices or email accounts had not garnered anything of great interest, and DI Aanya Patel's interview of Sophie's colleagues revealed only that everyone seemed to work effectively with each other. Similarly, the CCTV footage round Harvey and Blackman's office showed Alice leaving the building at exactly the times she claimed, and the High Street cameras confirmed her movements in Wanstead. DCs Green and Holloway had likewise nothing significant to report from their interviews at Barnaby Lewis.

DCI Templeman was growing increasingly frustrated although he stayed professional; as usual, not giving anything away. Flick, on the other hand, was growing increasingly excited as she began to realise that her team were the only people to have found out anything that would move the investigation forward.

"DS Featherstone - report on CCTV at Hitchen Road." requested Templeman in his normal succinct manner.

"Well, Sir, I've already met with DS Bebbington and DC Hussein who were on the ground. We have two images for you."

Flick circulated round the room an image of the Range Rover Evoque, explaining a possible link to the drug dealing in the street that had been established by Lucy and Hassan. DS Featherstone also explained why they had been unable at this stage to read the registration plate of the car.

"Okay - will need to ID that car and find out its movements," commented Templeman. "And the other image?"

DS Featherstone proceeded to circulate her image of a six foot, hooded man, calmy explaining how he had entered and exited Hitchen Road after having spent twenty-one minutes in the street."

"Excellent!" commented Bob. Flick felt like a contestant from 'The Great British Bake Off' who had just received a 'Hollywood handshake'! Bob Templeman was not a man prone to effusive praise, so an 'excellent' was a rare accolade which she would treasure for a short while at least.

"We need to ID that man as a matter of priority," announced Templeman, who then went on to allot further tasks that involved expanding the range of CCTV footage.

"We're also going to release that image of the six-foot hooded man to the press, to see if Joe Public can help us identify him. He didn't appear out of thin air, so someone must have seen him."

Templeman asked his team to reconvene at 1630 hours the following day and then went back to his office, followed by Sanna Malik. He was disappointed that there had not been a breakthrough in the case, but that was par for the course. Templeman reflected on the Thomas Edison quote which stated that 'genius was one percent inspiration and ninety-nine percent perspiration'. He reflected that it could equally be applied to detective work. Bob could sometimes find the one percent inspiration to get everybody pointed in the right direction, but normally it was the tedious investigation work that got them over the line, so that the Crown Prosecution Service had enough evidence to charge someone. He never underestimated the power of team work.

And with that team spirit in mind, he wondered whether his junior colleague could add anything to the picture:

"Okay Malik – what d'you think?"

"The man with the hoodie was in Hitchen Road when Chandler is estimated to have been murdered. And he stayed twenty-one minutes longer than any other pedestrian, so he's got to be our murderer."

"Indeed, unless another pedestrian went into the house, committed the murder, and was picked up by one of the cars that briefly stopped in Hitchen Road."

"I hadn't thought of that, Sir - a murderer and a getaway driver. But I still think the hooded guy is more likely to be the killer simply because he *was* hooded. He was obviously trying to hide his identity!"

"Yes – inclined to agree, Malik. Looks like my theory of two murderers may not be right after all."

"The guy with the hoodie is about six foot, Sir, and maybe he works out. Chandler was five foot seven and fairly light for a man. So if he was strong enough, I don't see why he shouldn't be the killer."

"Fair point Malik! Now what do you think we should do now?"

"You're the boss, sir!"

"Yeh, but what would *you* do?"

"I would be looking very carefully at CCTV footage to find out the movements of our hooded man."

"Yep – we're doing that. What else?"

Sanna wracked her brain wondering what Templeman was getting at. And then it came to her.

"Release Alice Chandler and Simon Bennett, sir. We've kept them here for almost twenty-four hours and we have insufficient evidence to hold them for any longer period of time."

"Yep - on the same page as me Malik. What advantage is there in doing that?"

Sanna thought for a moment and then her mind went back to their visit to Hitchen Road earlier in the day.

"We're pretty sure that the Chandlers knew the people or person that killed David....so we need Alice's help in leading us to them," proposed Sanna.

"Exactly," replied DCI Templeman grinning.

*****

"I tell you what – your food is shit!" announced a fed-up Sophie Chandler when she was brought into an interview room and found herself sitting opposite Bob and Sanna.

"Dinner was a sloppy cardboard-tasting lasagne, breakfast was a cheap muesli that makes sugar-free Alpen seem enticing and lunch was a cheese sandwich made by encasing something plasticky between two slices of bleached, processed bread. Hardly the sourdough I'm used to!"

"Welcome to my world," replied Templeman sardonically as Sanna muffled a laugh, "but you'll be glad to know that you won't have to suffer our cuisine anymore - we'll shortly be releasing you without charge."

"About bloody time too," replied Alice who was relieved but not altogether grateful. "You shouldn't have held us in the first place… and I can tell you DCI Templeman, you will regret having done so."

Bob had got used to Alice Chandler's hostility and was not particularly bothered by her threat. Nevertheless, he decided that now was a good moment to explain to her why her arrest had not been wrongful.

"Mrs Chandler, as you recall, we found you and Simon Bennett standing over the body of someone who had only just died – your mother-in-law Sophie Chandler. This established reasonable cause for suspecting you might have a connection with her death and by extension your husband's. As you might also recall, I gave you the option of 'helping us with our enquiries' by travelling in separate cars to Stratford Police Station. When you and your brother refused to cooperate with this, you left me with no option but to arrest you on suspicion of attempting to pervert the course of justice because you were obstructing police officers in the course of an investigation."

Alice was struggling to respond to this, but she was a lawyer after all, and although criminal law was not her speciality, her instincts were to take up the challenge she faced:

"DCI Templeman – suspicion in itself does not establish reasonable cause."

"Indeed it does not," replied Templeman quietly, "but suspicion on the basis of what a police officer has observed does establish reasonable cause. In this case, there were two police officers in attendance, observing you at the scene of a recent death in someone else's home which you had entered without the owner's consent. There were two of us observing you and your brother being uncooperative and potentially obstructing our work. I was perfectly justified in keeping you in custody until we had found out the cause of Sophie Chandler's death and had interviewed you separately about your husband's death. The post mortem seems to have established that she died of natural causes – a sudden and fatal cardiac arrest. Given, also, that I cannot see at this moment in time any public interest in charging you with attempting to pervert the course of justice, there is no reason to detain you further."

Alice was uncharacteristically silent. At that moment, the fight had gone out of her. She felt tired. Despite the pill she had taken, Alice had not had a full night's sleep. She was trying to keep it together even though her world had fallen apart in the previous two days. She wanted so much to be strong, but that was becoming increasingly difficult. Sensing her inner distress, Templeman changed tack:

"I know it's been a very difficult couple of days for you Mrs Chandler, so we will be making a family liaison officer available to you. And there's already been quite a lot of interest in your husband's death from the press."

"Those vultures!" responded Alice, rolling her eyes, "Makes me think I'd be better off here if it wasn't for the dire food. And no, I don't think I need a family liaison officer – I'll be staying with real family – my brother to be precise."

"I share your wariness of the press, but they can also be quite useful. We have identified a six-foot hooded man who we would like to find. Off the record, we think he might be the murderer. We'll be releasing an image of him to the media shortly."

Templeman also considered telling Alice about the further evidence gleaned from her husband's murder scene. On the one hand, it would be interesting to see her reaction to being told how precisely her husband had died and he needed her help in identifying recent visitors to her house. On the other hand, it was clear that Alice and her brother were tired and needed to get some rest before he threw anything else at them. He decided that it would be inappropriate to go further with the conversation without formally interviewing her and giving her a chance to have legal representation. He would talk to her tomorrow.

"Well, you're free to go, Mrs Chandler," he concluded, "although I'm still going to need your cooperation with the ongoing enquiry. We've already released your brother who's waiting for you in another room. And we'll give you both a lift back to his house. Hopefully, there'll be no journalists hanging around."

*****

"Well, I'm glad you gave me and Hassan some credit for the drug connection, Flick - I thought you were going to take all the kudos for yourself," commented Lucy.

Detective Sergeants Bebbington and Featherstone were sipping glasses of New Zealand sauvignon blanc in Jerry's Wine Bar located opposite the former Olympic park in Stratford City. They were chewing the cud after an eventful day. It was pleasant sitting outside whilst being warmed by patio heaters that kept the autumn evening chill at bay.

"Haha – yes, I was tempted to claim credit for it all, Luce. But it's not about me – it's a team effort."

"Are you sure Flick? When it comes to Templeman, it always seems to be about you and him!"

"Okay, I admit – I may be trying to impress him a little too much at times, but it's just a start – we've not got a huge amount to go on at this stage and there's still plenty of leg work to do."

"Yeh... I guess... now... hang on a minute..."

"What is it Luce?"

"Behind you, three tables away is a guy I recognize – sharp suit, lawyer, shortish and overweight. I saw him at the nick yesterday going into an interview room with Alice Chandler."

"Oh him," replied Flick who was determined not to turn round and look at the man in case it aroused suspicion, "That would be Blackman as in Harvey and Blackman. What's he drinking? Champagne?"

101

"No, he's got some sort of cocktail – looks like a Cosmopolitan. But the question is not what he's drinking, but who he's with. She's a stunner – brunette, at least twenty years younger. Lots of eye contact and holding hands – he's trying too hard for it to be his wife."

"Right, I'm going to the loo – I'll get a photo of them on my way back," announced DS Featherstone.

Flick left her seat, glanced at the couple and went into the interior of the bar. She found the ladies' toilets and decided that seeing as she was there, she might as well take advantage of the facilities. Afterwards, she picked up her phone, moved toward the exit and pretended to be looking at a phone message, whilst switching the camera on. As she passed Blackman and his companion, she surreptitiously managed to get a slightly askew but clear image of both of them.

"Got him! Your round Luce," Flick said conspiratorially as she sat down back at her table. The two friends giggled like school girls.

THURSDAY

FOURTEEN

DCI Bob Templeman drove to work the following day in his 1962 metallic blue Renault Dauphine Gordini. He loved this classic car largely because he could fit in it comfortably. Yes, the red interior was attractive and the shape of the car vaguely resembled a dolphin after which it was named. But he had liked the styling of many other vehicles only to find out that he was scrunched up inside them like Houdini doing a rope trick. The Renault Dauphine, however, had been designed as an economy, everyman car – suitable for all sizes, including his six-foot-seven frame. Two million Dauphine's had been manufactured over an eleven period in the 1950's and 60's, but Templeman hardly ever saw another one on the road. It never achieved the same fame or adulation as the VW Beetle or Austin Mini, but in Templeman's view, it was every bit as good. He had discovered a hidden gem, something that he was constantly trying to do as a detective. Even though Templeman owned the 'sporty' Gordini version of the Renault Dauphine, its performance was sluggish compared to modern cars. Yet this amplified its appeal in his mind. Templeman relished a challenge, and negotiating the Redbridge roundabout in a Dauphine was just that.

On arriving at Stratford Police Station, Bob was presented with some evidence that he had chased up the previous day - the phone records from David Chandler's mobile phone as well as the calls from his landline. His digital forensics team had carefully correlated the incoming calls and messages with the sender and discovered the recipients of outgoing calls and messages. This had been done for the three days prior to David Chandler's death and represented a reasonable amount of work, given that each telephone number had to be cross-checked with the national databases of mobiles and landlines. The only landline calls registered were two from Sophie Chandler's house. Bob wondered what the point of domestic landline telephones were for city dwellers given that they were rarely used anymore. He reasoned that most people continued with them out of habit and because they were a cheap add-on to a lot of broadband deals. In addition, a landline signified a 'settled' status which was reassuring to both the occupier and those who contacted them.

DCI Templeman grabbed his magnifying glass from his jacket pocket to look more closely at the small print of the records before him. Although not acutely long-sighted, he nevertheless found his magnifier helped him to see detail without having to resort to reading glasses. He knew he was fighting against the inevitable hyperopia of middle age, but his brass magnifying glass with a wooden handle had served him well over the years, so he saw no reason to change.

Templeman was able to match the calls and messages to known associates of David Chandler. He read entries from David's work What's App group, a couple of innocuous messages about cricket with an old school friend, and a text to his mother. He spotted a morning phone call to work on the day of Chandler's death and a private message to a colleague asking them to cover for an event that day. There was nothing of particular note apart from a mobile phone call the day before before his death from a number that did not appear on any of the databases. It seemed to all intense and purposes to be from an unregistered pay-as-you-go mobile. And it was this that peaked Bob's interest. There was no evidence that David Chandler had any criminal background or associates, yet someone who knew how to hide their identity by using a burner phone, had talked to him for four minutes on the afternoon of Sunday 15th October. Establishing the origin of this phone call was now high up on DCI Templeman's agenda.

*****

105

Flick Featherstone awoke with a sore head and recalled the two bottles of wine that she had shared with Lucy Bebbington the previous night. They had both got Ubers home but unlike Lucy, Flick had continued to drink at her flat until half-midnight. She inwardly berated herself for her heavy drinking on a week day. It was becoming an increasingly common occurrence, which had the potential to take the edge of her performance at work. Her mother had been an alcoholic and Flick swore that she would never follow in her footsteps. This morning, however, she reasoned that if she did not reduce her intake soon, she would soon be emulating Mum. Her father had been remarkably tolerant of his wife's drinking and it had not destroyed their relationship. But when her mother died of a brain hemorrhage in her late 50's, Flick sensed a certain level of relief come over her father. He had quietly carried the burden of his spouse's addiction for many years, and although he missed his wife, her death had been a weight of his shoulders.

Felicity was less forgiving – in her mind, there was no excuse for her mother's alcoholism. She had had it all; a kind, gentle and protective husband, two intelligent children and a three-bedroom semi in suburbia. There had never been money worries growing up and no major tragedies. Yet Mum, had become a selfish but semi-functioning alcoholic.

Flick, on the other hand, had been widowed at a young age and suffered from a post-traumatic stress disorder, but she was determined not to succumb to the addiction that her mother embraced. Nevertheless, she needed to be stronger, because recently, drink the enemy, had become too much of a friend.

DS Featherstone was keen to share the sighting of Harvey Blackman with Bob Templeman, so she arrived half an hour early to work and found herself in the loo brushing her hair and spraying herself with a slightly excessive dose of Tom Ford's 'Black Orchid' eau de parfum. As she looked in the mirror, it occurred to her that she was trying a little too hard to impress her boss, but she would play it cool when she saw him so as not to look pathetic.

"Come!" shouted Bob when Flick knocked on his office door. DS Featherstone entered to find DCI Templeman hunched over one of the photos she had distributed the day before. He was peering at it intensely with his magnifying glass. When he saw Flick, he placed the magnifier carefully on the desk, leaned back in his chair and raised his eyebrows:

"Got something new, Flick?"

"Well, err…yes, actually," responded DS Featherstone, thrown by Bob's seemingly telepathic skills. "How did you know?"

"Half-an-hour early for your shift – must be important."

Flick's intention to play it cool had been completely blown by her boss's knowledge of her shift patterns, but she decided that her knowledge was power too, so she replied,

"Not that important really Bob – it can wait. I'm more interested in the fact that you're looking at our photo of 'hoodie man'. Have you spotted anything?"

Templeman laughed out loud, amused that Flick was trying to turn the tables on him. He leaned forward, grinned at his colleague who was by now less than a metre from him and caught a pleasant whiff of her perfume.

"Okay, I'll go first," he announced. He turned the photo round and slid it to Flick who was sat the other side of the desk feeling a little aroused by his grin and boyish charm. Bob, then passed her his magnifying glass and said,

"Have a butcher's DS Featherstone – see if you can spot anything."

"I'm honoured DCI Templeman that you should let me use your magic magnifying glass – but I'm not sure if it's going to work for me." Flick was well aware that her powers of observation were not as finely tuned as her boss's, yet she was going to have a go, anyway. There was nothing unusual happening in the background of the photo, so she carefully examined the hooded figure. The face was covered by a black hoodie, slightly oversized, that looked in good condition as did the navy jogging bottoms which were also quite baggy. The black trainers he was wearing looked pristine as well.

"This outfit is new, Bob!" she proclaimed, "This is not normal attire for the man who is wearing it. If this is our murderer, he is not a young hoodie-wearer. I suspect he may be a little older, middle-aged even, trying to look younger, and of course hiding his identity."

"Good," replied Bob, "My thoughts exactly. And the clue is in the footwear."

"The footwear... Yes - brand new black trainers!"

"No, Flick, not black trainers! We assume that from the rest of the outfit, but look at the angle of his left foot – shows a thinner upper sole. Not wearing trainers – he's got loafers on. Seem to have quite high heels like a pair of trainers, but definitely loafers."

Flick studied the man's footwear carefully with Bob's magnifying glass. Yes, Templeman had spotted something she missed, which made her wonder whether she would ever reach the rank of Chief Inspector herself.

"So, we're looking for an office worker - an admin or professional person," she proposed.

"Quite possibly," replied Bob, enjoying the exchange. "Narrows it down slightly, but not much. Now your turn Flick – what have you got for me?"

"Well, I spotted a professional person we know at Jerry's Wine Bar last night with an attractive young brunette."

"You were drinking white wine with Lucy Bebbington," stated Bob matter-of-factly.

"Yeh, I was actually," replied Flick a little spooked again by her boss but reasoning that he knew that she and Lucy were best friends, and of course white wine is the most likely beverage to be consumed in a wine bar.

"And you saw Harvey Blackman," said Bob

"How the fuck?" Flick was becoming very unnerved by her boss's clairvoyancy.

"So who's the woman?" asked Templeman.

"That's the question, Bob! Who *was* the mysterious woman with Harvey Blackman? I took a photo so we should be able to identify her."

"It's Clare Davies, his secretary, Flick. DS Bebbington messaged me a copy of the photo last night. I sent it to DI Patel who was at Harvey and Blackman's yesterday. She recognised her."

If the floor had opened up and swallowed Flick at that moment, she would not have minded. She was simultaneously angry at her friend and embarrassed that she had, in her own mind, made a fool of herself.

"Oh, I'm such an idiot – I should have realised," commented DS Featherstone shaking her head.

"No, you are many things, Flick, but an idiot is not one of them," replied Bob grinning. "D'you think it has anything to do with Chandler's murder?"

"You tell me, Bob - you seem to know everything else. I'm guessing you've solved the murder too."

"No, don't know everything – that was a real question."

"I suspect it's just a middle-aged bloke having an affair with his young secretary – a bit of a cliché really," replied Flick.

"Fair point!" commented Bob.

A short pause ensued after which Flick said,

"Right, I'll get to work then." She got up to go and turned towards the door. Before she could open it, Bob said:

"Next time we have a drink, you should have white wine. I know you don't like real ale!"

DS Featherstone's face turned bright red, and as she was leaving the office, she flicked her hair and replied:

"If there is a next time!" With that, she was gone and Bob felt a tinge of guilt at having wound her up. But it had been fun!

FIFTEEN

"Didn't pick up on his affair then?" Templeman asked DI Patel. Aanya had barely sat down in his office and was not expecting Bob to start their conversation so abruptly. She was there to give him feedback from her visit to Harvey and Balckman's.

"No – that wasn't my brief. The task was to access Alice's email account and computer, and interview her colleagues. Although I met both Blackman and his secretary separately, I never saw them together."

"Must have got some idea of him as a person, Cracker!"

Aanya thought it inappropriate that her boss would use her nickname but reasoned that this was a man under pressure who would let his professional exterior slip when stressed. And with his rudeness came a wicked sense of humour, which she appreciated. Ignoring his continued abruptness, she replied:

"At first, I thought that Blackman may have psychopathic tendencies given his superficial charm and penchant for identification with victorious historic characters – he had a painting of Wellington at the battle of Waterloo on his office wall. But after talking to him for a while, I revised that opinion. I detected a man with an inferiority complex as a result of possibly an overbearing parent and as he revealed, older and even more successful siblings. Now that we know he is having an affair, we can assume that his marriage is dysfunctional as well. His secretary provides a much-needed confidence boost to his ego and adds an element of excitement to his life which is otherwise banal. His charm is not entirely affected – he seemed to have a good sense of humour and although a terrible snob, he is not a man devoid of kindness. In short, he is not someone I would automatically think was likely to commit murder or even conspire in one."

"Well analysed," replied Templeman nodding his head, "What about his colleagues?"

"Well, there was a male solicitor, Michael Sanders, family law expert, mid-forties. Nice guy, intelligent, seemed well-adjusted, straight-talking and married to his job. There was also a young guy there – Jack Bradbury, twenty-five, bit of a lad, but very intelligent. Head of family law was Fran Cohen, forty-five, cheerful, funny and astute. In charge of conveyancing was Jenny Wilson, fiftyish, very professional, unremarkable. Also in property was Jasmine Dhillon, twenty-four, recently qualified and keen to get on. That was it – only a small firm covering conveyancing and property, family law… plus crime which Blackman and Harvey do."

"Did they all have alibis for Monday around the time of the murder?"

"They were all in the office apart from two of them who said they were out of the office meeting clients."

"Which two?"

"Michael Sanders and Fran Cohen."

"Michael Sanders – what does he look like? His height, his build etc?"

"Yes, I can see where you're going with that one. Light brown hair, reasonably good looking but not exactly George Clooney. He was tall – just over six foot I would guess and average build. I suppose he could be the guy in the hoodie."

"Possibly – but a lot of six-footers out there. What sort of shoes was he wearing?"

"Black, I think, as he was wearing a dark suit and I would have noticed if he had brown shoes on. To be honest, I didn't really look closely – must have been leather uppers of some sort…"

"And Jack Bradbury. What about him?"

"He wasn't tall; may be five foot seven, and slim. He couldn't be Mr Hoodie."

"Right… mmm… and Stuart Harvey – what did you make of him?"

"He wasn't in yesterday. He was attending a funeral of a relative. But didn't you meet him when he came in?"

"Yep – represented Simon Bennett. Seemed alright – professional, not as arrogant as Blackman," replied Templeman.

"Do you think he could be our hooded man?"

"Nah – too short – can't be more than five-nine or ten, but Michael Sanders… I wonder…"

"We can keep an eye on him… discreetly… of course…"

"Yep – do that DI Patel. Check his alibi as well, and ask the tech guys to look at his social media accounts. And can you find Malik for me – no sign of her yet!"

*****

"You made me look like a right twat!" exclaimed Flick to her friend, Lucy Bebbington.

"Now, hang on a minute – you never said that you were going to get to work early and waylay Bob Templeman! I'm surprised you didn't WhatsApp that photo yourself!"

"I thought, as it was important, it was better to present the intel to him in person."

"Important! You call that Important! It's a dirty old man having an affair – that's all. D'you really think it's relevant to the case?"

"Well, you obviously thought it was important – you messaged him that photo pretty fucking damn quick."

"Haha, I was a little juiced-up and thought it would be fun to share it. And frankly Flick – you've got to relax, mate, and stop trying to impress Templeman!"

Flick paused for a moment. She knew Lucy was right – she was trying too hard with Bob, and in so doing, just making herself look foolish, or sad or desperate, or maybe all three.

"I'm not trying to impress him that much," she lied, "Okay, I could play it cool a bit more, but the job's important – it's my life. It's all I've got."

Lucy realised she had gone too far. She knew all that Flick had gone through. Losing her husband had almost destroyed Flick; she had no children, had few hobbies, and had not yet found a partner to match Martin. So, of course the job was at the centre of her life. Detective work was in any case more of an all-consuming vocation than a job.

Lucy had supported Flick for years. She had been a shoulder to cry on and a confidante throughout the years of bereavement. She had lost count of the times that Flick had crashed out at her house and the two friends had drunk excessive quantities of sauvignon blanc. They would play their favourite CDs loudly from the 1990s or in latter years streamed tracks from their phones on Lucy's Sonos. All the while, Lucy's husband, John, would try to sleep upstairs. He never once complained, as he knew how precious and life-affirming their friendship was. The alcohol would eventually lead Flick and Lucy to raid the larder and the fridge, or even start popping corn at two o'clock in the morning. Of course, they both suffered the next day for their excesses, but they knew it was worth it for the moments of joy and intimacy they shared the previous evening. Their friendship had kept Flick sane.

And Flick had been a steadfast friend when Lucy had gone through difficult times. Flick had comforted her when she had gone through a miscarriage and been a listening ear when her husband had strayed briefly. They had been there for each other since they met in their late teens.

"I know Flick – you're right - the job's important. Which makes it even more essential to laugh at stupid things like Blackman's affair with his secretary!"

Flick smiled and nodded, "Yep, I guess things could be a lot worse. At least neither of us is married to Harvey Blackman!

*****

By midday there was still no sign of Sanna Malik at Stratford Police Station. Templeman was beginning to worry, but reasoned that there must be a logical explanation for her absence. He felt it was a pity that she was missing out on his search for possible suspects, but knew that time waited for no one. He was pleased that there was at least one person at Harvey and Blackman who fitted the physical profile of the killer, but he had no evidence to link Michael Sanders to the crime. His next step was to see what had emerged from the interviews at David Chandler's place of work – Barnaby Lewis. Bob invited DC Amanda Green into his office to debrief him. He opened with an obvious question:

"Who did you interview at Chandler's work place, Green?"

"It's a big city firm, Sir, several hundred employees, so we narrowed it down to those who worked closest with David Chandler."

"Who were?"

"The Accounts Manager, Adam Butler, the Meeting Rooms' Manager, Marie Chevalier, the Admin Manager, Liberty Brown and Deputy Manager Charlotte Bagley."

"Describe them for me – age, physique, personality."

"Adam Butler is 40-something, average build, about six foot and a bit of a nerd. Polite, personable, and definitely a numbers man. Seemed open and honest and expressed surprise and shock about Chandler's

115

death. He's now been thrust into the role as acting Head of Business Services. Marie Chevalier is in her early 30's, average height and build, and a smart dresser. She seemed fairly open and honest as well. Liberty Brown is early fifties, quite tall, slim, business-like manner but friendly, and Charlotte Bagley – she was mid-twenties, curvy, polite and helpful."

"Who was most upset by Chandler's death?"

"They all expressed shock, but Adam Butler seemed the most upset. He mentioned that he valued Chandler as a friend, as well as a colleague."

"Did they all have alibis for Monday around the time of the murder?"

"Oh… I'm really sorry Sir…I forgot to ask them about that. I was pressed for time, and just wanted to get an impression of what they were like as people."

"That's a pity Green – make sure in the future you do the basics."

"Yes, of course, Sir,"

"Anyway, Butler seems our most likely suspect out of that lot – do you think this is him?"

Templeman passed DC Green the photo of the hooded man in Hitchen Road. Amanda had seen it in their meeting yesterday but had not spent much time looking at it. This time, she studied it more carefully, before saying,

"Can't tell. Probably the right height, but this guy looks a little fitter than Butler. Then again, that could be because of his outfit. I saw Adam Butler in a grey suit with black loafers."

"Black loafers?"

"Yes, Sir; black, leather, slip-on shoes."

"Were they like the loafers in that photo?"

DC Green did a double take and then had a closer look at the photo:

"I assumed this hooded guy was wearing trainers, Sir, but come to think of it, yes, they could be loafers. I can't say for sure they're the same shoes that Mr Butler was wearing, however."

"Fair point. But we need to find out a bit more about Adam Butler. I'll get the tech guys to look at his social media and we'll keep tabs on him for a while. Get a video of him walking. Want to see if his gait matches our hoodie guy. I'll also ask computer forensics to look at the social media of the others. Let's see if any of them have a closer connection with David Chandler than we might expect."

"Do you mean Charlotte Bagley, Sir?"

"Possibly, and the French woman - Marie what's-her-name…"

"… Chevalier, Sir."

"Yes. Need to look at Facebook in particular – how much they're liking Chandler's posts – that sort of thing."

"Yes Sir. Is that all?"

"Just one more thing - you're friends with Sanna Malik aren't you?"

"Well, I get on pretty well with her, Sir, but we're not exactly friends."

"Right… mmm… okay. Thanks Green."

"Sorry, Sir, but can I ask – is there something wrong?"

"Well… uh… Malik's a 'no show' so far today. Texted and rung her, but no reply. No sick call. Just wondered if you knew anything."

"No, Sir. Sanna's quite a private person – she doesn't really socialise with her colleagues. I know her partner's expecting a baby, but we haven't really talked much about it."

"Thanks Green. I'll give her wife a ring. Keep this one under your hat."

"Will do, Sir."

Bob was becoming more concerned about Sanna – something felt wrong, and it was time to chase up her absence. He picked up his office phone and rang Laura Sullivan on her landline. The phone was answered on the fourth ring:

"Ah, Good Afternoon Ms Sullivan, this is Bob Templeman from Stratford Police Station."

"Oh, hello Mr Templeman, is everything okay?" Laura was alarmed by Bob's call. She had also failed to get replies to a couple of messages she had sent to Sanna.

"Well… um… we were just wondering if Sanna had an appointment elsewhere today as she hasn't turned up for work."

A growing sense of panic started enveloping Laura.

"She left for work at 7.25 as usual this morning – are you saying she never arrived?"

DCI Templeman rapidly started processing the situation, regretting that Laura and not been contacted in person.

"That's right, and I'm sorry to have called you like this. I'll send a couple of colleagues round if that's okay, and I'm sure we'll find out where she's got to soon."

"Okay, but, bloody hell, this isn't like her. She must have had an accident or something."

"We'll look into that possibility. My guys will be with you shortly."

"Right – okay then!"

Templeman called Amanda Green back in and told her to go with DC Mark Holloway to Vardy Road where Laura lived. Then, he asked Flick Featherstone to contact local hospitals. Sanna Malik's disappearance was an unwelcome development, but he did not want it to derail his investigation into David Chandler's murder. He had already arranged a 1.30pm interview with Alice Chandler, her brother and Karen Bennett at Chipping Ongar, and he needed a fellow detective to accompany him. His choice was straightforward - he wanted someone who had psychoanalytic abilities. He needed 'Cracker'!

SIXTEEN

Simon and Karen Bennett lived in a three-bedroom cottage on the edges of the popular rural Essex town of Chipping Ongar. For those ignorant of the county of Essex, they imagined it to be a place where women wore designer sunglasses, had fake tans, hair extensions and breast implants. Similarly, they erroneously thought that men wore skinny jeans, designer trainers, had teeth veneers and coiffed hairstyles.

Whilst there were, indeed, people from the south west of the county that conformed to these stereotypes, most of Essex was countryside, in which people had a fairly unpretentious bucolic existence. The further away from London you got, the slower the pace of life became. A lot of people in Chipping Ongar worked on the edge of the metropolis, but surprisingly few commuted to the centre of London, as the town had no direct rail link to the city. The cost of property in this pleasant rural backwater was therefore surprisingly good value.

Simon and Karen had escaped from the city after selling their one bedroomed flat near Liverpool Street Station for a ridiculous amount of money the year before. They could have bought a manor house in Wales with the proceeds from the sale, but there was only the two of them and work tied them to the area. A smart, Tudor style cottage, originally built in the late sixteenth century, but extended sympathetically in the 1980's, proved a winner for them. The extension incorporated the white rendering and black beams that adorned the original dwelling, and a thatched roof added to its historic charm. Although increasing the cost of insurance, their roof also improved the insulation of their cottage, so the heating costs were surprisingly meagre.

DCI Bob Templeman and DI Aanya Patel were able to park the unmarked Ford Mondeo police car just a few metres from Simon and Karen Bennett's cottage behind a Porsche 911 Carrera.

"Nice property," commented DI Patel.

"Yes – escape to the country."

"Do you think that's their Porsche?"

"I was here on Tuesday and no sign of that thing then. Looks like Harvey Blackman's – saw it in our car park the other day."

It was Simon Bennett who answered the door and greeted them formally. He looked tired and drawn, but ushered them into the dining room where Alice Chandler and Karen Bennett sat, accompanied by Harvey Blackman. Bob had to duck to avoid a beam as he entered the cottage and then had to dodge another one as he approached the dining room. He had long since discovered the drawbacks of low-ceilinged properties, knowing that he would never own a house that was as unsuitable for a man of his dimensions as the Bennetts' cottage.

Bob introduced Aanya, which elicited from Alice a response that did not surprise him, but came as somewhat unexpected for DI Patel:

"So where's your normal sidekick DCI Templeman?" she asked.

"I don't have 'sidekicks' Mrs Chandler, I have 'colleagues'. Now we don't want to start on the wrong foot do we!?"

Templeman was determined not to discuss personnel issues with Alice or any other member of the public. But Alice was not finished yet:

"Just wondering why you've replaced a Detective Constable with a Detective Inspector. You're really pushing the boat out today!"

"You needn't worry Mrs Chandler, this visit is perfectly routine, as we need your help in trying to find out the person or persons involved in your husband's death. There's no hidden agenda here."

This finally brought an end to the initial skirmish, much to everyone's relief. Aanya was intrigued. She had not met Alice before and Bob had not filled her in on Alice's personality. Aanya was already forming a psychological profile of the widow before her: Not your typical smooth lawyer, rather very direct to the point of belligerence. This suggested someone who saw themselves as an outsider; who did not conform to the expectations of an ingroup – a high functioning, possibly borderline autistic individual, who had difficulty reading body language. She was unintimidated by authority, suggesting a high level of intelligence, original thinking and self-confidence. Aanya felt a kinship with Alice because, like her, she was unimpressed by the patriarchal power structures of society that they both had to negotiate as women. And DI Patel could tell that Alice knew one of these patriarchal structures was the Police service itself. Aanya liked Bob Templeman but she was not blind to his patronising ways and sense of entitlement as a white male. Neither, she realised, was Alice.

*****

At the same time as DCI Templeman and DI Patel were driving to the Bennett's cottage in Chipping Ongar, a dark cloud hung over East London. A cloud that was about to cast a long shadow over Templeman's investigation. The person who revealed this cloud was thirty-nine-year-old Keith Arnold, who outwardly seemed like a straightforward East End geezer, but in fact, was not entirely what he seemed.

Most people have secret fantasies and desires. It is perfectly normal. Think of all those billions of human beings that have lived before us, many of whom died having kept things hidden that they would not have wanted others to know. And, so it is was with Keith. Sometimes, these secret fantasies and desires lead a person to do things that are potentially hurtful to their nearest and dearest. Keith Arnold was seemingly happily married to his wife, Cathy, for ten years and was father to seven-year-old Jack and four-year-old Willow. However, he also led a double life.

At the exact moment that DI Aanya Patel was admiring Simon and Karen's cottage in Chipping Ongar, Keith was enjoying a sexual act with another man on Wanstead Flats. The 'Flats', as they are known, are not apartments, but a flat expanse of grass, copses, scrubland and ponds in East London between Wanstead, Forest Gate and Manor Park. They are at the southern end of the ancient Epping Forest that still exists north east of the Flats.

One of the larger copses in Wanstead Park was well known by locals and the Police as a popular place for gay men to meet and participate in activities that would be perfectly legal in private. This was where Keith and his male acquaintance were having oral sex. However, not many people were bothered by what went on in this small bit of woodland because, in general, the participants were discreet. The Police were far too busy dealing with more serious crimes to worry about cases of outraging public decency.

Once Keith and his acquaintance had finished their fellatio, they went their separate ways. As he was leaving the copse in a westerly direction, Keith's eye caught the sight of a human hand poking out from under a creeping willow bush. Thinking this strange, he had a closer look, spotting a large blood-stained area of grass in front of the shrub. As he approached, he started to make out the form of a human being lying face up in the creeping willow, and as curiosity enveloped him, a second later he found himself staring over the smartly clothed cadaver of a woman with multiple stab wounds around her head, neck and chest. He gagged, but somehow managed to stop himself from vomiting. Keith took the mobile phone out of his pocket and dialed '999'.

*****

Alice was crestfallen, Karen was sobbing quietly, Simon had his arm round his wife and Harvey sat expressionless, holding his Montblanc fountain pen, but not writing anything. DCI Templeman had just finished telling them about how David Chandler had been killed. He had broken it to them as kindly as he could, but there was no hiding the facts. The worst bit for Alice was the thought of David's unconscious body being hauled up on a rope like a piece of meat. She stared down at the oak dining table for a short while trying not to cry. A silence enveloped the room as everyone else waited for her to respond. Alice tried to piece together the information that she had just been told, but not only was she struggling with her emotions, she was also struggling with the facts. It just did not add up.

"I don't understand," she said.

"It's a lot to take in," replied Bob gently.

"No, not that! I don't understand why Dave had taken the day off. You told us that there was no sign of him having a stomach bug, so why did he not go to work that day?"

"That's a good question. I've thought about that myself and the only logical explanation I can think of, is that he had planned to meet up with someone that day, or was expecting his murderer to come round. It suggests that he knew and trusted his killer or, at least someone connected to them."

"But I can't think of what would be so important that he needed to take the day off work."

"That's still to be determined Mrs Chandler. We don't know at this stage either."

"The other thing I don't understand is how the person who killed Dave managed to inject him with a syringe that was in my bathroom cabinet First Aid case!"

"Can you explain further Mrs Chandler?"

"Well, there was no sign of a struggle so logically they must have overpowered Dave and injected him with the insulin as soon as he answered the door. They can't possibly have gone upstairs, grabbed the syringe, put insulin in it and then gone back downstairs to kill him.

They must have had the syringe ready, full of insulin, before Dave answered the door."

Bob and Aanya were impressed, both thinking simultaneously that Alice would make a very good detective if she ever chose that career path. DCI Templeman had of course already gone through the same process of logic as Alice, so his answer was already thought through:

"You are absolute right in your thinking Mrs Chandler. I, too, am drawn to this theory. Another idea we have is that the person who killed your husband threatened him with a gun, led him upstairs and made him fill up the syringe with insulin. It's not a pleasant thought, I know, but we mustn't rule anything out."

"So which do you think is more likely DCI Templeman?" replied Alice, managing to suppress her emotions, and even feeling a small amount of enjoyment at going through a problem-solving exercise with Bob.

"On balance, I think your theory is more likely. Which is why we need your help today. If the syringe was removed from the house before David's death, we need to identify everyone who has been in your house in the last few months and eliminate each one from our enquiry until we find a connection to the crime. I'll need a list of names from you."

"You'll have to give me a little while to work out who was visiting us and when they were there, but yes, I can do that."

"Of course," replied Bob, "but I'm afraid we do need to move this investigation along as quickly as possible, so do you think you can get that done by tomorrow?"

"DCI Templeman," interjected Harvey, "We really don't want to put undue pressure on Alice at the moment – it's been a very stressful...."

"....it's alright Harvey," interrupted Alice, "I want this solved as soon as possible too, so, yes, we'll get names and dates to you by tomorrow, Bob."

125

Templeman was a bit taken aback by Alice using his first name, but not at all displeased. He viewed this as a breakthrough in their relationship; a sign that Alice, for all her previous hostility, was now on the same page as him. He needed her and she needed him if they were both going to find out who was responsible for the death of David Chandler.

"Thank you, Alice," he replied, reciprocating her familiarity, as his mobile vibrated in his jacket pocket. "Here's my work email address, so you can contact me directly." He handed Alice his card.

The vibrating in his pocket soon stopped and as the meeting broke up, he quickly looked at his phone to see who had rung. A message came up from Flick Featherstone which read: "Urgent – please call me now." A feeling of nausea grew inside him as he started to consider the possibility that something terrible had happened. In his distracted state, he hit his head on the beam outside the dining room, and the sharp pain caused him to suppress a yelp by gritting his teeth hard.

"What is it?" asked Aanya when they got back into the Mondeo. It had been impossible for her not to notice the change in his demeanour.

"Don't know, but it's not good. Need to ring Flick Featherstone."

"What's up?" he asked as soon as Flick answered the phone.

"Oh fuck - that's terrible," heard Aanya.

"Good… Yeh – well done… Yep…going to need every spare person we've got… and yes – we'll head straight over." DI Patel was getting increasingly frustrated not knowing what was being talked about.

Bob came off the phone and stared momentarily into thin air.

"So what's happened?" asked Aanya.

"Sanna Malik has been found stabbed to death on Wanstead Flats. They've shut the area down. The Super knows and is on the phone to the Commissioner. It's a shitfest, Patel. And we're going to the scene now."

126

SEVENTEEN

Templeman was normally fine with dead bodies – he had encountered many in his time as a detective. He remembered his first one – a woman who had been the victim of domestic violence. It had been difficult, but he had managed the situation well.

It was Thursday and Templeman had already seen two cadavers since Monday. This would be his third. Despite being accustomed to death, it was a high unusual week. Nevertheless, he was a Police detective, and that meant being able to switch to a professional mode that suppressed his emotion and enhanced his observational and logical thinking skills. If he wasn't able to deal with the macabre, he was in the wrong job.

But this time it was different. There was a personal element to this that magnified the horror of it all, so for the first time in a very long while, he wondered whether he would be able to cope. Bob had known Sanna, had liked her and mentored her. She had been a talented detective with her whole life ahead of her. And she was about to become a mother.

As he looked down at her lifeless body, he reflected on the transience of life. He had interacted with her the previous day, seen her eyes light up when she was working something out. He had seen her smile and laugh. She had been so alive, so positive, so much herself! Yet hours later her existence had been snuffed out suddenly and brutally. Her future had been stolen. With their frenzied attack, the murderer had created tragic ripples which would extend far beyond Sanna's home in Vardy Road.

"You carry on DI Patel – I just need a moment," said Templeman after viewing the scene. Bob wandered off on his own to get some air and collect his thoughts. He was not someone to show emotion in public, but he suddenly felt overwhelmed by the fragility of life and the

127

dangers that he and his colleagues put themselves through on a daily basis. This could have been any of them; it could have been him. The police had lost one of their own and that fact did not sit well with him.

*****

Dr Pat Newton arrived at the scene with another senior forensic investigator and four colleagues. It was not long before they had tents set up and were directing their team's painstaking work. Flick Featherstone had already shut down a large area of Wanstead Flats and was in the process of organising uniformed officers and community support officers in preparation for a fingertip search. The murder weapon had yet to be found. Local CCTV was being looked at to trace Sanna's movements and those of her killer. Events were moving forward at breakneck speed. And sitting in a Police car in the now blocked-off Lake House Road, was the man who had found the body – Keith Arnold.

It was DI Patel who told Bob where Keith was. He was their only witness, so they were keen to interview him straight away. Mr Arnold did not argue when they suggested going to the Police station, for he knew he hadn't killed anyone, and as for his other activities – well, they were irrelevant. Rather than interviewing Keith in an interview room where the conversation would be recorded, Bob Templeman decided that he and DI Patel would talk to him in his office.

"So you found the body at about 1315 hours – is that correct Mr Arnold?" asked Aanya.

"Yeh, that's right, Miss."

"And you called emergency services straight away."

"Yeh, as soon as I saw she were brown bread, I got on the dog and rang '999'."

128

Templeman was momentarily offended by Keith's use of the cockney rhyming phrase 'brown bread' to mean dead. It seemed to lack respect for his colleague. But he realised that Keith was only using the slang he had been brought up on. Even Bob himself used some of the phrases, often saying 'Let's have a butcher's' meaning butcher's hook – look.

"Just talk us through exactly what happened," requested DI Patel as she reflected on Keith's use of the phrase 'on the dog' to mean on the dog and bone – phone.

Keith proceeded to explain how he had walked through the copse and spotted Sanna's hand and then her body in creeping willow as he left the trees.

"Did you touch the body or disturb anything around it?"

"Nah – no point."

"Tell me, Mr Arnold – why were you walking through the copse at that time?" interjected Bob.

"I was walking from Manor Park to me 'ouse in Forest Gate. It were me lunch break, Guv."

"Where do you work in Manor Park?"

"Park Motors – I'm a mechanic."

"Now that copse is hardly the most direct route to take, is it?"

"Well, it's lovely round there, so it's good to take different routes y'know – it stops them balls from being boring."

"Balls? What do you mean?" interjected Aanya.

"Ball of chalk – walk, Miss. It's slang like."

DI Patel wondered whether Keith's use of 'balls' was a Freudian slip, indicating what he was really doing in the copse! But before she could continue, Bob leaned forward in his chair, looked down intently at his interviewee and said:

"Okay, Mr Arnold. I'm going to level with you, and I want you to level with me. The body that you discovered is that of a Police detective who I was working closely with yesterday, so this crime is going to attract a lot of publicity. It may well end up being the lead story in tonight's Ten O'clock news. The press are going to be crawling all over this and I would not at all be surprised if they took an interest in you as the man who discovered the body next to a copse which we know is a popular place for gay men to meet. This could be very embarrassing for you Mr Arnold and very upsetting for your wife."

" 'Ow d'you know I'm married?"

"Mr Arnold – you may have removed your wedding ring, but where it normally sits on your ring finger, the skin is noticeably a different colour."

Keith had deliberately placed his wedding ring in the small, zipped left-arm pocket of his bomber jacket. In his mind, his marital status was not relevant to his homosexual activities.

"Now, I'm not interested in what you were doing in that copse, Mr Arnold, but I am keen to know who you were with or may have seen, as they are potential witnesses who may have information that could help us catch the killer."

By this stage, Keith was beginning to panic. He found Templeman's height and size intimidating, especially when he leaned forward towards him. He did not want his double life exposed and moreover, he didn't think he had anything useful to tell the Police. A long pause ensued as he tried to work out what to say. Eventually, he came out with:

"I don't want no barney - you wouldn't give me name to the papers, would you?"

"Barney?" asked Aanya

"Barney Rubble – trouble, Miss."

"Of course, we wouldn't give your name to the papers Mr Arnold," responded Templeman, "We try to protect witnesses! But then again, there are ways in which the press can find things out."

Aanya was squirming in her chair. Templeman's veiled threat was something that she knew could cause him problems if it came out. Yet, she understood why he was doing it, and reasoned that Keith had more to lose than Bob.

"Okay, yeh…I was with another geezer in that copse," admitted Keith.

"And what was his name?"

"Umm… I dunno… we didn't swap names… 'e were standing by a tree, I saw 'im, 'e saw me, and then we did what we did."

Templeman put his right hand on his forehead and rubbed it slowly. He did not understand or appreciate how someone could have a sexual encounter with another human being without even knowing their name. Bizarrely, Bob understood murder, rape, fraud and a whole range of other serious crime a lot better than he could comprehend the peccadillos of promiscuous men.

"And then what happened?"

" 'E went out of the copse t'wards Lake 'Ouse Road, Guv, and I went t'wards Dames Road."

"So he didn't witness anything?"

"Nah - couldn't of."

"So were there any other people around?"

"Not in the copse, but I saw a couple of dog walkers free or four hundred yards away – that's all."

"So that was your only visit to the Flats that day?"

"Yeh, apart from my ball to work."

Templeman rubbed his forehead again, thinking that he was wasting his time with Keith, who he found strangely genial despite his obvious flaws. There was, however, one line of questioning left:

"So, Mr Arnold. What time did you walk to work?"

"I left me house at seven thir-ee-five, Sir, and got to work just before eight. It's about twenny minutes."

"Did you see anything unusual this morning on your walk to work?"

"Umm… let me think… yeh, I did!"

"Please explain."

"As I was crossing Middle Road, a jam jar went into the car park and some geezer jumped out. 'E ran across the road and over the Flats."

"In what direction?"

"Sort of t'wards Lake 'Ouse Road."

"In the direction of the copse where you were later?"

"Yeh, sort of."

Templeman felt he was finally getting somewhere. Was it possible that Keith Arnold had found Sanna's body and seen her killer earlier? It would be an unlikely coincidence but not beyond the bounds of possibility.

"Was there anybody else in the car?"

"Nah – think 'e was on 'is Jack Jones."

"Okay – describe this man for me."

"I didn't get a good view of the geezer's boat, but 'e were about five-nine, dark brown Barnet and wearing a grey jacket with blue jeans. That's about it."

"What was his build? Was he slim, medium, large?"

"Normal I'd say - 'e ran pretty quick!"

132

"Did you notice his ethnicity – was he black, white, Asian?"

"Nah, not black. 'E weren't wearing turtles or nuffing and 'is Germans weren't black. Could have been Asian I s'pose or white."

DI Patel was struggling with Keith's cockney rhyming slang. She knew that on his Jack Jones was 'on his own', boat was boatrace - face, and Barnet was Barnet Fair – hair. She guessed that turtles meant turtledoves – gloves. But what were 'Germans'? She could contain herself no longer.

"Sorry, Mr Arnold, you'll have to forgive my ignorance but what are 'Germans?'"

"German bands - 'ands, Miss."

"Perhaps this geezer was just exercising," suggested DCI Templeman, inadvertently adopting Keith's vocabulary.

"Nah, 'e got out of 'is jam jar too quick like, as if he'd seen somefing and wanted to chase it."

"Was he carrying anything?"

"Nah. Didn't see him carry nuffing."

"What sort of car was it?"

"It were a silver BMW 3 series."

"Did you get the number plate?"

"Nah – but it were the fourth model. They were around between 97 and 2006."

"How can you be so precise?" asked DI Patel.

"I told you, Miss – I'm a mechanic – I know all them jam jars."

Aanya felt stupid. For all her psychoanalytic abilities, even she sometimes made rooky errors. Templeman looked briefly amused and then decided to wrap up the proceedings. He thanked Keith for his help and explained how he would need to provide a statement which included both an account of finding the body and what he had seen on his way to work.

"I don't need to mention the other geezer, do I?"

"That's up to you Mr Arnold. Personally, I don't think it's relevant, but we will be looking in that copse for evidence, and I suspect we might find quite a lot of DNA there, including yours!"

Keith gulped and appeared a little panicked. Bob looked out of his office window to see a large group of journalists and camera crews congregating outside the front of the station.

"And when we've finished taking your statement, we'll let you out the back way," concluded Templeman.

After Keith Arnold had left Bob's office accompanied by a uniformed police constable ready to take his statement, Templeman turned to DI Patel and said:

"Right! Go straight over to Middle Road car park and get that CCTV footage. Need the reg. for that BMW pronto."

EIGHTEEN

"The Commissioner is going to make a statement for tonight's news," announced Detective Superintendent Karen Michaels to DCI Templeman as he sat grim-faced in her office, "but we're still going to have to deal with the press outside here and at the murder scene."

"Can you deal with them, Karen - got a lot on my plate with Malik's death and the Chandler case."

"Yes, I was coming to that! I want you to pass the Chandler case over to DI Patel and concentrate on investigating Sanna's murder. It's high profile, desperately tragic and we need to find the killer ASAP. I need my best man on the job, Bob. Whoops! - didn't mean that rhyme!"

Templeman sniggered. Despite, or maybe because of the tragic circumstances, he enjoyed any moment of amusement or light relief that came his way. But he also regretted showing weakness in front of his boss.

"With respect, not prepared to give up the Chandler case. Got a feeling it might be a tough one to crack."

"Mmm – look Bob, as good as you are, you can't do everything, so I'll tell you what – you can choose which one you're going to lead – Malik or Chandler. You decide."

"If I chose Chandler, who'd do the Malik case? As you say - it's high profile."

"I would lead it myself, Bob, but I'd need DI Patel as my deputy and we're getting some guys from Redbridge to help out too. We're stretched as it is."

Templeman thought for a moment. He knew that DSU Michaels was right – he couldn't head up both cases at once. Of course, finding Sanna's killer was a priority for everyone, but there was at least one good reason to continue with the Chandler investigation. His mind was made up.

"DC Malik and I started the Chandler case together. Owe it to her to finish it. But I'd like DS Bebbington as my deputy."

"I thought you'd be asking for DS Featherstone, but I can imagine that would be awkward."

Templeman remained silent.

"Yes, Bob, we've all noticed what's been going on between you two. All I'm going to say is… tread very carefully."

Bob knew that to protest too much would be counterproductive, so he ignored what his boss had said and responded with:

"So is that agreed? You and Patel cover Malik's murder and I'll continue Chandler with Bebbington?"

"Yes, that'll work…. So, I guess I'd better get up to speed with Sanna's murder then."

Templeman proceeded to update DSU Michaels on developments, recounting the interview with Keith Arnold and his description of a possible suspect and vehicle. He explained how he had already sent Aanya Patel over to Middle Road in the hope of identifying the car.

"That's a bloody good start," commented DSU Michaels. "Anything else?"

"Just one thing," replied Templeman.

"What is it?"

"Yesterday, did that press statement out there in front of TV cameras on the Chandler case. The one you asked me to do. Appeared on ITN London News – briefly caught a glimpse of it myself."

"Yes, I saw it – you skillfully managed to say very little indeed."

"Mmm… Yes… and DC Malik was standing next to me - clearly visible in camera shot as well."

136

"Oooh, now that's interesting!"

"Yep! Maybe first time she'd been on TV. Got a hunch someone in the London area who knew her, saw her in that report, and it set something off in their mind."

"Go on…"

"Maybe… they found out where she lived, tracked her down and killed her. As with most murders, reckon she knew her killer."

"So you don't think it was a random attack?"

"No – too frenzied – twenty plus stab wounds. No sign of rape or sexual assault. Suggests a crime of passion – someone who felt strongly about her. And premeditated."

"Do you think it could be an ex-lover?"

"Wounds were deep – suggests a male attacker, and she was married to a woman. Might have a history with men – Laura would know."

"If not an ex-lover or admirer, then who?"

"Close friend or family member – father's deceased so best guess would be brother, uncle or cousin."

"But what would the motive be?"

"With ex-lovers, could be jealousy, rejection, pride or any combination of those. If family, could be her lifestyle. Homosexuality isn't popular with Muslims!"

"So you don't think there's a connection with the Chandler case? Could it have been the same person?" asked Karen.

"Very much doubt that, but you can never rule anything out. Suspect both Chandler and Malik were killed by people they knew, but can't see an obvious connection between them."

"What if Malik had come across the murderer in her investigation of Chandler, and then they had murdered her because she was getting too close to the truth?"

"Unlikely. Frenzied attack – suggests someone she'd known for a long time. In any case – don't think she knew anything more than I did about the Chandler case."

"That sounds reasonable. Anyway, good job, B... I mean... good thinking! Wonder if you're right...Now, I'd better give the press a statement outside and head over there myself."

*****

"Over here, Ma'am!" shouted Police Constable Nick Pond, raising his hand. He was in a line of uniformed officers carrying out the fingertip search of Wanstead Flats initiated an hour earlier. Pond was bent over in long rye grass, fifty metres east of where Sanna Malik's body still lay. He knew what he was looking at, but touching or disturbing it was not an option.

DS Featherstone ran over to him and asked the obvious question:

"What have you got, Nick?"

"It looks like a blood-stained kitchen knife, ma'am."

"Right – don't move, and I'll get forensics over."

After photographing the knife and then carefully putting it in a transparent evidence bag, a forensics expert showed it to Pat Newton who confirmed the possibility that it was the murder weapon.

"The blade certainly looks the right size. It's a brand new Wüsthof 20cm chef's knife – an expensive and very sharp piece of kit" she said, "but I'll need to do further tests with an identical knife if we can find one. Otherwise, I'll have to wait for the DNA and fingerprint evidence to be gleaned from this one."

At that moment, DSU Karen Michaels arrived at the scene to assess the state of the investigation. First of all, she talked to Dr Newton, who briefly showed her the murder weapon in its evidence bag. Pat then led Karen to the cadaver spending some time explaining to her how the wounds on Sanna's body were caused. Dr Newton was already fairly certain the murderer was right-handed given that the majority of the twenty-three wounds were on the left side of the body. Detective Superintendent Michaels had not seen a murder victim for some time, and it had never been part of the job she relished, but she swallowed hard and managed to stay focused and professional throughout.

After seeing Pat Newton, Karen had a word with DS Featherstone who was continuing to direct the fingertip search of the area.

"Well done on finding the murder weapon Flick, and good to see your eye is much better."

The swelling round Flick's right eye had diminished and she had disguised the bruise with carefully applied make-up. DI Featherstone was not in the mood for small talk:

"Thank you, Ma'am. Yes, we think the murderer attacked DC Malik by that copse over there and then headed East towards Middle Road, dropping the knife on their way."

"My thoughts too Flick! Please carry on with your good work and can you tell me where DI Patel is? – I need to talk to her!"

"She's over at the car park the other side of Middle Road, Ma'am."

"Excellent – that's where I hoped she'd be!"

At the car park, DI Patel was excited as she had just managed to access the footage from the CCTV camera going back to 0742 hours that day. She was able to see it all exactly as Keith Arnold had described it to them. The footage showed the BMW 3 Series car coming to a sudden stop and a man in jeans and a grey jacket jumping out quickly. He ran in the direction of Middle Road and then was out of camera shot. What pleased her the most was the fact that she could read the registration plate of the car.

Aanya ran over to a colleague's car and asked the officer inside to search for the name and address of the '05' registered vehicle. Just as Karen Michaels arrived, he handed her a piece of paper with the information she had requested. DI Patel read it open-mouthed.

"Ah, Aanya – just the person I was looking for," said DSU Michaels

"I've got it Ma'am – I've got it!" replied Aanya excitedly.

"I think I know what you're talking about – Bob Templeman filled me in. You've got the name and address for our suspect's car, haven't you?"

"Yes! Here it is!" Aanya passed the scrap of paper to DSU Michaels.

Karen's eyes widened as she read what was written: 'Jafar Malik – 24 St Edmund's Road, Chingford E4 8XT'.

"Malik! Must be a relation – a brother or cousin. Bloody Templeman – I reckon he already had this one solved! No wonder he wanted to stay on the Chandler case!" she exclaimed.

"He is our best detective, Ma'am," stated DI Patel needlessly, for Karen Michaels was already well aware of the fact.

"Quite so. Now Aanya, you go over to that address and nick this Jafar Malik. I'm going to visit Sanna's wife, to see if she can tell us anything about him."

*****

The majority of Newham's CID and uniformed Police officers were working in and around Wanstead Flats, leaving a skeleton staff at Stratford station to deal with other emergencies. So, when Bob Templeman arrived at his 1630 hours briefing for the Chandler case, there were only three colleagues in the incident room. They were sitting round two desks that backed on to each other. The room lacked

140

its normal daytime buzz with so few people occupying it, and those that were present spoke in hushed tones. They were discussing the shocking events that had befallen them, without their normal bravado and laughter.

Fortunately, the three officers that were assembled, happened to be the colleagues Templeman most wanted to see. Bob pulled up a chair and sat down opposite them.

"Know there's not many of us here, but time for our 1630 briefing on the Chandler case," announced Bob.

"I thought the meeting was cancelled, Sir," piped up Detective Constable Richards.

"Didn't officially cancel it, Richards, but, yep, events have overtaken us."

"I thought you'd be down at the Flats, Guv," commented DC Sam Smith.

"I was, but I'm here now," responded Bob.

"So what next?" asked DC Mike Tyrrell.

Templeman could see how lost his colleagues were. Sanna had not been high-profile in the department, but everyone had worked with her and respected her. Losing a fellow officer in such circumstances was a bitter blow for all of them. Bob was upset too, but he knew that introspection would not serve him well at that moment. Yes, he had to recognize the tragedy, but his job was primarily to rally the troops. He did not have a speech prepared but he knew what he wanted to say, and this time he *would* bother with pronouns and verbs:

"Losing one of our own is absolutely dreadful – we're all affected by this. And Sanna Malik was a dedicated officer who left no stone unturned in pursuing a case. I'm confident that our team down at The Flats, led by Karen Michaels, will find Sanna's killer very soon. But DS Malik was working on the Chandler case. She was with us only yesterday doing so, determined to see it through to its conclusion.

141

Therefore, I think that the best tribute we can pay to her, is by continuing the work she started. And that's why I'm here at 16:30 with you guys – to move the investigation forward just as Sanna would have wanted. So, chaps, what have we got on CCTV for that Range Rover and the hooded man?"

There was a short pause as Bob's colleagues digested what he had said. It was DC Sam Smith that spoke first:

"We got the number for the Range Rover from a CCTV camera in Dames Road, Guv. It's registered to a Kyle Price of Northwick Road, Canning Town."

"Okay – good - does Mr Price have form?"

"He certainly does," continued DC Mike Tyrrell, "He served two years for possession and intent to supply Class A drugs. On that occasion he was done for Cocaine and MDMA. He also has a previous conviction for possession and intent to supply a Class B drug – cannabis."

"Looks like Hitchen Road *is* popular with drug dealers, but I don't think Price is a killer – well not directly, anyway. What have we got for hoodie man?

"That was a bit more difficult, Sir," replied DC Richards. "CCTV showed him crossing Dames Road from Wanstead Flats on the way to the murder, and then back the same way after he left Hitchen Road."

"So, he went back into Wanstead Flats after the murder and could have gone anywhere?"

"Yes, but I had a hunch that after murdering Chandler, he might of gone through the flats towards Aldersbrook Road," continued Richards.

"Were you right?"

"Yes – CCTV showed him walking out of The Flats along Aldersbrook Road briefly, and then crossing the street and walking into Dover Road."

"Doesn't that lead to Wanstead Park?"

"It does, Sir. And that's where he went. A CCTV camera in Northumberland Avenue picked him up going into the park."

"Then what?"

"We don't know, Sir. We thought he might of gone through the Park up towards Wanstead tube station or the High Street. That's the most direct route to an underground station. So we checked the CCTV camera in Overton Drive that leads to the station, and the station cameras themselves, but there was no sign of him. He just disappeared."

"Mmm – you mean there was no sign of a six-foot guy wearing a black hoodie and jogging bottoms."

"That's right, Sir."

"But what if he took his hoodie and his jogging bottoms off?" suggested Templeman, "Assume he works in an office and is wearing ordinary trousers and a shirt. He disguises himself by putting a hoodie and joggers on over his work clothes, murders Chandler, walks back across Wanstead Flats and goes into Wanstead Park. He discards the hoodie and jogging bottoms there and casually walks back to work in his work trousers and shirt."

"So we're looking for a man wearing ordinary trousers and a shirt. That could be anyone!" interjected DC Mike Tyrrell

"Not if we can narrow it down to a certain time and place, Tyrrell," responded Bob. "So, chronology – what have we got?"

"Mr Hoodie leaves Hitchen Road at 12:48, crosses Dames Road at 12:50, crosses Alderbrook Road at 13:12 and enters Wanstead Park at 13:16," explains DC Richards.

"How far is it from there to Overton Drive?"

DC Smith was the first to look at Google Maps on his phone and said:

"About three quarters of a mile, Guv - across the Park."

"So, he takes his hoodie and joggers off and probably puts them in a bin or throws them in a bush. Then walks into Overton Drive between 13:30 and 13:40, before going back to the tube station or High Street," suggests Templeman.

"So we need to look at CCTV between those times," concluded DC Tyrrell, frantically scribbling down the relevant details in his notebook.

"Yes, but need to go back in time too, and track his walk to the murder, assuming he took the same route to Hitchen Road. What time did he cross Dames Road before the murder?"

"12.25, Sir. Arrived at Hitchen Road 12:27," replied Bill.

"Right… umm… 40 to 50 minutes back in time gets us to 11:35 to 11.45."

"So we also need to look at CCTV between those two times in Overton Road. He's wearing work trousers and a shirt and coming from the direction of the tube station before going into the park," concluded Smith.

"Yes, and carrying – some sort of bag containing a hoodie and jogging bottoms! Must have put them on in the park, on the way to the murder, and discarded the bag," concluded Templeman.

"That makes sense," commented DC Tyrrell

"It's all we've got chaps! Contact Redbridge Council to find out where they put the park bin rubbish, and get on to the blower to their station to see if they can help out with a ground search – it's their patch. If he's discarded his hoodie and trackie bottoms in the bushes, they'll probably still be there! If we're lucky, we might even find the bag as well! See you all tomorrow, back here at 1500 hours."

NINETEEN

DSU Michaels was relieved that no one had followed her to Vardy Road. Thankfully, the press had not yet encamped themselves outside the house. They knew that a female police detective had been found murdered, but Sanna's name had only just been released. Karen reckoned she had maybe twenty minutes at most before Vardy Road became the focus of much journalistic attention.

Inside the house, DSU Michaels observed that there were an excessive number of people in the property. DCs Amanda Green and Mark Holloway were still there as was a police family liaison officer. Laura's mother had come round to support her daughter and Sanna's brother, Amin, had also turned up after the Police had informed him of his sister's murder an hour earlier. The lounge-diner of the small two-bedroomed maisonette had reached capacity.

In the middle of this congregation was Laura herself - red-eyed, weeping and in shock. She seemed in no fit state to be suddenly exposed to the further bad news that DSU Michaels brought with her. Laura had barely computed the fact that her beloved wife had been murdered. Karen wondered how she was going to broach the subject of Jafar Malik with her, but fortunately she could see another option standing before her – Laura's brother Amin.

Karen quietly beckoned DCs Green and Holloway outside and quickly briefed them on recent developments. They, in turn, informed her of what they had discovered from Laura, her mother and Amin. Karen then sent DC Holloway back to Stratford Police station, explaining to him that he would be needed there to debrief his colleagues. Just by reducing the number of officers at Vardy Road by one, created a little more room for her to manage the situation. She would have moved DC Amanda Green on to other duties as well, but she needed her for the most pressing matter in hand – interviewing Amin Malik.

Sanna's brother was perfectly amenable when Karen asked him to step outside with her and Amanda. DSU Michaels knew that this was going to be a difficult conversation but one that could not be delayed. Fortunately, the small garden belonging to the maisonette, contained some garden furniture and an enclosed area that offered sufficient privacy for the interview to take place.

"Mr Malik – we are very sorry for your loss. Your sister was a talented police detective of whom you must have been very proud," commenced Karen.

"I was proud of her. I can't really believe what's happened – it just makes no sense."

"And DC Green tells me you were such a loving brother to Sanna, that you provided the gift of life that enabled her and Laura to conceive a child."

"Yes, it was something that I wanted to do for them, but now she won't be able to be the great mother I know… oh fuck…sorry…" Amin began the tearful and unrestrained weeping that men succumb to in extreme circumstances. He placed his hands on his face to contain his tears and mute the sound of his distress. Instinctively, Amanda Green leaned forward, put her arms round him and let him cry on her shoulder. It lasted less than a minute, but was the emotional release he needed in order to compose himself.

"I'm sorry – it's just that…"

"… no need to apologise Mr Malik – it's totally understandable how upsetting this is." Karen was struggling with her own emotions as well, but was determined to remain professional.

"Now, I know this isn't a good time to question you, but this investigation is moving at a very fast pace and we do need your help right now Mr Malik," continued DSU Michaels.

"Of course, I will help you in anyway I can, but I'm not sure I will be of any use."

"Well, I just really want to ask you one question: What can you tell me about Jafar Malik?"

"Jafar? My brother?"

"Oh, he's your brother – I thought that might be the case. The thing is Mr Malik: Your brother, Jafar, is our prime suspect for the murder of Sanna."

"But that's impossible!"

"What do you mean?"

"It's impossible – Jafar is dead!"

*****

It was early evening when Bob Templeman finally managed to meet with Lucy Bebbington in his office to discuss the Chandler case. He was keen on getting her up to speed with the investigation.

"Right, Bebbington - need to fill you in on the Chandler case."

"Sorry, can I stop you there," replied Lucy.

"Beg your pardon?" Templeman was perplexed by the detective sergeant's response.

"The thing is DCI Templeman, I'm uncomfortable with you calling me 'Bebbington'. Now, I respect the fact that you are my boss and you like traditional ways, but I prefer a more… uh… twenty-first century form of addressing colleagues. So, seeing as we're going to be working closely together, would it be possible if you could call me Lucy, and I could call you Bob? … at least in private conversations, that is?"

"Umm…. Urr… Yes… of course… didn't mean to offend you." Templeman had not really considered that it might be inappropriate to address junior colleagues by their surname alone. He had been doing it for years because that's how he had been addressed as a young officer himself. In his mind, that's how the Police service worked. Then again, he made an exception for DS Featherstone, calling her Flick. But that was different.

"I know you didn't mean to offend me. And, yes, I am keen to be updated on the case," replied Lucy magnanimously.

Templeman quickly regathered his thoughts and briefed Lucy about the Chandler investigation, right from the beginning up to the most recent developments. At the end of it, DS Bebbington said:

"Okay, so we know of a couple of possible candidates that could be our hooded murderer: Michael Sanders who works with Alice, and Adam Butler who worked with David Chandler. But do we have a motive?"

"No - can only speculate about that. Possible that Alice was having an affair with one of them, and then broke it off. Obsession can lead to extreme behaviour, Lucy."

"But you also said that Sanna suspected David Chandler was having an affair."

"Also possible – may be with one of his colleagues – Charlotte Bagley or Marie Chevalier."

"So, maybe Bob, our hoodie guy is a partner or ex-partner of one of those women. Or perhaps the partner of a more junior female member of staff who wasn't interviewed."

"Yep – that's another possible line of enquiry. But we suspect that our murderer has been to Hitchen Road very recently and removed the syringe from the bathroom cabinet. So, more likely someone close to the family."

"Or perhaps the murderer had been *conspiring* with someone close to Alice and David Chandler," suggested Lucy.

"Indeed! To narrow it down, we need that list of who has been to Hitchen Road recently. Key to solving this is Alice Chandler."

*****

The early evening sun hung low in the sky, creating long menacing shadows across the street. Plane trees were dotted in the pavements at regular intervals, complementing the architectural grandeur of the mostly large Edwardian properties. Several of these had been split up into flats, which provided a lucrative rental income for local property developers. One such rented apartment in the Chingford street, had a brass-numbered '24' on its front door.

Just opposite this flat, parked in the road, was the '05' registered BMW car that had been driven by DC Malik's suspected murderer. A CCTV camera in the street had shown the driver getting out of the vehicle and entering his residence earlier in the day. There was no indication that he had left, so the police were confident that he was still ensconced inside. They had cordoned off the road at both ends and then quietly knocked on all the doors except for the suspect's place. They had asked the inhabitants to remain in their houses out of sight.

As an unusual and nervous calm descended on the street, a police armed response unit prepared to storm 24, St Edmund's Road. Detective Inspector Aanya Patel was crouched behind a plane tree with a pair of binoculars and a police radio, watching from a safe distance. Crouching next to her was DC Steve Cook who had accompanied her to Chingford from Wanstead Flats. Steve was looking on with fascination and not a small amount of glee. This was even better than watching his beloved Rugby Union.

DI Patel was the most senior officer present, so it was up to her to give the instruction to enter the flat. However, being relatively new to such operations, she was happy to be guided by Police Sergeant Simon Russell who was in charge of the armed unit.

The police team had discovered that number 24 was a first floor flat with a ground level entrance facing the street. Inside, opposite the

149

front door, was a small hallway and stairs that led directly up to the apartment. At the back of the property was a first-floor back door, connected to an exterior steel staircase leading down to a communal garden. PS Russell had positioned two armed officers at the back of the building and three at the front, with two further officers holding a ram in order to bash in the lock at the appropriate moment. All members of the unit were wearing full body armour with helmets and bullet-proof visors. The armed officers were carrying Heckler and Koch G36C assault rifles.

"PS Russell – is all your team in position and ready to go?" asked Aanya over the radio.

"Affirmative," responded Simon.

"Okay, proceed at your command," instructed DI Patel, who was extremely nervous but exhilarated by the situation. Aanya loved intellectual problem-solving, but she also enjoyed action on the ground, with its visceral rawness and adrenaline-filled excitement.

Ten seconds later, the ram had smashed through the locked front door of the property, allowing the armed response team to enter the building and swiftly move up the stairs into the suspect's apartment. The officers moved with stealth and precision, covering each other as they entered first the kitchen, then the sitting-dining room, followed by the bathroom and spare bedroom. But it was in the master suite that they found him. He was there, kneeling on his prayer mat and facing South-East in the direction of Mecca. He was dressed in his thawb, the traditional Arabic garment, and on his head was a white taqiyah. He had only recently commenced salat al-maghrib, his early evening prayers.

"Police – hands on your head!" shouted PC Andy Willocks as he and two other officers trained their gun sights on the back of the suspect's cranium. His hands did not have far to go for they were already by his ears as he knelt reciting the traditional refrain commencing with 'Allahu akbar'. The police officers showed no respect for his religious

150

devotion as they unceremoniously grabbed him, pulled him up on his feet, frisked him and cuffed his hands behind his back. They were not going to be gentle with their suspect. Why should they be? In their minds, he was a cop-killer.

TWENTY

"Dead? Your brother Jafar is deceased?" responded Karen Michaels incredulously.

"Yes, he went to Syria in 2014 and fought for Islamic State. He was killed by an American drone strike the following year."

"That must have been very difficult for you, but how was his death confirmed?"

"A friend of his in Syria contacted us and told us about him being killed. Eventually some of his personal effects were returned to us as well."

"What sort of items were returned to you?"

"His wallet with his credit cards, and a metal bangle he wore that had his name inside. It was an eighteenth birthday present – he always wore it."

"Did the authorities ever get in contact or interview you about this?"

"Oh yes! We went to them initially in 2014 and told them of our concerns about Jafar. They traced him to Syria and when I told them we'd heard he was dead, they investigated that as well."

"And did they confirm his death?"

"Well no, not initially, but when we showed them his personal effects, they seemed fairly convinced that he *had* died. It was brutal out there – that's what happened to a lot of them."

"Yes, I can see that. So... um... you've never had official confirmation that Jafar is deceased?"

"No, but getting his bracelet and wallet was confirmation enough, and we haven't heard from him in the last three years."

"Okay, Mr Malik. I'm going to tell you where we are at with your sister's murder investigation, as you certainly deserve an explanation for my line of questioning. The thing is – the suspect that we think killed your sister, drives a car that is registered to a Jafar Malik in Chingford. Now, it could be an amazing coincidence that he shares a name with your deceased brother. But, I think it's considerably more likely that our suspect *is* your brother."

"What!? You're saying my brother is still alive! Surely, it could be someone else, who has stolen his identity."

"That is a possibility as well, but… why would someone who has done that, kill your sister?"

"And why would my brother Jafar kill her? That's crazy!"

"And did you think Jafar was crazy for going to Syria?"

"Yes! Fuck… everything's crazy at the moment." Amin rubbed his eyes with his right hand and wiped away a few tears. That day he had found out that one of his siblings who he thought was alive, was dead. And then discovered that his other sibling who he thought was dead, was alive.

"Now we have to decide how we talk to Laura about this Mr Malik. She needs to know, but we've got to do it in the right way."

Karen proceeded to discuss with Amin how they were going to approach Laura with what was going to be her second big shock of the day. She was relieved that the widow was surrounded by the support she was going to need, yet DS Michaels could not help thinking that the strategic management she normally undertook was a good deal more straightforward than this situation. Being on the ground was maybe more exciting, but she was also aware of just how rusty she had become. Despite consulting with Amin, Karen could not see any way in which she would be able to sugar-coat the news she was about to impart.

153

Tentatively, DSU Michaels re-entered the maisonette, pulled up a dining room chair, and spoke gently to Laura:

"Ms Sullivan, I'm so sorry about your loss. I can't imagine what you're going through."

"It's a nightmare," snivelled Laura, "I can't believe this has happened."

"Indeed - it is a nightmare. You'd known Sanna for quite a long time I understand."

"Yes, we met at a church youth group when we were both nineteen. We just clicked straight away."

"And when did you get married?"

"Three years ago – not long after gay marriage was made legal."

"And Amin here helped you conceive your baby – that must have been a wonderful thing."

"It was…" Laura dissolved into tears and was enfolded in the arms of her mother.

"Now, I'm afraid I need to ask you about another member of the family. I know this might seem strange, but have you seen Sanna's brother, Jafar, recently?"

"No, I thought he was dead. I've never met him and Sanna told me she hadn't seen him for about six years ago."

"Well, I'm really sorry to tell you this, but we would rather this came from us than from the news. The thing is… we think Jafar is alive… and may have killed Sanna…"

*****

Detective Inspector Patel was surprised to see her suspect being brought out of 24 St Edmund's Road dressed in a thawb and taqiyah.

154

The CCTV footage she had seen earlier showed him wearing a grey jacket and blue jeans. She wondered therefore whether the armed response unit had arrested the correct man. As they started leading their detainee to a police van, Aanya decided to intervene:

"Come on Steve, let's get our man."

DI Patel proceeded to march up to PS Russell, closely followed by DC Cook. She thanked Simon for his team's 'excellent work' and said:

"So, have we verified our suspect's identity?"

"Yes, he had on his person a wallet with a driving licence – it's in the name of 'Jafar Malik' and the photo matches his face."

"Great – I'll take him to Stratford then."

"Not in your car, you won't – he'll have to go in a van."

Aanya quickly psychoanalysed PS Russell: He was probably from a dysfunctional family background with an absent or domineering father, she judged. A sense of insecurity and powerlessness as a young child was overcompensated for, by an obsessive controlling nature later on. This in turn meant he was a stickler for rules as they provided clear parameters for attaining the security and control he craved. In short, there was no point arguing with him!

"Of course! Detective Constable Cook will accompany him in the van to Stratford" replied Aanya.

*****

Anaya was in a state of shock and deep in thought as she drove back to Stratford Police Station on her own. She had received a text from Karen Michaels confirming that their suspect was Sanna's brother. She wondered why a brother would kill a sister, and the only thing she could think of, was that it was some sort of 'honour killing.' Yet, she hated that phrase because she could not imagine how killing could ever

155

be honourable. 'It should be called out for what it is – family murder,' she thought to herself.

Aanya's parents came from the North of India and although rare, family murder for cultural reasons, did take place there as well. Aanya had experienced the coercion that families attempted on their children. She was the eldest of three and had resisted a couple of attempts to pressurise her into arranged marriage. She was not against the tradition if the daughter or son were consulted properly, but it was not something to which she was drawn. No, she was quite happy to be single and mostly enjoyed her work as a detective. Today, however, was proving to be one of the most emotionally and professionally challenging days of her career so far.

When Anyaa arrived aback at the station, Jafar Malik had already been brought into the station by DC Steve Cook and was being charged with murdering Sanna Malik 'contrary to common law'. He was photographed, had his DNA and fingerprints taken, and then transferred to an interview room. Having got back from Vardy Road more than an hour earlier, Karen Michaels was keen to talk to the suspect straight away

"Is he co-operating?" she asked DI Patel.

"Yes, Cookie said that Jafar is not insisting on legal representation and apparently says he has nothing to hide."

"Great, this is our chance to interview him before SO15 gets their hands on him."

"SO15 – Counter Terrorism? I thought he was wanted for murder?"

DSU Michaels proceeded to tell DI Patel about her conversation with Amin Malik. Aanya realised then that what they were dealing with was not only a family murderer, but someone who had been radicalised into an extreme form of Islam.

"I think this is going to be weird, so brace yourself!" she exclaimed.

Both detectives prepared themselves mentally, looked at each other nervously, and nodded. Then they entered the room. Jafar Malik was sitting calmy, still wearing his thawb and white taqiyah, and staring aimlessly into space. After cautioning Jafar and introducing themselves and their suspect for the audiovisual recording, DSU Michaels commenced the interview.

"Mr Malik, can you please confirm that you are the brother of Sanna Malik, the victim of today's murder?"

"She has not been my sister for a very long time, but we were born siblings."

"And you have a brother - Amin Malik."

"Yes."

"Is it alright if I call you by your first name?"

"As you wish."

"So, why did you murder Sanna on Wanstead Flats this morning, Jafar?" asked Karen.

DI Patel was a bit taken aback by her colleague's directness. 'She's not hanging around,' thought Aanya, but it was getting late in the evening, so it made sense to keep the interview as short as possible.

"I did not murder her, but she was an apostate and fornicator."

"What do you mean?"

"The qur'an says 'Those who reject Faith after they accepted it, and then go on adding to their defiance of Faith, – never will their repentance be accepted; for they are those who have gone astray.'"

"So are you saying she deserved to die because she no longer followed the Muslim faith?"

"She became a Christian. The prophet – peace be upon him – said 'whoever changes his religion, execute him.'"

"And you said she was a fornicator as well. What do you mean by that?"

"The prophet – peace be upon him – said that if a woman has sexual relations with another woman, then they are both guilty of zina."

"Zina? Could you explain that for me, please?"

"That is fornication."

"Okay, so why now? Why kill her now?"

"I received a sign."

"A sign?"

"The Qur'an says 'Praise be to Allah. He will show you His Signs and you will recognize them.'"

"What sort of sign?"

"A sign that I had to submit to the will of Allah."

"And punish Sanna for being an apostate and fornicator?"

"Yes, Islam means submission to the will of Allah. That is the purpose of my life, but Sanna had gone astray. She no longer followed the righteous path. There is no greater sin than apostacy."

"What about murder, Jafar, isn't murder worse than apostacy?" Karen Michaels was struggling to stay calm whilst she had to listen to the twisted religious logic of the man before her.

"I did not murder her – I was following the will of Allah and fulfilling the words of the prophet Muhammed – peace be upon him – that an apostate is executed."

Sensing that her colleague was about to lose her temper, DI Patel decided to intervene:

"Jafar, you stabbed Sanna 23 times round her head, neck and chest. How can that be the will of Allah?"

For the first time, Aanya could see a flicker of human weakness in Jafar Malik's eyes.

"I do not recall that many, but, yes, I executed the apostate according to the will of Allah."

Karen was relieved that Jafar had confessed, but angry that he was not able to see the depravity of his actions. DSU Michaels wished that she had the photos of Sanna's mutilated body to shove in Jafar Malik's face. But she tried to control her emotions and changed tack:

"Tell me Jafar, which mosque do you attend?"

"Al Salam Mosque in Godfrey Avenue"

"That's in Edmonton isn't it?"

"It is."

"And do they know that you were in Syria"

"You have been talking to Amin."

"Yes, he thought you had been killed in Syria. I'm surprised you, yourself, have not converted to Christianity, seeing as you seem to be resurrected from the dead."

Ignoring Karen's sarcasm, Jafar replied, "I do not wish to talk about this."

"You fought for Islamic State in Syria, didn't you Jafar?"

"No comment."

"You killed other innocent people there as well, didn't you?"

"No comment."

"Is that where you learnt to stab people to death?"

"No comment."

DI Patel could see that Karen's anger was real and in danger of making her say or do something that she would regret later. She had a vision of DSU Michaels suddenly getting up and trying to slap some sense into Jafar, who was clearly a religious extremist. She decided to intervene before things got out of hand:

"You've got a lot of questions to answer haven't you, Jafar?"

"No comment."

"But we seem to have gone as far as we can with you today, so we will now contact the Crime Prosecution Service. I anticipate, that you will be charged with the murder of your sister and appear in court tomorrow."

Jafar Malik was led away while the two detectives momentarily sat in their chairs stunned, and in silence.

"This job never fails to amaze me," commented DSU Michaels.

"Yes, it's been a very tough day," replied DI Patel.

"So what do you think, Aanya?"

"Would you like a theological or psychological assessment?"

"I didn't know you were an Islamic scholar."

"I'm not, but I did study a module on the psychology of religion as part of my degree and have read widely about Islam.

"Okay, – give me the religious assessment."

"As far as I can make out, he's being very selective in his interpretation of the Muslim faith."

"Go on, Aanya - I'm interested."

"Well, when he says Muhammed told people to execute apostates, that's not something that is in the Qur'an and we can't be sure that it's supposed to be taken literally. It's in the Hadith which is a collection of discourses from Muslim authoritative figures who lived many years after the prophet. Of course, apostacy, is seen as a serious sin in Islam, but a lot of more liberal Muslim scholars would argue that people will be judged in the next life for their lapse in faith and it's not for us to judge them and then kill them."

"Okay – what about lesbianism. What's the Muslim view on that?"

"Well, the Qur'an doesn't talk about Lesbianism and his quote about it being zina – fornication – is also in the Hadith. It is regarded as Haram – a forbidden act – by most Muslims, but generally seen as less serious than gay sex. To be honest, just like with Christians, homophobia amongst Muslims is not just to do with theology but with socially conservative attitudes generally."

"In other words, he was taking the most extreme possible interpretation of the Muslim faith!"

"Yes."

"So, what did you make of him psychologically, Aanya?"

"Well, it's a bit beyond me to be honest. He needs to be assessed by a clinical psychologist which is not my expertise. He obviously has mental health issues and has been brain-washed. He certainly needs to follow a deradicalisation programme. It could also be that he is suffering from a form of dissociative amnesia as he could not recall stabbing Sanna twenty-three times. Frankly, we… umm… or rather, he, needs professional help."

"Mmm, yes…. I'm sure he will be assessed by a clinical psychologist – the defence will make sure of that. And maybe he does have a diagnosable mental illness. But my fear is, that he will get away with manslaughter by reason of diminished responsibility. So, we do need to hand him over to SO15 to see what they can charge him with. If he can be shown to be a threat to national security as well, they'll never let him see the light of day."

"So where do we go with the investigation, Ma'am?"

"That's a good question. We need to get a team down to Al Salam Mosque to find out what they have to say. It could be that there are others involved. Let's track his movements for the last couple of weeks and interview all his known associates, including his family. I want to make sure there are no other cop killers out there connected to Jafar Malik."

TWENTY-ONE

At twenty past ten that evening, Bob Templeman sat in his office finishing off some paperwork. He was tired, sad, stressed, and more than ready to finish work. Some of his colleagues had gone to a local pub to drown their sorrows after what had been a tumultuous day for Newham Police. Other members of staff had gone home in search of succour from their families. As Bob looked out of his office window, he could see The Shard on the south bank lit up like a glass Christmas tree, dwarfing The Gherkin and Walkie Talkie north of the river. He looked directly down and was struck by how quiet it was outside the station. Only a few cars were parked in the bays, including his blue Renault Dauphine that always looked incongruous next to modern vehicles. And the journalists that had been encamped at the front earlier, were now gone. He imagined they had moved on to Vardy Road instead.

There were not many colleagues left inside the building either, apart from the night staff that manned the desk and cells downstairs. But, with his office door open, Bob caught a glimpse of Flick Featherstone walk by in the dimly lit corridor. Before he knew it, he had got out of his chair and was standing at the threshold beckoning her:

"Flick – fancy a chat," he said.

DS Featherstone had noticed he was in his office, but she was still smarting a little from the way he had wound her up in the morning. When he spoke, however, she turned round to see his face devoid of its normal vivacity. There was something different about him tonight in the half-light – his boyish grin was replaced by a sad puppy-like stare. Gone was his normal swagger and he appeared somehow smaller – diminished by the weight of events. Flick was not someone who bore grudges for long, so sensing his vulnerability, her heart melted. She responded to his call:

163

"Yeh, okay – it's been a tough day for all of us."

Bob slowly sat back down in his desk chair and Flick gingerly entered his office, shutting the door behind her. She sat down, facing him in the same chair that she had occupied that morning. Only Templeman's desk separated them. They looked at each other with sad, tired eyes, their faces etched with melancholy. A brief, but intimate moment of empathy was shared, so intense that Flick had to look away to stop herself from bursting into tears.

"Sometimes, this job is just too much Flick," said Bob ruefully.

"I know," she replied.

"I mean…it's fun… love the cut and thrust of it…wouldn't know what else to do… but when shit happens, shit really does happen."

"Yes, it really hit the fan today. Sanna was here yesterday, part of the team, and now she's gone – just like that! It's a hell of a shock for everyone, and terrible for her wife and family."

"How did you cope Flick – when your husband died?"

Flick was not expecting this question, but she could see that Templeman was preoccupied with grief, something she had too much experience of for a person of her age. She rarely talked about Martin, but she loved and trusted Bob, so did not want to hold back from him.

"I didn't cope. I immersed myself in work. I drank. I socialised with friends, and had flings. I did everything I possibly could, to avoid the pain and guilt that I felt, because it was too much to face up to."

"Guilt? Why did you feel guilty?"

"I loved Martin, but it was tough when he got ill. I was unfaithful to him, I said nasty things to him, I wasn't patient enough with him. I wasn't good enough. I should have been better."

"You mean, you felt guilty for being human, for being fallible like the rest of us."

"Yes, that's exactly what I came to understand after two years of counselling."

"Didn't you have any support from your friends and family during that time?"

"I did. Lucy kept me going. She supported me throughout, but grief is a lonely place, Bob, especially when it's your other half. They're part of you, and when they go, a part of you goes with them."

"Gosh – you talk so poignantly… I have much to learn..."

Flick felt closer at that moment to Bob than at any other time. She was seeing a different Templeman to the expert, patronising sleuth and arrogant piss-taker that she had witnessed earlier. She had caught glimpses of this more sensitive, humble and vulnerable Bob during their 'quiet ones' in The King's Arms, but their conversation had never before reached this level of intimacy. It was therefore natural, rather than affected, when she asked Bob:

"And how did you cope when your marriage ended?"

"That was different," he replied.

"Was it? It was another form of loss. Grief takes many different guises you know."

"True, but it was less final. Emily's still alive, I think, although I don't have contact with her anymore."

"So, if you don't have contact with her anymore – it is final! – at least for you, Bob."

"Yes, I see what you're saying. Looking back there was grief, and certainly guilt for the way I treated her. And anger at the way she behaved. So, in the end, the overwhelming feeling was one of relief!"

"Oh, there's always relief. I watched Martin die over a three-week period and it wasn't pretty. It was certainly a relief when he finally passed away – relief that his suffering was over and relief that I didn't have to watch him suffer. But the pain of loss was intense. I still miss him so much…"

Flick started weeping, putting her hands over her eyes and face, in an attempt to contain her tears and hide her quivering mouth. Bob grabbed a handful of tissues from the box that he routinely kept on his desk and came round to her. He gently placed the tissues in her grasp with his right hand, and rubbed her shoulder with his left.

"Sorry, Bob, I'm just…"

"…It's okay… it's okay."

Flick wiped her eyes and mouth clean with the tissues and then turned her head upwards to look at his handsome face, whilst he massaged the top of her back. At that moment, they both knew in which direction the situation was going but neither of them wanted to draw back.

She gripped his left arm and gently, but firmly, pulled him down towards her as both of them stared intently at each other. Bob had to bend his tall frame a long way to reach her face. Finally, their lips met. They shared a long passionate kiss that contained all the intensity of the day and the desire they felt for one another. Their bodies automatically responded to the stimulus. Bob could do nothing to stop the erection that he knew was causing a protrusion in his suit trousers, and Flick sensed a growing warmth spread inside her vagina. She instinctively felt for his bulge, massaging it slowly. She then stood up, unzipped his flies, put her right hand inside his briefs, and enveloped his phallus. In response, he undid the buttons of her blouse and slid his right hand inside her bra to feel her ample left breast. The nipple automatically hardened to his touch.

Nothing was said between them as they quickly slid off their shoes and removed their trousers and underpants. Flick propped herself on the edge of the desk, grabbed Bob's buttocks with both hands and pulled him towards her until his erect penis had found its desired destination. She rubbed her clitoris with her right hand to intensify the pleasure whilst his thrusts inside her become harder and more frequent. Their desire for each other was overwhelming, and their intercourse all the more pleasurable for its danger. It was not long before they experienced intense simultaneous orgasms. Yet both suppressed the cries of ecstasy, which would have given themselves away.

Afterwards, they dressed swiftly. Then he wrapped his long arms around her in a gentle embrace, as they stood in his half-lit office. Bob felt the stresses of the day fall away like curtains dropping from a magician's vanishing box. Flick experienced a profound contentedness in the gentle, protective strength of the giant man. It was as if they had finally come home to port after a long voyage at sea.

And then reality suddenly kicked in! Bob needed to sleep in order to gain strength for the following day, but he feared that Sue would smell the scent of his infidelity. But he had to go home, otherwise it would arouse Sue's suspicions. And if he went to Flick's place, he knew they would repeat their love-making to such an extent, that they would both be completely useless in the morning. In his heart, he knew his future lay with Flick, but he could not suddenly abandon Sue. It would have to be a managed retreat; done as humanely as possible.

He resolved to go home, remove his suit and put it in the boot of his Renault Dauphine (which was actually the bonnet as the engine was in the boot. He would drop his suit off at the dry cleaners in the morning). He would then have a shower and slip into bed next to Sue. Bob had previously been unfaithful to Emily, so he knew that the worst part of an affair was deceit. The sex was great, but having to lie to one's partner was soul-destroying. As Bob thought through his plan, he felt as if he had become one of the criminals he loved to thwart. And moreover, it all depended on Sue having gone to bed at her normal time. She hadn't!

*****

Flick was happy as she drove back to her flat after her liaison with Bob. She understood why he had to go home to his long-standing partner that night, but she was now convinced that she had her man. There was no way she was going to let him slip out of her grasp. And their sex had been great, so great that just the thought of it made her want to masturbate.

But then reality kicked in. Flick suddenly felt guilty for her happiness as she remembered that one of her colleagues had been brutally murdered earlier in the day. And what if Bob just used her as a fuck-buddy whilst going home every night to Sue. Flick knew that this would send her spiralling once again into a state of depression. It would be another bereavement and a blow to her confidence, that she feared she would not survive.

And then there was the work dimension. If anyone found out that she and Bob had shagged in his office, they could both end up being disciplined or sacked and the last thing she wanted was for Bob to lose his job. It was, from a disciplinary perspective, 'gross misconduct' although in her mind it was 'fucking amazing misconduct'! Yes, tonight had been wonderful, but she could not stop doubt and insecurity invading her happiness.

When Flick finally got home to her one-bedroomed apartment in Canary Wharf, tiredness hit her. The adrenaline that had kept her going during the day, and the oxytocin that had surged through her during love-making, had both subsided. She had done enough thinking for the day. She had a quick shower, changed into her night t-shirt and slid under the duvet of her king-size bed. She was so knackered that it was not long before she fell soundly asleep. Twenty minutes later she was awoken by her mobile phone ringing.

*****

When Bob parked his Renault Dauphine outside his three-bedroom 1930's semi in Loughton, he felt nervous. He was nervous because everything had changed that evening and he knew there was no going back to normalcy at home. He was nervous because he feared that the ever-perceptive Sue would spot his infidelity straight away. And he was nervous because he feared that if she did not, she would want him to make love to her so soon after his intercourse with Flick.

He got out of his car, walked the few paces to his front door and turned the key in the lock. He let himself into the house as quietly as he could so as not to wake her up. He was about to take his suit jacket off when Sue suddenly emerged from the kitchen and approached him.

"Oh Bertie – you must have had a dreadful day. I saw it all on the News!" she exclaimed. Bob never told his colleagues that Sue called him Bertie. It was an affectionate diminutive of his name, but one that he feared would bring him derision at work.

"Yes, it's been a real shitfest today," he replied.

Sue embraced him lovingly and put the side of her head gently on his chest. She could feel his heart beating abnormally quickly.

"It's good to have you home, Ber… hang on a sec… is that women's perfume I can smell on you?!"

Sue stepped back from him and looked up at his face. Bob tried to affect a half-smile as if nothing was wrong and he was glad to see her.

"No, no, that's just something we were playing around with at work today."

"Don't lie to me Robert. You've been with a woman – you've fucked someone, haven't you?! It's written all over your face, and you smell of sex."

Bob knew then that the game was up. Despite being a brilliant detective, he was a lousy liar. At that moment, he realised why he was in the police and not part of a criminal gang.

"Umm… ur… okay… yeh… I have"

"And do you love her?"

"Mmm… ur…. maybe… I don't know."

"GET OUT. GET THE FUCK OUT OF MY HOUSE!" shouted Sue.

Bob was taken aback by the sudden anger of his partner. She was a life coach and normally so laid back. He had never seen her so irate, but then again, he had never before been unfaithful to her. He knew he could not leave the house immediately for he needed his tooth brush and clothes for work. So he had to try to manage the situation in order to buy some time.

"I'm really sorry Sue," he said in a futile attempt to placate her anger.

"SORRY! Sorry doesn't cut it! I knew there was someone else – I knew it! Now, fuck off back to your whore!"

"Okay, I just need to go upstairs and pack a few things," he replied awkwardly.

"Right – you've got five minutes, Fuckface!"

In just a minute Bob had gone from being 'Bertie' to 'Fuckface'. That summed it all up in his mind.

Sue marched into the sitting room, banged the door shut and as Bob began to climb the stairs, he could hear her crying loudly. He knew this was his opportunity to go to her, to plead with her; to tell her he hadn't meant it – it was just a moment of weakness. He could tell her how much she meant to him, and that he didn't want to split up. Halfway up to the first-floor landing, he stopped. It was painful to hear Sue weep – it made him feel like a bastard, a cad. He felt dreadful.

Yet his mind was made up. His desire for Flick trumped all that he had shared with Sue over six years. All the laughs and the tenderness, all that they had done to make a home together. All of it faded into insignificance compared to what he felt for the widowed Flick

Featherstone. And he knew he had to choose Flick because she needed him most. Sue would suffer for a while, but she was strong and independent. In a year, she would have moved on. But that evening, he had been touched by Flick's vulnerability and her backstory of grief. The depth of their connection and the intensity of their lovemaking had won the day.

Bob went to the master bedroom, took his suitcase out of the walk-in cupboard and quickly packed enough clothes to last a week. It took more than five minutes, but within ten he had left the house that he and Sue had bought in Loughton more than four years ago. Bob thew his luggage into his Renault Dauphine, fired up the engine, drove half a mile down the road and stopped. Then he took his mobile out to phone his lover.

"She's chucked you out, hasn't she," commenced Flick before he could say anything.

"Yes."

"Well my address is…"

"… it's alright Flick, I know your address."

"Good! I'll see you very soon then."

FRIDAY

TWENTY-TWO

The next morning, Bob and Flick agreed that they would leave for work at different times and in their own separate cars. Bob joked that as they were now living and working together, they should be making more of an effort to save the planet. But it was certainly not the right time to go public with their relationship.

The two lovers were deliriously happy together, and completely exhausted, after a night of very little sleep but plenty of physical exercise. Bob's only irritation with staying at Flick's apartment, was the cost of underground parking in Canary Wharf for his Renault Dauphine. He resolved to work out a way of continuing to drive the car to Stratford Police Station, without having to keep it in such an extortionate location.

Templeman was the first to leave the flat and was pleasantly surprised to find that his drive to work was seven minutes faster than from his house in Loughton. Despite his tiredness, he felt motivated to move further forward with the Chandler case. He had a feeling that today would be a productive one. Yes, he was exhausted, but with plenty of coffee and the stimulation of problem-solving, he would get through the day. In any case, it was Friday, and tomorrow was a day off. If required, he would go in to work on Saturday, but he would try his best to ensure that he and Flick had a leisurely and intimate lie-in.

Templeman's first task of the day, as always, was to check his emails on his work laptop. He opened his account and started his routine deletion of subscription messages. It would have been quicker in the long run to just unsubscribe from the organisations that contacted him, but like most people, he had an addiction to the waste paper bin icon. Finally, he found an important message; Alice Chandler had emailed him the information that he sought on recent visitors to her house. He opened it immediately and printed out half a dozen copies of the email on his Hewlett Packard laser printer. He picked up the top one, and read it very carefully:

Dear Bob,

Here's a list of all the visitors to 15, Hitchen Road for the three-month period from Monday 17th July to Monday 16th October. I have included all people who came into the house at that time apart from David and me:

Sunday 23rd July: Sophie Chandler round for lunch.

Thursday 27th July: Alan Colston from AJC Plumbing to fix a leaking tap. Stayed one hour.

Friday 4th August: James and Claire Edwards stayed for weekend (friends of David).

Sunday 13th August: Simon and Karen Bennett round for lunch.

Sunday 20th August: Sophie Chandler for lunch.

Saturday 26th August: Simon and Karen Bennett came back for cup of coffee after the four of us had lunch in Wanstead.

Between Saturday 2nd September and Saturday 9th September, David and I were on holiday in Cephalonia, Greece. Simon and Karen have a key to the house but tell me they didn't go round.

Friday 15th Sept.   Adam Butler came back to the house after going out for Friday night drinks with David.

Sunday 17th Sept.   Sophie Chandler for lunch.

Sunday 1st October: Simon and Karen Bennet for lunch.

Sunday 8th October: Adam Butler round for lunch.

Below, you will find my contact details if you have any further questions.

Kind regards, Alice Chandler

Bob found the document interesting. He knew that David and his deputy, Adam Butler, worked closely together from having read their communications on WhatsApp. He had accessed these on Chandler's phone. Bob did not know, however, that they socialised together in their private lives and that Alice also knew him. Adam Butler had just become a person of extreme interest. But Bob needed more. He required feedback from the digital forensics team about Butler's use of social media and he needed to talk to DCs Green and Holloway in more depth about their interview of Butler. He also wanted to find out if they had discovered anything about his other main suspect, Michael Sanders. Bob picked up his mobile phone and rang Lucy Bebbington. He explained the new development and asked her to set up a meeting urgently.

Immediately after finishing his call, Bob heard a knock on his office door and then the 'click' of the handle, as someone entered without his permission. He looked up to see Karen Michaels standing the other side of his desk. The detective superintendent stood there for a short moment with a surprised expression on her face. Then, while sitting down opposite him, she said:

"Morning Bob – you were right, you know."

"Yes, I heard. You've arrested Sanna's brother and he confessed to killing her."

"Yep – just had a phone call from The Commissioner. She's mightily relieved and impressed that we caught him so quickly. And I put a good word in for you, Bob. I told her it was thanks to an interview that you conducted with a witness. She sends her congratulations."

Bob was completely indifferent to what The Commissioner thought. Unlike Karen, he had no ambitions to advance any further up the greasy pole. The idea of being a pen-pusher and politician did not

175

appeal to him at all. In his mind, he was already required to do more than enough paperwork and man-management.

"Thanks Karen – good to know she's pleased," he replied, as his eyes twitched with tiredness.

"And we've now referred Jafar Malik to SO15. He's being transported to Paddington Green as we speak. I don't like that place – there's something a bit sinister about it, but they seem to do a good job. There's a rumour going round that they're going to close it soon."

Bob was sort of half-listening to Karen. He could tell she was energised and in a good mood after her call from the Commissioner, but he was exhausted, and not particularly interested in what she was saying. His mind wandered to an image of the fellatio that Flick had performed on him at 2am in the morning.

"Are you alright Bob?" asked Karen.

"Yeh... fine," replied Templeman.

"It's just that you look really tired this morning. I don't suppose it has anything to do with the... ur... pair of black women's underpants lying underneath your desk."

Bob's eyes widened in shock and before he knew it, he had bent down to look under the table. There they were - Flick's black knickers - lying under his desk where she had discarded them the night before. 'Shit!', he thought. He grabbed them, and hurriedly stuffed them in the right-hand pocket of his jacket. Karen could not contain her laughter as she said:

"I've seen it all now! But seriously, Bob, are you mad?"

"Well... ur... maybe... it's sort of... um...complicated. It was a one-off. It certainly won't happen again."

"Right, Bob. This stays just between us. Officially, I didn't see that item underneath your desk, and I don't need to know how it got there. However, I *am* going to make a suggestion."

Bob was completely blindsided and highly embarrassed! He had put himself in a very vulnerable situation and was now reliant on the charity of his superior officer. The only thing he could do, was be compliant.

"Open to any suggestions you might have," he replied.

"I think it would be best if DS Featherstone asked for a transfer to Redbridge. I hear they're looking for a good detective sergeant."

Bob knew that Karen did not want to lose him, and given a choice, she would much rather see Flick transferred. He was also aware that it was not kindness that motivated his boss, but the fact that his success as a senior detective was beneficial to her. And, of course, DSU Michaels was right. His relationship with Flick did create a conflict of interests that would best be resolved by a transfer. Yet of one thing he was sure – Flick's future could only be decided by Flick.

"Okay – I'll level with you. Yes, I am in a relationship with DS Featherstone and agree that one of us needs to be transferred to another borough. But I cannot make decisions on Flick's behalf. I'm not the person you need to be talking to, unless of course, you want *me* to put in for a transfer."

Karen paused for a moment, before saying:

"This can wait 'til Monday. I'll have a chat with Flick then. In the meantime, perhaps you can find out for yourself what she wants to do."

"Fair enough," replied Bob.

"Right – I'll let you get on with your work. By the way, I've handed over the Malik case to DI Patel to complete. There's still plenty of evidence gathering to do, so she'll be coordinating that… Oh yes…and one more thing… how come you didn't see that item under your desk when you came in this morning? – you're normally so observant!"

"Height, Karen. You came in and saw it straight away. I noticed your look of surprise as you entered. But you spotted it only because you

177

are a foot shorter than me, which allowed your angle of vision to see further under the table than mine."

Karen nodded, bade farewell, and left. After she had gone, Bob retrieved Flick's underpants from his jacket pocket, put them against his nose, and deeply inhaled the scent of his lover. He then placed them in the top drawer of a filing cabinet.

*****

"Right, Chapman, let's start with Michael Sanders. What have you got on his social media use?"

Templeman had convened his urgent meeting to discuss the latest development in the Chandler case. Jim Chapman was Head of Digital Forensics. A typical geek, he was slightly overweight, had long hair and glasses, and wore an old check jacket with leather patches sewn on to the elbows. What he lacked in sartorial elegance, he made up for in outstanding computer skills.

"Nothing, I'm afraid. Sanders seems to be quite a private guy. He doesn't have Facebook, Instagram or LinkedIn Accounts. Of course, he may be using a pseudonym, but I looked at possible contacts of his and could not find any links back to him."

"Mmm…interesting…that's unusual. And he says he was seeing business clients on Monday. I asked DI Patel to chase this up, but she's now working on the Malik case. DS Bebbington – can you look into that, please?"

"Of course - I'll do that this afternoon."

"Let's move on to Adam Butler. What have you got on him, Chapman?"

Jim had with him, a record of Butler's social media use, which he had written down on an iPad. He pressed on the screen and started reading out from his notes:

"Adam Butler has Facebook, Twitter, Instagram and LinkedIn Accounts. He hasn't used his Twitter account for two months, his Instagram for five months and his LinkedIn for nineteen months. However, he is a regular user of Facebook. I managed to get into his account and found out that he is forty-one years old, has a birthday on the 8th of August and lives in Snaresbrook. His posts on Facebook are fairly uninteresting – a couple of selfies in the last year, a few jokes, some references to Quentin Tarantino films and the football team he supports – West Ham. There are several photos in his account. I printed off one of them, so you can see what he looks like."

Jim proceeded to hand round copies of a full-length photo of Adam with his arm around what appeared to be his female partner. Chapman explained how the photo was tagged with a location of Leyton Flats, near to Butler's home in Snaresbrook.

"Certainly looks about six foot. He can give his girlfriend six inches," said Templeman.

"I'm sure he can!" commented Lucy as everyone laughed. Bob rolled his eyes and slapped his head with his right hand, wondering whether his Freudian slip was due to his own recent sexual exploits.

Jim Chapman continued with his analysis:

"I also looked at his 'sent' and 'received' messages on Facebook messenger. There weren't any recent ones, and nothing of interest in his archived messages. I'm guessing he uses WhatsApp instead. I then looked at his search history on Facebook – that's usually a good indication of people's interests. I found out that he had recently searched three female friends' accounts, including Alice Chandler's. Interestingly, they were all young. The other two were Sarah Brideswell, aged 25, and Lauren Charles, aged 19. There was no evidence that he had searched his male friends' accounts recently. The most searched for person was the nineteen-year-old. He is in a relationship with a forty-year-old librarian called Janet Ashworth, but there's no record of him searching for her Facebook account or liking any of her posts for the last four months. As for 'likes', he tends to 'like' a variety of things, especially other people's jokes, comments about West Ham and posts made in his old school's Facebook page. He has liked the last three posts by Alice Chandler. She's not a frequent user of the platform – only made five posts in the last twelve months. He has also liked eleven posts by the twenty-five-year-old and a whopping thirty-seven by the nineteen-year-old. That's about it."

"Okay – comments please!" said Templeman.

"So, I guess we can conclude that he likes nineteen-year-old females but not forty-year-olds," suggested DS Bebbington.

Once again, everyone laughed at Lucy's quick wit. Bob realised that his colleague's brain was working a good deal faster than his that day.

"Yes, it's strange that a nineteen-year-old uses Facebook so much - most of them seem to be more into Instagram and Snapchat," commented DC Amanda Green.

"There doesn't seem to be anything particularly incriminating there," observed DC Mark Holloway.

Templeman reflected for a moment and then said:

"Mmm, yes. You're right Holloway. Nothing incriminating on social media. But you and Green interviewed him. Did he mention anything about socialising with David Chandler or even going to his house?"

"No, Sir, he didn't," replied Amanda, "He did, however, say that he liked David and that he would be missed. I got the impression they got on really well. He seemed very upset by his death. With hindsight, we should have asked about whether he had been to the Chandler's house, but we didn't."

"No worries, Green. Also asked you to do some observation of Butler. Did you manage that?"

"No Sir," interjected Mark, "we both got caught up in DC Malik's murder, so that didn't happen."

"That's understandable. Now, you've all had a few minutes to look at the email from Alice Chandler. Any comments?"

"Two things, Sir," replied Amanda, "Firstly, what do we know about James and Claire Edwards who stayed the weekend with the Chandlers? And secondly, on the 8th of October, Butler went for Sunday lunch with them on his own. Why didn't his girlfriend go with him?"

"Very good questions, Green. Need to do some covert following of Butler. Get that video of him walking. And Chapman - you need to check social media of the Edwards couple. I'll ring Alice Chandler, to ask her about Butler's girlfriend. So, that's it then."

"Not quite, DCI Templeman," interjected Jim Chapman.

"There's more?"

"Yes, I've kept the best until last."

Chapman suddenly had everyone's attention.

"I was also asked to look at the social media activity of two other colleagues of David Chandler's – Marie Chevalier and Charlotte Bagley."

Everyone stared intently at Adam, whilst he proceeded to explain:

"As regards Marie Chevalier, I didn't discover anything of particular significance, but it was a different story when it came to Charlotte Bagley. I won't bore you with all her 'likes' and posts on Facebook, but Messenger was… um… a lot more revealing. I've printed all the relevant messages off for you – there's quite a few pages of them, but I think I got them all."

Jim Chapman opened an A4 folder and passed round to each of the four detectives, six pages of messages that had been shared between Charlotte Bagley and David Chandler. Nobody said a word as they avidly read the contents of each message. She had a nickname for him – 'Washy' and he had a nickname for her - 'Bagels'. Their messages were always affectionate, invariably funny and sometimes explicit. As they scanned through the content, all that could be heard was the rustling of paper. There was an awkwardness about their voyeurism, especially as they were reading the words of a ghost and a young woman so evidently connected to him. But they were detectives, and their job was evidence gathering. And contained in these six pages was more than enough proof that Charlotte Bagley and David Chandler had conducted an affair. This time, Lucy Bebbington did not crack a joke.

"How come none of this was on his mobile phone, Chapman?" asked Templeman.

"David Chandler didn't have a Facebook account, but I'm assuming he had downloaded the Messenger App on to his phone using his mobile number. The last message between him and Charlotte was six week ago, after which he must have deleted the App. We could have easily retrieved the App and his messages if he had backed up his phone properly, but he hadn't. Nevertheless, we could have still found everything if we had dug deep enough, but that would have taken time, and you would need to know what you're looking for."

"Why does she call him 'Washy'?" mused DC Holloway.

"I don't know," replied Chapman.

"A reference to his initials, I imagine" commented Bob. "He's DC which is short for Washington DC, so hence 'Washy'"

"And Bagels must be a corruption of Bagley," added Lucy.

"Certainly makes things more interesting – good work Chapman," announced Templeman. "Think we'll be taking a trip down to Canary Wharf; to interview Miss Bagley."

TWENTY-THREE

At 1.12pm, Detective Sergeants Bebbington and Featherstone were both drinking lunchtime cappuccinos in 'Alessandro's' coffee shop, just a couple of hundred metres from Stratford Police Station. When Alessandro, the owner and manager, was present, their cappuccinos would be complimentary as he knew what the two detectives did for a living. However, on this occasion, he was not, so the plainclothes officers retained their anonymity and paid for their beverages. It was a distinct disadvantage of working in CID. Uniformed officers could enter numerous establishments and be provided with free food and drink in each one. On the other hand, plainclothes police generally had to pay for everything, and could only claim expenses if they were on an undercover job.

As Lucy sipped her cappuccino, she wondered whether there was anywhere else in London that could match the quality of Alessandro's coffee. It was imported directly from Italy, and brewed to a specific method that Alessandro carefully trained his baristas to reproduce each time.

Lucy also reflected on how unusually quiet Flick was. Normally, their conversation flowed liberally like the Sauvignon Blanc that they drank at Jerry's wine bar. But, this afternoon, not only did her friend seem distracted, but her eyes were full of fatigue.

"You look knackered, Flick – didn't you sleep last night?"

"I'm fine, Luce," replied Flick yawning, "Just found it hard sleeping after all the trauma of yesterday. Such a waste…"

"Yeh, it's always grim losing one of our own. I think Bob Templeman had trouble sleeping last night as well – he looked really fucked when I saw him this morning."

Flick said nothing in response to Lucy, which seemed odd to DS Bebbington as normally the mere mention of Bob elicited some sort of response from her friend. And it was simply this - Flick's silence after the mention of Templeman - that aroused Lucy's suspicions. DS Bebbington wondered whether there might be another reason for Flick and Bob's joint tiredness. And then Lucy understood why her friend had a diverted gaze, as if her mind was in a completely different place to her body.

"Hang on a minute! You've slept with Bob, haven't you?"

"Don't tell anyone!" responded Flick who was not at all surprised that her best friend had worked it out. They had known each other for so many years that they could almost communicate telepathically.

"Hahaha – of course I won't! But you've gotta fill me in. I mean…When? How? What happened?"

"Oh, Luce, I don't want to go into details, but it sort of started in his office and then back at my place."

"What? You had sex with him in his office? That's hilarious! And bloody risky! What were you thinking of?"

"It just happened. I know it was reckless, but it was also kind of… great!"

"Right, Flick. We certainly do need to keep quiet about this. God… this is complicated."

"Mmm, yeh…it is."

"I mean… what about his partner? … if she found out about this…"

"…she did! Bob's now staying at my place."

"Bloody hell Flick, that was quick… what are you going to do? It's going to be difficult back at work?"

"Yeh, I know. I'm going to have to get a new job – may be in Hackney or Waltham Forest or Redbridge."

"What about Tower Hamlets? – You live there!"

"Nah, anywhere but Tower Hamlets… far too political for me."

"Anyway, can you make sure he gets plenty of kip over the weekend! I've got to work with him, and he's going to be even more of a grumpy old man than usual if he continues to have sleep deprivation!"

"I'll try!" replied Flick, smiling wistfully and with a twinkle in her eye.

*****

Shortly after lunch, Templeman drifted off to sleep in his office chair. He had grabbed a roast chicken, bacon and mayonnaise sandwich from the Tesco Express near to the station, together with a packet of ready salted crisps, and a bottle of water. His 'meal deal' was enough to keep him sustained, but also brought on a drowsiness, exacerbated by his lack of sleep. He gently snored, undisturbed in his chair, until the high-pitched ringing of his desk phone awoke him. He shook his head, rubbed his eyes and grabbed the receiver.

"Templeman," announced Bob gruffly to the caller, whose number he did not recognise.

"Ah, Good afternoon, DCI Templeman, this is Neil Chazelle from telephone surveillance. You put in a request yesterday to identify the location of a pay-as-you-go phone."

"Yes, I did!" responded Bob, suddenly feeling a lot more alert and sitting up straight in his chair.

"Well, one of our ISMI-catchers identified the phone number you provided us with, and gave us a location for where it had last been used."

Templeman was not quite sure how an ISMI-catcher worked, but was aware that they were increasingly being used by the Metropolitan Police for surveillance of people's mobile phone activities. He was

185

grateful for any technology that made his job easier, even if it was controversial with civil liberties campaigners.

"Okay, fire away," said Bob.

"Just to check, DCI Templeman, you're interested in the phone call made from the mobile at 1549 hours on Sunday 15th October, which lasted four minutes and six seconds."

"Have you got any other data from the phone?"

"No, we haven't. The phone looks as if it was only turned on shortly before the call and turned off straight afterwards."

"So where did that call come from?" Templeman was waiting with bated breath, hoping that this would be the breakthrough he had sought all week.

"We've tracked it down to the West side of Eagle Pond in Snaresbrook."

"Snaresbrook?"

"Yes, DCI Templeman. We can be pretty accurate by measuring the strength of the signal."

"Thank you - that's very useful."

Templeman finished off the conversation and then sat in contemplation. He felt remarkably refreshed after his power nap and more confident than ever that he had found David's murderer. Everything was now pointing towards Adam Butler. It could not possibly be a coincidence that the phone call from a burner phone, was made a few hundred metres from where Butler lived in Snaresbrook. Whilst staring at his office wall, Bob thought through a solution to the Chandler case:

Adam Butler had been obsessively in love with Alice Chandler for some time. He had stalked her on Facebook and liked her three most recent posts. But his main route to contact with Alice was not Facebook (which Alice seldom used), but through her husband David.

186

He would manufacture ways of seeing Alice by going out for a drink with Dave and then getting an invitation back to the house afterwards. He may even have started having a covert affair with Alice. By September, Adam's obsession with her had become so extreme, he decided that the only way he could possess her, was by killing her husband. He hatched a plot to murder David, which would make the death look like suicide. So, when he went round to the Chandler's house for lunch on Sunday 8th October, he removed the 10ml syringe from the bathroom First Aid case and discovered there was a tow rope in the shed that he could use for the hanging.

At the same time, Butler had found out that David was having an affair with Charlotte Bagley. Using an anonymous burner phone, he rang Chandler the day before the murder from Eagle Pond in Snaresbrook, just a few hundred metres from his home. He threatened to expose David's affair to Alice unless they met to discuss things at his house the following day.

On the day of his murder, David pretended to have a stomach bug so that he could meet Butler at his house. Adam went to work as usual but used the excuse of a business meeting to take time off work during the day. Butler got on The Underground at Canary Wharf carrying a bag containing an oversized hoodie, jogging bottoms, some disposable vinyl gloves and the syringe full of insulin. He took the Jubilee Line to Stratford, changed to the Central Line, and travelled three stops to Wanstead. He got off the Tube, walked along St Mary's Road, into Overton Drive and found his way to Wanstead Park. Once there, he put the hoodie and jogging trousers over his work clothes and placed the gloves and syringe in the pockets of his hoodie. He discarded the bag, walked across Wanstead Park, and then across The Flats, finally arriving at 15, Hitchen Road just before 1230 hours.

When Adam knocked on the door, David Chandler was expecting him. Butler was invited in, but before entering, he politely slipped off his loafers and left them on the door mat. Whilst he was led to the sitting room, he put on the disposable gloves. Once inside the sitting room, he suddenly took Chandler's arm and injected him with a massive dose of insulin. He overpowered the smaller man, holding him still with his hand over his mouth. Within minutes, David was unconscious.

Butler rushed to the shed, fetched the tow rope and then fashioned a noose. He moved the unconscious Chandler to a sitting position leaning against the French doors and put the noose around his neck. He was just tall enough to feed the other end of the rope over the top of the curtain rail. He then hauled David up until his legs were dangling about eighteen inches off the ground. He put the fingerprints from David's left hand on to the syringe and then placed it near to the sofa as if it had dropped from Chandler's fingers. Butler took a stool from the kitchen and placed it on its side just to the right of David's now dead body.

Adam took some paper towel from the kitchen and quickly cleaned the French door windows where David's sitting body had been propped. He then discarded the paper with the other rubbish. Butler opened the front door, put his loafers outside and then picked up the door mat. He stepped out of the house, slipped his loafers back on and then shook the door mat. He carefully placed the door mat back in its position and shut the door behind him. He removed his disposable gloves and put them back in his hoodie pocket.

He then walked back along Hitchen road the way he came and crossed Dames Road to Wanstead Flats. Adam Butler travelled back to Canary Wharf the same way as he came, making sure that he disposed of the hoodie, gloves and jogging bottoms before he exited Wanstead Park.

Templeman's thought experiment pleased him. He was now expecting the imminent feedback from the CCTV cameras in Overton Drive and Wanstead Underground Station to confirm this scenario. Bob hoped to have Adam Butler arrested and charged before the end of the day. He was looking forward to his Saturday morning lie-in.

TWENTY-FOUR

Templeman was in a cheerful mood when he met with DCs Richards, Tyrrell and Smith. Life was good! He was in a new relationship with someone who he found totally irresistible, and who understood exactly what he had to go through in his work life. And he was about to solve the Chandler case which had been frustrating him all week. All he needed now was some hard evidence to corroborate his solution. Templeman knew he was outstanding at his job, and he very rarely got anything wrong. Mainly, because he was a good deal more intelligent than his criminal adversaries. He was aware that he sometimes made mistakes, but not as many as the killers he tracked down. He prided himself on his ability to sniff out any small error they made, and then pounce on them at the appropriate moment.

"Okay, guys, we've got a name for our six-foot suspect," announced Templeman, "Adam Butler, colleague of Chandlers, forty-one, lives in Snaresbrook and works at Canary Wharf. Here's a photo of him." Templeman proceeded to pass round the picture of Butler with his partner.

"So, let's start with CCTV in Overton Drive. What have we got?"

"Well, we looked at CCTV for the times when we were most likely to spot our guy," commenced DC Tyrrell, "That's 11.35 to 11.45 going to Wanstead Park and 13.30 to 13.40 for coming back from the park. In fact, we expanded the time frames from 11.25 to 11.55 and 13.20 to 13.50."

"And?"

"Nothing, Sir," replied DC Richards.

"Nothing?"

"Well, we spotted some dog walkers, a few elderly people, a couple of kids (don't know what they were doing out of school), and one short guy (about five foot six) in the 11.25 to 11.55 slot. And it was similar for the 13.20 to 13.50 time period. But no sign of a six-foot bloke or anyone who looks like this Butler guy."

"Did you see any of the same people in both time frames?"

"No, Sir."

"What about CCTV at Wanstead Tube?"

"We didn't bother with that, Guv," replied DC Smith, "There's hundreds of people that go in and out of the station, and as we had no suspect to follow, there was no point. But we can get right on to it straight away, now that we have a photo."

"What about the ground search at the entrance to Wanstead Park?"

"Yes, we contacted Redbridge, and they sent some uniforms down there to do a search. I went as well and had a look myself," replied DC Tyrrell.

"And?"

"Once again, we drew a blank. They found a couple of supermarket carrier bags and other bits of rubbish, but no sign of a hoodie or jogging bottoms."

"And the Council rubbish?"

"They do daily collections of the bin rubbish in the park, Sir," responded DC Richards, "but it goes to the landfill site on a Tuesday morning. We could, of course, do a search of that, but it would be a very costly and time-consuming exercise."

"Okay, let me think!" Templeman sat in thought for a moment. He no longer felt so upbeat, but his frustration made him all the more determined to find some hard evidence that could identify the murderer. He had a suspect, but he was beginning to think that Butler was even more cunning than he had thought. He needed to get into his mind and think like the killer.

"Where are the other exits from Wanstead Park?"

"Well, there's another way in from Park Road, just off Northumberland Avenue," commented DC Tyrrell.

"So he could have doubled back on himself?"

"Yes."

"And there's an exit on to Blake Hall Road to the West, Sir," proposed DC Richards.

"Or you could go East, Guv, and take the pedestrian bridge over the dual carriage way to Ilford," commented Smith.

"Right, need to expand our search guys," announced Templeman, "We've been assuming that our suspect took the most direct route back to Wanstead, but he could have gone East to Ilford and then took the Overground. Or gone West out of the park on to Blake Hall Road and took a longer route to the Tube. Organise an urgent search of all entrances of Wanstead Park, and look at CCTV around Blake Hall Road and that footbridge."

"We'll get on to that straight away, Sir," replied Richard.

"Yes, and one other matter. Our suspect made a phone call from a burner phone on the west side of Eagle Pond in Snaresbrook, between 1549 and 1553 hours on Sunday. Must be a CCTV camera around there. See if you can get an image of that. He's a clever bugger this one, but we'll get him."

*****

It was Detective Sergeant Lucy Bebbington who drove to Barnaby Lewis at Canary Wharf. Detective Chief Inspector Bob Templeman

191

sat in the passenger seat next to her. They were on their way to interview Charlotte Bagley. They had already phoned ahead and found out that the young woman was at work until 5pm. It was already 4.18pm, so they were keen to meet her as soon as possible. Templeman had insisted on taking a marked police car, much to the surprise of his colleague.

"So why didn't we take an unmarked car, Bob?"

"Have you ever parked in Canary Wharf, Lucy?"

"Once or twice. Why do you ask?"

"Bloody extortionate – what they charge. Much better to take a marked car, drive into the drop off point, and get free parking!"

Lucy smiled to herself. She knew that Bob was now staying at Flick's apartment in Canary Wharf, and could sense his frustration at the parking situation. There was no way she was going to mention her friend to Templeman. She knew that Bob and Flick had copulated in his office, but suspected that he was not yet aware that Flick had confided in her. It was not for Lucy to share their earlier conversation with him.

The whole thing was in fact quite awkward for her. Lucy could not help but have an image in her mind of Templeman thrusting his large frame against Flick. And it was not a particularly pleasant thought. Bob was definitely not Lucy's type. She was struggling to understand what Flick saw in him. Maybe it was his height, but he was too tall in Lucy's opinion. Perhaps, Flick was drawn to his authority and status, but whilst respecting Templeman's ability to do his job, DS Bebbington was far from starry-eyed about his rank. Lucy quite liked Bob; she thought he was a good man, but for her, he lacked the sex appeal she found in her husband.

"Did you check out Michael Sander's alibi, Lucy?"

"No – I thought we were concentrating on Butler. I know we want to interview Charlotte Bagley, but why don't we just arrest Adam while we're at it, and interview him back at the nick?" asked Lucy.

"Would love to, but so far, all the evidence we have is circumstantial. Pretty certain he's our man, but need some hard evidence to arrest him. Haven't got enough yet to satisfy the CPS, and don't want to alert him to the fact we're on to him."

Lucy parked the police car at the front of the forty-two floor skyscraper in the drop off point, just as Templeman had suggested. It was only twenty metres from there to the main entrance of Barnaby Lewis.

The two detectives went straight inside and introduced themselves with their warrant cards. The downstairs reception was a cavernous, brightly lit area with sofas, chairs, several desks and pass-card operated turnstiles that led to the elevators. They were escorted into one of them and transported in a few seconds up to the fourth floor where Charlotte worked. They were greeted by Adam Butler.

"You must be DCI Templeman and DS Bebbington," he said, offering his hand. They each responded by shaking it. Bob was not surprised that his murder suspect was being so conspicuously friendly. It suggested that he was the killer. Chandler's murder had been carefully planned, and the person who committed it, had to be very intelligent, cool, and confident. Adam Butler seemed to possess all these characteristics.

"I understand you want to speak to Charlotte. She's in a meeting room waiting for you, so I'll take you straight there. You won't be disturbed."

Templeman observed Butler's stride as he led them to the room, trying to see similarities between his gait and the video he had seen of his hooded suspect. Bob decided that this was not his area of expertise. When they arrived, Butler opened the conference room door for them and then quietly closed it after they had entered. There, sitting behind a desk, was Charlotte Bagley looking surprisingly composed.

Bob automatically started comparing Charlotte to Alice in his mind. He was struck by how youthful she looked. She was twenty-five, just three years younger than Alice, but looked more like twenty-one. He saw that she did not have Alice's blonde hair. It was dark brown. Bob considered Alice to be handsome, but Charlotte was prettier. He also noticed that she had a fuller figure than Alice. He could see why David Chandler might have been attracted to her appearance-wise, but what Bob was really interested in, was whether she could provide some evidence against his suspected murderer.

After introducing DS Bebbington and himself, Templeman commenced the interview:

"Miss Bagley, I understand that you work closely with Adam Butler, Liberty Brown and Marie Chevalier. Could you recall what each of you were doing between 10am and 3pm last Monday?"

"Marie and I were here doing meeting rooms. I remember seeing Liberty in the Admin Office during that time, and I think Adam was working from home."

"Does he often work from home?"

"Once or twice a week. He's the Accounts Manager so it's not essential that he's here all the time."

"Okay… and David Chandler…What was your relationship like with him?"

"We got on very well. We worked effectively together. He was an excellent boss."

Bob and Lucy were struck by how confident Charlotte was in both her speech and demeanour. Templeman, however, suspected this might change once he dropped his bombshell on her. But before he could do that, DS Bebbington interjected:

"Did you have a sexual affair with David Chandler, Miss Bagley?" Lucy decided that such a direct question might be better coming from another woman, although Bob was a little disappointed that he had missed out on the pleasure of asking it.

"I'm sorry, that's a very odd question," replied Charlotte. "No, of course I didn't – he was my boss… and married."

"So how do you explain this then?" asked DS Bebbington waving Charlotte's Facebook messages in front of her.

"What's that?"

"This, Miss Bagley, is six pages of 'love messages' exchanged between you and David Chandler over a five month period, starting in April this year and ending in September. You refer to him as 'Washy' and he refers to you as 'Bagels'. Would you like me to read them out?"

"That's private – how on earth did you get hold of those?"

"Miss Bagley, we're detectives, so our job is to detect," interjected Templeman.

"Well, you must have hacked into my Facebook account to get those. Did you have a warrant for that? I'm not sure that's legal."

Templeman was impressed by Charlotte's fighting spirit but he was not going to be defensive:

"How we obtained those messages is not your concern, Miss Bagley. The fact that they exist, is. Now, I'm going to level with you. You have not, as far as we know, done anything criminal. If Mr Chandler had not been murdered, we would have no interest at all in your relationship with him. However, we want to catch the person who killed him as soon as possible and believe that the murderer might have found out about your affair. So, what we need from you is this: Who did you tell about your relationship with David Chandler? Or who might have found out about it?"

Charlotte paused for a moment, reflected on what Templeman had said to her, and decided to cooperate with him.

"To be honest, I never told anyone about it. I never discussed it with friends or family or work colleagues. It was our secret and we both tried our very hardest to keep it that way."

"But, is it possible someone found out about your affair?"

"There was one time. We were having a drink together in The Red Lion in South Woodford one evening, back in May. We were holding hands and being quite romantic with each other. And then one of our colleagues came in."

"Which colleague?"

"Adam Butler. I'd forgotten he lived down the road in Snaresbrook, otherwise we would have gone somewhere else."

"And did he see you holding hands?" asked Templeman.

"I don't think so, but it's possible. We saw him at the bar and then he saw us, and he joined us for a drink, and we pretended we had gone there after a meeting with a client. He seemed to accept it and wasn't suspicious or bothered."

"Do you think he could have seen you together as soon as he came into the pub… when you were being affectionate with each other? And then turned to the bar to buy a drink?" asked DS Bebbington.

"Yes – I suppose that's possible, but there was no indication from him that he thought we were on a date."

"And has he mentioned anything about your relationship with David since? or did he mention seeing you in the pub to anyone else at work?"

"No, not at all. Quite the opposite. Since then, he's never talked to me about David and never discussed that evening. Even today, all he said was that you were coming to interview me. He never mentioned David's murder enquiry… but then… maybe it was obvious that's why you wanted to see me."

"And you're sure there's no other incident when someone might have witnessed you on a date with David?" continued Lucy.

196

"Yes, I'm sure. We were very careful. We never socialised together in Canary Wharf or West India Quay, or Stratford, or anywhere else near work. And after that evening in South Woodford, we used to go even further out – to places like Chigwell and Brentford."

"Now, these messages we found seem to have ended in September. It looks like David deleted Facebook Messenger from his phone at that point. Is that when your affair with him ended."

"Yes, it finished a few weeks ago. I think it had just run its course and David said he wanted to have another go at making his marriage work. But, of course, I was disappointed – I loved David."

"Of course," interjected Templeman. "Just one more question, Miss Bagley. Whilst you were having an affair with David, were you in a relationship with another man, or did you consider yourself 'single'?"

"I don't know what you're trying to imply there DCI Templeman. No, David was my only relationship. For me, there was no one else."

"Right. I think that's all we need to ask you today, Miss Bagley. We would appreciate it if you didn't mention the contents of our meeting with anyone else. I'm sure you want to keep your affair with David Chandler as private as possible."

"But *is* that possible? Surely it's all going to come out in some future court case!"

"Well, the future is something not yet known," concluded Templeman.

The two detectives left the meeting room and headed back to the escalators. Before they were able to enter them, Adam Butler appeared seemingly from thin air and said:

"Thank you for your visit DCI Templeman and DS Bebbington – I do hope it was helpful."

Templeman looked at the well-dressed and smiling man, and said simply:

"Thank *you* Mr Butler. It was indeed very helpful."

197

After they had left the Barnaby Lewis building, DS Bebbington climbed into the driver's side of the marked police car while Templeman squeezed into the passenger seat. Lucy drove out of Canary Wharf, past Billingsgate Fish Market and into a rush-hour traffic jam.

"Right, let's not hang around," exclaimed Bob as he leaned over and turned on the siren. Almost instantly, the traffic parted, like the Red Sea opening up for Moses, and DS Bebbington was able to slice through the tailback rapidly. As they sped back to Stratford, Templeman asked:

"What did you make of Charlotte Bagley?"

"Quite a cool customer really. She was confident, composed, didn't show much emotion, and was able to defend herself well."

"My thoughts exactly. Reminds me of someone you have yet to meet, Lucy."

"Who's that Bob?"

"Alice Chandler!"

TWENTY-FIVE

Immediately after DCI Templeman and DS Bebbington had finished interviewing Charlotte Bagley, Adam Butler left the Barnaby Lewis building. He descended the elevator at Canary Wharf Station to join the Jubilee Line. He changed to The Central Line at Stratford, taking the Epping train, and alighted ten minutes later at Snaresbrook. He then started walking the six hundred metres to his flat – 52, Isis Grove.

Waiting for Butler in an unmarked Ford Focus police car, were DCs Amanda Green and Mark Holloway. They were parked at the front of Isis Grove, a development that consisted of three blocks of apartments. Adam's flat was in the block furthest from the road, so they knew he had to walk across their field of vision to reach the communal entrance. As Butler emerged from the street, Amanda grabbed the Canon single-lens reflex camera from the centre console, turned the setting to 'video', and filmed him as he strolled past them.

"We've got him walking!" she exclaimed, whilst observing Butler turn his key in the lock.

"I guess we can go then," commented DC Holloway.

"Not yet, Mark. Let's hang around for a while to see if he goes out again. It's Friday night – he might be meeting up with someone."

"Yeh, I know it's Friday night, Mandy. I'm supposed to be out on the razzle with some mates later."

"I'm sure you'll make it…*now*… who's this?"

A young woman with long, straight blonde hair came into view, walking in the direction of Butler's block of flats. She was wearing a denim jacket and jean shorts with mid heel black shoes buckled at the front. She was sort of half walking, half skipping, like a child. She pressed the button of number 52, and quickly, a buzz followed. She entered through the communal door and headed up the staircase.

"Was that Butler's flat she pressed?" asked DC Holloway.

"Not sure – can't see from here."

"Do you think it might be that nineteen-year-old he's been stalking on Facebook… Laura James…or something!"

DC Green removed her notebook from her top pocket and found the appropriate page.

"Lauren Charles, Mark."

"Right – I'll find her online."

DC Holloway removed his smartphone from his pocket, pressed on the Facebook App icon and then typed 'Lauren Charles London' into the search bar. He scrolled down, clicked on the first girl with blonde hair, and brought up her details. He could not see many of her posts, but the profile picture was unmistakably the same girl that had walked past them a minute earlier.

"It's her," he said, showing Amanda the photo on his mobile.

"Oooh, that's a bit pervy; a forty-one-year-old bloke going out with a nineteen-year-old girl."

"Is it? Imagine if it was the other way round; a nineteen-year-old boy sleeping with a forty-one-year-old woman. We'd probably say he was just sowing his wild oats and she was a cougar!"

"Maybe, but women are more vulnerable, particularly young women. How do we know he doesn't like fourteen-year-olds, as well!?"

"We don't! But they're both adults, and as long as she consents, who are we to judge?"

"Mmm… it still feels wrong Mark… I mean she's basically a child."

"In her mind maybe… and that's the problem. She's much younger than him, so her life experience is going to be far less. There's a generation gap and a different way of looking at things. It's very difficult to maintain a relationship when you don't have much in common."

"And if he's our murderer, you certainly wouldn't want your daughter hanging out with him. We need to tell the boss about this. She may not be a minor, but we still want to protect her."

"Okay, I'll give him a call."

*****

DCI Templeman knew what he was going to do when he returned to Stratford Police Station. And he was keen on DS Bebbington being party to it. But it required the quietness of his office. When he invited Lucy inside, she could not help wondering where in the room, her boss and Flick had performed a sexual act. She looked at the large armed desk chair and imagined Bob sitting at the edge of it with Flick astride him. She envisaged him lying flat on the floor with her friend in a kneeling position on top of his large frame. And then she visualised Flick lying on the desk while he thrust himself inside her. She then conjured up an image of her friend performing fellatio on Bob. And then, her mind was invaded by a scene, involving Templeman stimulating Flick's clitoris with the tip of his tongue. It all became a very unpleasant muddle of different postures and orientations. Lucy suddenly wished that Flick had not been so honest with her. It just encouraged her vivid imagination to run riot.

"Okay, where are we at with Butler?" asked Bob.

Lucy blinked, wiped her mind of her lurid thoughts, and applied her brain to analysing the Chandler case:

"You told me DC Green had seen him wearing black loafers. He's six foot tall, he's been to the Chandler's house recently, so he could have stolen the syringe. We know he was stalking Alice on Facebook and

201

suspect he was obsessed with her. He also knew about the affair between Chandler and Charlotte Bagley. The phone call last Sunday came from Snaresbrook, where Butler lives. In addition, we know he was supposedly working from home, so he doesn't have a work alibi. Therefore, we have means, motive and opportunity."

"Excellent Lucy – couldn't have put it better myself."

"So, do we have enough to arrest him now?"

"Almost. Need to ring Alice Chandler first."

"Now?"

"Have arranged the call for now!"

Bob picked up a copy of Alice's earlier email and dialed her mobile number on his desk phone. He then switched to speaker mode. After introductions, Templeman asked Alice:

"I see from your email that some friends of David's came to stay with you on the weekend of 4th August – James and Claire Edwards. Can you tell me about them and how that weekend went?"

"James and David were at school together and were very good friends. James was best man at our wedding. He's perfectly pleasant, as is his wife, Charlotte. To be honest, I find her a bit boring, and I could have been a bit more sociable that weekend, but they seemed to have a good time with David."

"Thank you. You also mentioned Adam Butler coming back to your house on Friday 15th September. Can you tell me what happened on that occasion?"

"Well, they'd had a lads' night out. When they got back, they were both a bit drunk and were laughing. I was on the laptop in the dining room, so they went into the sitting room and had a whisky."

"How was Adam Butler that night? Was he friendly?"

"Oh yes. He's always friendly when he's sozzled."

"Was he overly friendly with you?"

"I don't know what you're trying to infer Bob. If you must know, Adam Butler has always been very polite and gentlemanly. He knows I'm not a very physical person, so he never hugs me or touches my hand or anything."

"I'm sorry – that question may have come out the wrong way."

"I don't think you are sorry, Bob. I think you intended that question exactly how it came out."

Lucy smiled to herself. She was warming to Alice Chandler. Templeman was riled. Alice was proving herself once again to be more than his equal. Ignoring her comment, he asked:

"What about when Mr Butler came round for lunch on Sunday 8th October. Why didn't he turn up with his partner, Janet Ashworth?"

"I can see you've been doing your homework, Bob," replied Alice. "I'm getting the impression that Adam Butler is your prime suspect. If that's the case, then I'm afraid you're far off the mark. He was a good and loyal colleague and friend to David. He would never have killed him."

"Alice, is it possible you could just answer the question about where Janet Ashworth was, please?" asked Bob, almost pleadingly. Lucy suppressed a laugh.

"Her Dad was ill in hospital, so she had to visit him. And if you're thinking that she and Adam don't have a good relationship… once again, you've got that wrong. They've both been round for lunch on, I think, three occasions. They are a very well-matched and united couple."

Templeman was annoyed by Alice's tone, but found her responses interesting. He ended the conversation, turned to Lucy, and asked:

"What d'you think?"

"Wow – she doesn't take prisoners!

203

"Indeed!"

"But, she's obviously taken in by Butler. Do you think he might be a sociopath who convinces others that he is normal, when he isn't?"

"Possibly, but Alice Chandler is very astute. You said it – she doesn't take prisoners."

At that moment, DCI Templeman's mobile phone started vibrating. It was DC Mark Holloway. Bob took the call. It was only a brief conversation but one that made him reflect on the situation. So far, he had no firm evidence that Adam Butler was the six-foot hooded suspect and based on his conversation with Alice, he now had reason to doubt that Adam Butler was the murderer at all. Yet, if he were the killer, what harm might he do to a young woman barely out of her childhood? When he told Lucy about the latest intelligence, he was not at all surprised by her reply:

"What more do you need, Bob? The guy's not only a murderer, but a paedophile, too."

"That's a bit strong, but, yes…think we've got enough now. We'll arrest him straight away, and search his flat and place of work."

※|◇|※|◇|※

When Adam Butler opened the front door of his first-floor apartment to Lauren Charles, they hugged each other and she followed him into the sitting room.

"Do you want a drink, sweet pea?" he asked.

"What have you got?"

"Tea, coffee, coke, white wine, beer, whisky – take your pick!"

"Urgh… whisky, no thanks – don't know how you can drink that stuff."

"It is an acquired taste...one that I've acquired."

"I'll have a glass of white wine, please!"

"Okay - on its way!"

Lauren sat down on the sofa and looked round at the sitting room, with which she was so familiar. She noticed that there were spiders' webs in a top corner of the room, which stood out more against the white ceiling than the grey walls. The beige Berber carpet was fairly new, but had not been vacuumed recently, whereas the curtains either side of the large rectangular window, were much older and had seen better days. There were some DVDs spread on the coffee table with a TV guide, and either side of the gas fire, stood a couple of tall, three-foot wide bookshelves. These were crammed with a variety of different sized publications, some of which were placed horizontally on top of the others. There were a couple of Banksy prints on the wall and an acrylic cityscape. And a large television was positioned in the corner, not far from the window.

In no time at all, Adam returned with a glass of Chardonnay for Lauren and a can of pale ale for himself. He passed her the white wine, drew the curtains and then sat down next to her.

"So, Kill Bill Volume 1 this week," he announced.

"Yeah," replied Lauren, "That's cool, that one... Tarantino showing us how much he loves martial arts!"

Adam went over to the coffee table, grabbed a bright yellow DVD case, took out the disk and placed it in the Blu-Ray player. He picked up the remote control and hovered his thumb over the 'play' button.

"Ready?" he asked

"Yeh, Go for it."

Each of them made themselves comfortable by using the cushions on the large sofa. The haunting title song - 'My baby shot me down' - filled them with anticipation, and they immersed themselves in one of their best-loved movies. They relished the escapism of Tarantino's over-the-top cartoonish violence, and the vengeful heroics of the main character – Beatrix "The Bride" Kiddo. The film violently moved towards Lauren's favourite moment, when Beatrix kills one of her most sinister adversaries - the coquettish and sadistic school girl - 'Gogo Yubari'. Just as an image of the dying girl's blood-streamed face came into view, a loud 'bang' filled Butler's apartment. Despite being immersed in the violence that occupied the fifty-five-inch screen of Adam's LED television, they both jumped. Lauren and Adam stood up and looked at each other.

"What the hell was that?" said Adam.

Before Lauren could answer, two armed police officers were in the sitting room with their guns trained on Butler's head, and shouting:

"Police! Show us your hands!"

For a split-second, Lauren thought she had been transported into a Tarantino movie herself, but then it struck her – this was for real. She screamed loudly as DC Amanda Green barged past the armed officers, and embraced the shocked and shaking nineteen-year-old.

"It's alright Lauren – everything's going to be fine," said Amanda trying to calm and reassure the young woman.

"It's not fine," replied Lauren tearfully. "I don't understand… what do you want with my uncle?"

TWENTY-SIX

Charlotte Bagley loved Chinatown, mainly because she had a penchant for chicken chow mein and prawn dumplings. On a Friday night, it was not uncommon for her to take the Tube to Leicester Square and then walk the two hundred metres to her favourite restaurant – 'Shanghai Dumpling' in Lisle Street. She invariably chose 'Set Menu B', because it was made up of all her preferred dishes, including crispy duck with pancakes and hoisin sauce, as well as salt and pepper squid. Of course, it also contained the chicken chow mein and prawn dumplings Charlotte craved.

The inside of Shanghai Dumpling was unpretentious. It had simple wooden tables, benches and chairs. The soft orange and yellow lighting made it cosy, and at the far end, there was a nook cut off by a partitioned wall. The nook contained one table which was big enough to accommodate four, at a squeeze. On it, sat a small, leaf-patterned glass and iron candle holder, in which was placed a tealight. This was the table which Charlotte always requested when making a Friday night reservation. And - as a regular who knew how to get her way - this was the table she always got. The intimacy of the nook appealed to Charlotte, because it provided an ideal setting for conspiracy. The twenty-five-year-old loved scheming and manipulation. She considered herself an expert at it.

Although not an academic highflyer at school, Charlotte was bright enough to attain three average-grade A-Levels and then advance to London Metropolitan University. There, she achieved an under par 'Desmond' (2:2) degree in Business Management. She might have done better if she had spent less time on sugar daddy dating, pretending to enjoy the company of older, rich men. However, she felt she had learnt more about business management from this extra-curricular activity than she had from any form of study. It taught her everything she needed to know about transactions. Give as little as possible of yourself, in terms of time and effort, in order to achieve the maximum monetary award.

She was very discerning about which sugar daddies she dated, preferring the older, less virile men who paid her a handsome allowance. And although they bored her, she had plenty of time and energy left, in order to sleep with younger and more exciting male specimens. She left university with the ability to put a fifty percent deposit down on her first London flat.

With Charlotte, everything was a means to an end. And her goal was to be rich, successful and at the top of the pile. On the way, she wanted to have lots of fun, plenty of sex, and loads of chow mein. She did not care whose dead body (literally and metaphorically) she walked over to achieve her goals. She had no conscience. Charlotte Bagley was a psychopath.

Charlotte rarely went out to dinner on her own. She had one or two friends who shared her interest in food, drink, men, and gossip. But most of her relationships rarely lasted a long time, as it would not be long before her lies and backstabbing came to light. People instinctively knew that Charlotte hated personal rejection evenly though she herself could end a relationship instantly and brutally. So, knowing the danger she posed, people did not usually dump Charlotte as a friend suddenly, but gradually withdrew from her sphere of influence. When, this happened, Charlotte would simply use her powers of persuasion to find someone else to dine with.

On this particular Friday night, Charlotte was in Shanghai Dumpling with her lover. He was a successful and wealthy man in his forties, who shared elements of Charlotte's psychopathy. He knew how to lie without his lies being found out, and he was a specialist at covering his own backside at work.

He wasn't a total sociopath like Charlotte, for he did sort of love his wife and sixteen-year-old son. But, like Nazi death camp commanders, he was able to compartmentalise his life between being an outwardly normal father and husband at home, and being a ruthless operator in the outside world. He enjoyed wielding power. He had the superficial charm of a psychopath but lacked the narcissism of one. He was surprisingly lacking in vanity, did not seek the lime light, and was quietly spoken.

His one weakness was sex. He liked Charlotte Bagley because sleeping with her was fantastic. She knew how to do things to him that he had never imagined would be so pleasurable. Although he kind of cared about his wife, he had long since lost interest in her sexually, so taking a lover filled a big hole in his life. He did not, however, entirely trust Charlotte. He knew she was liar and had already decided that their relationship was going to be temporary.

He was not a natural risk taker, and on his own, without the encouragement of Charlotte Bagley, he probably would not have murdered David Chandler. But their lives had collided and they had a mutual interest in killing him. He didn't enjoy ending David's life, but he saw it as a necessary act. And now he was convinced that he would get away with it. His planning and execution had been meticulous, and in addition, he had managed to frame Adam Butler for the crime. He could tuck into crispy duck with pancakes and hoisin sauce without needing to worry too much about watching his back.

"So how did the interview go today?" he asked Charlotte.

"Oh, fine, just as we had planned. I maybe should have shown some emotion, but I sort of got into it and enjoyed the exchange. That Templeman fellow is huge – I wouldn't mind riding his cock!"

"Haha – now, now Charlotte. You wouldn't want to get too close to the Met's finest. That could be risky!"

"Maybe not, but at least we've got something to celebrate – I reckon they'll be arresting Adam Butler anytime now."

Charlotte picked up the bottle of Veuve Clicquot champagne and poured each of them a glass. It was not her favourite – she preferred a vintage Dom Perignon – but it was the best wine that Shanghai Dumpling stocked and, besides, she was there primarily for the food.

"Chin-chin!" she exclaimed as she raised her glass.

"Prost!" responded her lover as they clinked glasses.

*****

Darkness had descended on Stratford when the hand-cuffed Adam Butler was brought to the station. It had been a miserable journey for him in the back of a police van - he was feeling shock and confusion at the violent and sudden nature of his arrest. He was wondering why the police hadn't just interviewed him about David Chandler's death, instead of treating him like a dangerous criminal. And he felt terrible that his niece, Lauren Charles, had been subjected to a trauma that came completely out of the blue. He wondered whether they would, ever again, be able to indulge in their joint love of Quentin Tarantino movies. He knew he was innocent of the murder, but having seen numerous documentaries on miscarriages of justice, he was aware that he could not take anything for granted. He needed a good lawyer, and fortunately he knew one – Harvey Blackman.

Adam Butler found the rituals of being arrested humiliating, but he had no option but to give his fingerprints, have his mouth swabbed for DNA and listen to the duty sergeant explaining to him why he had been arrested. He was led into an interview room where DCI Templeman and DS Bebbington were waiting for him. He knew who they were, for he had met them a few hours earlier, but this time he was dressed in chinos and a tee-shirt, not his work suit.

"Good evening Mr Butler," said Bob politely.

"There's nothing good about it, DCI Templeman. Excuse me for asking, but was all that really necessary?"

"All that what?"

"Breaking down my front door, arresting me at gunpoint in front of my niece, and then dragging me here in a police van."

"Your niece?" exclaimed Lucy Bebbington incredulously.

"Yes, my niece - Lauren." Then the penny dropped for Adam Butler. "You were watching me, weren't you, and thought that she was my underage girlfriend. Is that why you raided my flat?"

Lucy wondered why DCs Green and Holloway had not pre-warned them about Adam's real relationship with Lauren. She would talk to them later.

"No, it wasn't, and I can imagine that it was indeed a shocking moment for Lauren, Mr Butler," commenced Templeman, "And we will be offering her counselling to support her. But this is a very serious crime you are accused of, so, unfortunately, we had to be robust in our actions."

Adam Butler was not an argumentative person so accepted Bob's explanation without coming back at him. He had made his point politely and did not want to upset the two detectives unnecessarily.

"So, Mr Butler. Perhaps you'd like to tell us about the murder of David Chandler. It must be playing on your mind, and I'm sure it would be helpful to talk about it."

Adam Butler appreciated Templeman's polite and calm approach, but he knew what he was trying to do. And he was determined not to play along.

"I cannot talk about something I did not do DCI Templeman, and I'm sure you appreciate that I don't wish to answer any further questions without legal representation."

"As you wish," replied Templeman, "We'll ask the duty solicitor to join us."

"No, I'd like to be represented by Harvey Blackman, if I may, please."

"Okay. You're allowed a telephone call. And I understand that you wish to appoint your own counsel. So, we'll stop here and continue with our conversation tomorrow."

Adam Butler was led away, leaving Bob and Lucy sitting briefly in silence. Templeman was glad that his initial dealings with him had been brief. Bob was not at his best, and he needed the break to reflect on his doubts, and the current state of his investigation:

"Glad we've finished for today Lucy – feeling a bit tired."

DS Bebbington knew exactly why Bob was so exhausted, but replied simply:

"Yes, it's been another long day and a terrible week."

"Yeh – poor Sanna," sighed Templeman feeling suddenly very melancholy.

Lucy was touched by Bob showing her an emotional side that he usually kept hidden. It gave her a small insight into why Flick was so head over heels in love with him. Lucy knew that Bob was a kind and fair man, but she found his abrupt style and patronising approach grating at times. She had enjoyed working with him that day and was beginning to form the opinion that they could make a very good team. She also realised that he could teach her a lot. Yes, he was a bit of a dinosaur, but the most successful dinosaurs were intelligent predators that invariably caught their prey.

"So, what d'you think?" asked Templeman.

Lucy was once again irritated by Bob. All she could think was: 'Why does he always have to come out with 'what d'you think?' all the time? He just wants to steal all your good ideas and then come out with some sage-like comment!'

But, rather than challenging her boss, she decided that she would let this one play out. So, she made a fairly predictable response to his question, knowing that he would come up with something cryptic:

"Mr Butler is polite, reasonable and intelligent, which tells us nothing really. And I'm sorry about my reaction to Lauren Charles – couldn't help it," she said.

"Yes – I was surprised as well. Things are not always what they appear to be in this job. Got a feeling that Adam Butler might be innocent."

TWENTY-SEVEN

When Templeman got back to Flick's apartment that evening, she was cooking him steak and chips.

"How did you know that was my favourite?" he asked, as he grabbed her waist from behind and then slid his large hands up the side of her body towards her shoulders. He gently massaged her for a moment while she closed her eyes enjoying the feeling of his thumbs caressing the erogenous zone at the back of her neck. He kissed her behind the right ear, undid her bra strap and then let his hands wander back down to the bottom of her back. Still standing behind Flick, Bob felt under her top, slowly making his way up the front of her body from just below the navel towards her 34F bosom. The bra loosened as his hands slid under both cups and gently massaged each breast simultaneously.

By this time, Flick was so aroused that she abandoned dinner, turned round to face him, and grabbed his erect penis, still encased in his trousers. She kissed him full on the mouth, undid the buckle of his trouser belt and then virtually ripped open the top of his trousers. She encircled his phallus with her right hand and started to masturbate him - slowly at first, and then quicker.

"Stop," he said, "I'm going to come if you carry on like that!"

Flick took his right hand and guided it under her skirt towards her moist vagina. He was aroused simply by the fact that she was not wearing any underpants. The tip of his finger slightly touched her clitoris, which was all the encouragement she needed for her to push him backwards out of the kitchen into the sitting-dining room and on to the leather sofa. She mounted him as he lay horizontally across the full length of the two-metre couch. Bob's penis effortlessly slid inside her, as she put both her hands flat on his chest and rode him like a horse. He wanted to lick the nipple of her left breast but he was too

214

tall to reach with his mouth. So, he used his right index finger and thumb to tweak it gently. He climaxed before her, his eyes rolling back to reveal the whites. But he managed to retain his erection until Flick, too, orgasmed with a loud, high-pitched cry of pleasure.

Afterwards, they sat at Flick's dining table eating dinner with a bottle of Beaujolais Village. They were both exhausted, but experiencing that post-coital feeling of relaxation that banishes any stresses of the day.

"How's Sanna's murder investigation going?" asked Bob.

"Well, we've completed the search of the Flats and his apartment, and I think forensics have got everything they need. We're now in the process of tracing Jafar Malik's movements in the run up to the attack, and interviewing known associates. It's fairly painstaking, but we'll get there. What about your day?"

"Mmm… interesting you should ask me that! Not such a great start when Karen Michaels came into my office… and saw a pair of your knickers under the desk!"

"Fuck!" exclaimed Flick open-mouthed.

"It's alright, she's not going to say anything, but suggested that you transfer to Redbridge."

"How did she know the knickers were mine?"

"The enormous size, probably!" joked Bob, laughing.

"You bastard!" commented Flick, sniggering and punching him playfully on the arm.

"To be honest – think we've been spotted together in The King's Arms. Problem with working in CID is… detectives tend to notice things…"

"No shit, Sherlock! Anyway, I'd already realized that I'm gonna have to put in for a transfer."

"Fair enough. She said she'd be talking to you on Monday."

215

At that moment, Templeman's mobile phone rang. It was DC Mark Holloway. Bob took the call and discussed with his colleague new evidence that had been discovered at the scene of Adam Butler's apartment block. Flick was intrigued, so after Bob had ended the conversation, she eagerly enquired what was going on.

"Three things have emerged Flick," replied Bob.

"Which are?"

"They've found the hoodie and jogging bottoms in our suspect's black bin."

"Great news! What else?"

"Someone vandalised all the CCTV cameras around his flat last weekend. Still haven't replaced them."

"Well, that would have been him – to hide his movements!"

"Maybe."

"What's the third thing?"

"They can't find a laptop, PC or tablet in his flat. Would have also told us whether he was at home or elsewhere on Monday."

"Perhaps he's left his work laptop at work?"

"Yes - thought of that. Which is why I've arranged a search of his office at Barnaby Lewis."

"What about his mobile phone?"

"Oh, we've got that, and it might help, or might not."

"How do you mean?"

"Well, if he were the murderer, he would have left his phone at home and then claimed he was in his flat all the time. If he's not the killer, he might not have used his phone at the time of the murder because he was on his laptop. However, if he was using his mobile from home at the time of the murder, that might clear him."

"Unless someone else was using it from his home!"

"Unlikely, but possible. Of course, if he sent an email from his laptop at the time of the murder, that might also clear him."

"Unless it was a pre-scheduled email," commented Flick.

"In which case we would need to look at his laptop, which has disappeared or is at work."

"So, if he's managed to get rid of all the evidence that would have implicated him in the crime, then he's got a defence. Or, he would have, if they hadn't found the hoodie and jogging bottoms. That's pretty damning," concluded Flick.

"Mmm… but was it him who put them in the bin? Would make more sense if had burnt the clothes or disposed of them elsewhere. But just chucking them in your rubbish – that's sloppy. Doesn't add up."

"What are you suggesting?" asked Flick.

"I'm suggesting that Adam Butler is not the murderer. I think he's being framed!"

"So, if he isn't the killer, who is?"

"I have no idea, but I think I've met someone who can tell me."

"Who's that?"

"Charlotte Bagley."

"Who's she?"

"Chandler's colleague. He was having an affair with her. Interviewed her today and she was very plausible. Too plausible, and strangely lacking in emotion. Thought she might be hiding something."

"Oh right… that's interesting…so, what are you going to do now?"

"Going to call Smith and Tyrrell. Need to start following Miss Bagley straight away."

"You're not going back to work are you?"

"No! After this phonecall, I'm going to bed with you! And won't be going back in 'til 10.30 tomorrow morning."

"That sounds like a plan to me," said Flick, smiling broadly, as she reached for Bob's arm and pulled him towards her.

*****

After Charlotte Bagley and her lover had finished eating their Chinese meal in Shanghai Dumpling, they went for a drink in 'The Plumpton', a popular city pub between Leicester Square and Charing Cross underground stations. The theatres had not yet finished their evening shows, so they were able to find a table quickly. They shared another bottle of Champagne, after which Charlotte had attained an unusually high level of inebriation.

"How about coming back to my place, Tiger," she suggested, slurring her speech.

Her lover was sorely tempted by the offer. He had been staring at her cleavage all evening and knew what treasures lay underneath. But, despite his desire for her, he knew that it was too risky. It was not so much he was worried about his wife. She was long suffering and gave him a free rein. No, it was more that he didn't want to be seen with Charlotte in Stratford – it was too close to home. He had been careful all week, and had taken a calculated risk by agreeing to dine with her. But what she was suggesting now, was just one step too far for him.

"I'd love to, Charlie," he replied, "But it's too soon after what happened on Monday. Too risky. But, how about this coming Monday, when our man will be… in the news!?"

Charlotte knew that alcohol increased her already substantial sexual appetite, but even she, in her inebriated state, could see that what he was saying, made sense. Yet, she had, at that moment, a strong desire to fuck someone. So before she answered him, she thought about who she might be able to telephone at short notice, to satisfy her needs. Once she had worked this out in her mind, she replied:

"I see what you're saying. Monday it is then."

They finished their drinks, left the pub together, and went in different directions. On the way back to Leicester Square underground station, Charlotte took her mobile out of her handbag, and arranged her late evening shag.

*****

Charlotte Bagley lived in a thirty-eight-storey luxury development in the heart of Stratford, just opposite the former Olympic Park, and two hundred metres from the Tube. Her substantial two-bedroomed apartment was ideally situated for accessing Central London, Canary Wharf and Essex to the East. Situated on the twentieth floor, it had magnificent views across the city. She could see all the major landmarks including The Shard, The O2 (formerly The Millennium Dome), The London Eye and The BT Tower. Of course, her flat had cost her the best part of a million pounds, but she was practised at obtaining money for investment. And, she had recently acquired a substantial inheritance from a rich aunt who had died in mysterious circumstances, orchestrated by Charlotte herself.

Watching the main entrance to the recently completed development, were DCs Mike Tyrrell and Sam Smith who had just arrived in an unmarked police car. They were dressed in casual evening clothes which for both of them involved jeans, a teeshirt and a leather jacket, albeit of different styles and colours. They were disappointed that they had to work on a Friday night, especially to do a dull stakeout job, but they were used to being called out at short notice, so took the overtime in their stride.

"Are you sure she lives here, Mike?"

"That's the address we've got!"

"She must be minted! Those flats cost the best part of a million quid, and God knows how much you'd have to pay in rent. I think I'm in the wrong job!"

"Me too! But I guess we'd better find out whether she's in her flat."

"How are you going to do that?"

"The old pizza trick, Sam."

"How does that work?"

Mike Tyrrell proceeded to unzip the main compartment of his backpack and take out a baseball cap and a thermal insulation bag.

"I'm going to pop across the road to that pizza place, order an extra-large pepperoni pizza with chicken dippers, and then pop them into this bag."

"Then what?"

"And then I'll buzz her number wearing this cap, and, if she answers, I'll just say 'Pizza delivery'. She'll be able to see the bag on her intercom but not my face."

"What if she answers and says 'Come on up?'"

"I'll go in, hang around for a while, and then leave."

"But won't she be suspicious that you didn't deliver the pizza?"

"No – she'll assume the pizza was for someone else because she didn't order it."

"But, what if she had, by coincidence, ordered a pizza?"

"Then that will be delivered by someone else. She might be a bit confused but won't suspect anything, because people are having pizzas delivered all the time on a Friday night."

"And we get to eat the pizza! I like it!"

DC Tyrrell put his plan into action, came back twenty minutes later with his order and stated simply that Charlotte wasn't in. The two detectives proceeded very rapidly to demolish an extra-large pepperoni pizza and chicken dippers with garlic sauce.

One hour and forty-three minutes of boredom later, Charlotte Bagley returned to her apartment block. Her fuck buddy was waiting for her. DC Smith grabbed his Nikon camera, to which he had fitted a telephoto lens, and started taking rapid snaps of both Charlotte and her acquaintance.

"She's grabbed his crutch!" laughed Mike.

"Looks like it might be his lucky night!" replied Sam.

"I wonder who he is?"

"Haven't got the foggiest, but we can always ask our colleagues."

Sam chose a close-up photo of the man's face, downloaded it to his mobile phone via Bluetooth, and then posted it on the Newham CID WhatsApp group. 'Confidential – please PM me if you recognise this man,' he wrote. Five minutes later, he received a private message from DI Aanya Patel.

"It's a chap called Jack Bradbury. He works at Harvey and Blackman, apparently," Smith announced

"That's where Alice Chandler works, isn't it?"

"Yep. And Charlotte Bagley worked at Barnaby Lewis with David Chandler."

"So, there must be a connection through Alice Chandler somehow."

"Yes! I'd better let the boss know."

SATURDAY

TWENTY-EIGHT

DCI Templeman arrived at Stratford Police Station at 10.26 the following morning feeling a little more refreshed than he had done the previous day. DS Bebbington was already there, surprisingly enthusiastic for a Saturday. She was keen to get on with the job.

"So when do we start interviewing Butler?" she asked Bob as he came into the main incident room.

"Shortly, but something else we need to do first."

"What?"

"Find out what's turned up in our search of Wanstead Park."

"Is that more important than interviewing Butler?"

"Yes. Told you yesterday – think Butler is innocent."

"But that was before they found the hoodie and jogging bottoms in his bin. That's hard evidence. It's got to be him."

"Not necessarily. Could be that someone planted those items to frame him for murder."

"Are you joking?"

"We'll see. I've asked DC Richards to join us. Ah… here he is."

Lucy looked up to see the six-foot-three lean figure of Bill Richards coming through the door. He greeted DCI Templeman and DS Bebbington politely, pulled up a chair and sat opposite his colleagues.

"Let's start with CCTV, Richards," commenced Bob, "What did it show around the entrances of Wanstead Park?"

"To the West, there's a CCTV camera in Blake House Road that shows everyone going in and out of that entrance. And there's also one by the bridge over the dual carriageway to the East. We looked at both of those for the most likely times, but there was no sign of our hoodie man, Sir."

"What about the entrance off Northumberland Avenue in Park Road?"

"There's no CCTV on that one, Sir."

"Okay. Any sign of six-foot men going into the park carrying a bag around 11.45am?"

"Nope, we only spotted one guy carrying a bag on CCTV, from the Blake Hall Road entrance, but he was shorter than our suspect."

"Any six-foot guys in work trousers and a shirt leaving the park later?"

"No, Sir."

"Mmm. What d'you think, Lucy?"

Lucy was waiting for Templeman to ask her this, and furthermore, she was ready for him:

"This is what I think. I think Butler took his car down to Park Road and left it by the entrance where there is no CCTV. He then went into the park, and came back out by the other entrance in Northumberland Avenue where there was CCTV. He committed the murder and then came back the same way. He got into his car, still wearing the hoodie and jogging bottoms and drove home, where he disposed of the clothing."

"That's possible, and logical, given the evidence," commented Templeman.

"Yes, I like that theory too," added Richards.

"So," continued Lucy, "He never changed into and out of the hoodie and jogging bottoms in Wanstead Park, and never had a bag. He simply drove to and from the park knowing that there was one entrance without CCTV. I bet you didn't find a bag in the park, did you Bill?"

"No, we didn't."

224

"Very good Lucy," commented Templeman patronisingly. "Think we should go with this theory. Richards – go back to Park Road with a picture of Butler's car and do some door-to-door. Find out if any local residents have seen it. And get Tyrrell to look at CCTV in that area – want to know if we can spot our suspect's car."

After Bill Richards had left, Lucy turned to Bob and said,

"Have you changed your mind now about Butler?"

"No - still think he's innocent."

"But, how can you? My theory fits all the facts we have."

"All the facts we have so far."

"So why ask Richards and Tyrrell to look for his car?"

"To rule Butler out, Lucy. You're right - the killer probably did park his car by the entrance without CCTV, but that doesn't mean the killer was Butler."

*****

Adam Butler had managed about three hours' sleep. He had been shocked and stressed after his sudden arrest, and had lain awake for hours in his cell. His inability to sleep was exacerbated by the constant noise of crying, yelling, singing and the banging of doors. It had been a normal Friday night for Stratford Police, and that meant locking up an array of drunken fools for fighting, petty thefts and possession of drugs. By two o'clock, things had started to calm down and by three o'clock, Butler had fallen asleep out of sheer exhaustion. By six o'clock, he was awake again and thinking about the difficult day ahead.

It was 12.15pm before DCI Templeman and DS Bebbington were ready to interview Butler, by which time, Adam was starting to drift off to sleep again. The noise of someone opening the door, startled him, but he felt a good deal of relief when he was finally led out of his cell. He was taken to an interview room, where his lawyer was waiting for him.

His phone call, the previous night, had not gone exactly as he had expected. Harvey Blackman spoke to him from Brighton where he claimed he was having a school reunion. This was also the excuse he had fed his wife. Harvey was telling the truth when he said he had gone to Brighton. But he was not there with his old school friends. He was enjoying an adulterous weekend with his young secretary. Harvey assured Butler that he would find him a very capable criminal lawyer to replace him, and fortunately, his partner, Stuart Harvey, was available. Adam had met him once before, and knew from his reputation, that he was a very capable lawyer. Stuart stood up when his client entered the room and shook his hand:

"Okay, Adam, I'm assuming you didn't do the crime of which you are accused. Am I right?"

"Of course – I'm completely innocent."

"Excellent. I'm sure you have nothing to worry about then. All you need to do, is be completely honest, establish your alibi and cooperate fully with their questioning. I'm sure we'll have you out of here in no time at all. If they try anything silly, I'll intervene. Don't worry - you'll be absolutely fine, Adam."

Butler was mightily reassured that he had Stuart by his side. Despite the terrible ordeal he had been through, he felt for the first time since his arrest, that there was light at the end of the tunnel.

When Templeman came in with DS Bebbington, the first thing he noticed was how tired Adam looked. Bob had never spent Friday night in the cells, and had no desire to do so, but he had enough imagination to understand why this would have been a difficult experience for Butler. He introduced all those present, and then started the interview:

"Mr Butler, where were you between 11am and 2pm this last Monday – that's the 16th October?"

"I was in my flat at Isis Grove in Snaresbrook."

"And what were you doing there."

"I was supposed to be working from home, but things didn't work out as I had planned."

"How do you mean?"

"Well, just before eleven, about 10.50, my laptop started doing funny things. I couldn't do anything with it. As soon as I opened a file, it would go dead. The internet wouldn't work – it was really bizarre. I suspected it was being hacked."

"What did you do?"

"I rang our IT department at work and managed to get them to work on it remotely. They said it might take a while to sort out, and so it transpired. It was gone two before it was back to normal."

"Did you ring them initially on your mobile?"

"Yes – I don't have a landline."

"And did you ring them regularly after that to see what was going on?"

"I would have done, but then my phone went dead. The phone signal went down as if a local mast had failed."

"Or someone was jamming the signal?"

"Yes."

"So what did you do?"

"I watched a film – 'Pulp Fiction.'"

"Okay. Did you use your phone at all during that time?"

"Yes, I could still use it through Wifi. I sent one or two Whats App messages, looked at the BBC website briefly. That's about it."

"What time did you do that?"

"Just after eleven, I think."

"And then you didn't use your mobile after that for a couple of hours while you were watching 'Pulp Fiction.'"

"Longer than that – it's a good two and a half hours, that film."

"Did anything else strange happen this week?"

"Well, apart from being arrested at gunpoint – No!... except for one thing…"

"What was that?"

"My phone went missing from work the following day – on Tuesday. I thought I'd left it on my desk, but then it was gone. Someone could have taken it when I went to the loo. I tried ringing it with my office desk phone, but I couldn't hear it. Shortly after that, I had to go to a finance meeting, and when I came back, it was there again."

"So someone took it, checked it and returned it."

"I suspect so – yes."

"Mmm… you've got a problem, Mr Butler."

"What's that?"

"You've got no alibi for the time of David Chandler's murder, and I can't see how you're going to establish one."

*****

Detective Constable Bill Richards was not having a productive day around Park Road in Wanstead. He had knocked on all the doors at the lower end of the street and then the nearby houses in Northumberland Avenue. He had even tried the first few in Woodlands Avenue.

Nobody had seen Butler's car or anything like it. It was a very distinctive vehicle – a 1980 red Mercedes-Benz SL convertible, so

Richards reasoned that if it had been around the park, someone would have spotted it. Bill thought the car was quite cool and wondered why Butler had chosen that model. The truth was that Adam was obsessed with the red Chrevolet Chevelle convertible from Tarantino's 'Pulp Fiction', but could not get one of those. So he drove something that sort of resembled it. He also knew that a Mercedes-Benz SL had featured in another of Tarantino's movies – 'Jackie Brown.'

DC Richards had discovered one interesting thing from a local resident. They complained to him that there was an itinerant man camping out in the trees that were just a few metres from their back garden. Bill did not think this was likely to be significant but wondered whether the itinerant gentleman in question might have witnessed his hooded killer on Monday. Richards wandered round the back of the houses, and sure enough, he found a tent with various objects outside, including some aluminium pans and a gas bottle with a cooking ring attached. He was hesitant about looking inside the tent, so he found himself calling politely:

"Hello, anyone at home?!"

The entrance of the tent was half unzipped and a man's head emerged from inside it. He had a dark beard with streaks of grey, and even from several feet away, Bill could smell that he had not showered for some time. But more noticeable than his odour, was the fact that he was wearing a black hoodie. The hood was down, but could still be seen from where Bill was standing.

"I'm a police officer," said Richards, politely, showing the man his warrant card.

"Fuck awff," replied the itinerant in what Bill thought was a surprisingly posh voice. The man disappeared back into his tent and zipped up the door.

"It's alright, Sir, I'm not here to move you on or arrest you. I just need your help. I'm a detective, and I think you could be the man I need, to solve a murder case."

There was a brief silence, and then, the itinerant unzipped his tent door, and poked his head out again. He looked quizzically at Bill and said in an educated voice:

"Normally, people are offering me help which I do not want. I can't remember the last time someone asked me for my help. So, how can I help you?"

"You're wearing a hoodie, Sir. It would be very helpful to my murder enquiry, if you could tell me where you got it from."

"I found it in that bin over there," replied the itinerant, pointing towards Park Road.

"And, can you remember when you found it in the bin?"

"About four or five days ago. What day is it today?"

"Saturday, Sir."

"So that would be Monday or Tuesday afternoon."

"I'm sorry Sir – my name is Bill. What's your name?"

"Stephen. That's my name. You can call me that if you wish."

"Okay, Stephen. When you found the hoodie, did you find anything else with it?"

"Yes, I did, Bill. I found a pair of track suit bottoms as well. They're very comfortable. I'm wearing them now."

"Are they navy blue?"

"Yes, they are."

"Right, Stephen. I'm really sorry, but I'm going to need those items. They could be vital evidence in our murder enquiry."

"But they're mine now, Bill."

"Yes, I know, but by giving them to us, you would of done the most helpful thing in your life."

TWENTY-NINE

Adam Butler was feeling worried. DCI Templeman was right – he did not have an alibi for the time of David Chandler's murder. Nevertheless, he was still wondering why he was a suspect in the case. Yes, he was a friend and colleague of David's, but he had no reason to kill him. Before he could ask the obvious question, Stuart Harvey intervened for him.

"But DCI Templeman - why would my client need an alibi? What evidence have you got to link him to the alleged murder of David Chandler?"

Templeman did not reply to Stuart. Instead, he looked at Adam, and asked:

"Mr Butler, did you see the image we released earlier this week of the suspected murderer - a man in a hoodie and jogging bottoms? It was in the news."

"Yes, I remember that. Wednesday, wasn't it?"

"Indeed! The thing is, Mr Butler. We've found an identical hoodie and jogging bottoms in your black bin at Isis Grove."

Adam Butler was shocked. He could not believe it.

"In my bin? Number 52? That doesn't make sense."

"Yes, here are the photos that were taken at the scene.

Templeman passed Adam and Stuart photographs of the hoodie, jogging bottoms and his black bin. There were several pictures, including a photo of the black bin with a 'number 52' clearly visible. There was also a picture of the black binbag, in which the clothing had been placed, and one of the position they were found in the bin. There was a photo of the items laying just inside the opened black binbag, and finally, the clothing pictured on top of the refuse bag. There was no denying it – the hoodie and jogging bottoms had been discovered in Adam Butler's bin.

"These items could have been planted," asserted Stuart Harvey.

"That's entirely possible," replied Templeman, "But, why would the murderer want to frame you Mr Butler? Doesn't it seem more likely, given the evidence that we have found, that you are the murderer?"

Adam Butler put his head in his hands, shook his head, and just said:

"I have no idea why someone would to do this to me."

"My client is clearly tired, and needs a break DCI Templeman. Can we adjourn for a little while?" requested Stuart Harvey.

*****

The forensics team had put two tents up at the entrance to Wanstead Park. One was for the itinerant, Stephen Maingot to change out of the hoodie and jogging bottoms, and the other around the bin where he had found the clothes. There was a small team of police officers doing a second search of the park, and joining DC Richards was DC Tyrrell who had completed his initial CCTV search for Adam Butler's car, without success.

Bill had managed to source some buckets, soap and water for Stephen, as well as a change of clothing, which a uniformed colleague had purchased from Marks and Spencer's in Stratford City. Richards liked his new-found acquaintance, and was keen to make him feel that his contribution was central to the murder investigation.

Stephen had lived a nomadic existence for seven years. He was not an alcoholic or a substance abuser. He was just someone who had dropped out of society due to the breakdown of his relationship. He had always possessed a hankering for the eremitic lifestyle, so once he was free of responsibilities to another human being, he headed outside.

Stephen found living al fresco liberating, and had adapted to life amongst the trees. He had a lot of money in savings, but only went to shops to buy essentials that he needed to survive. Sometimes, he was refused entry, but there were a few places where he was treated like the anonymous person he liked to be. Stephen was often moved on from the sheltered spot he camped in, but he would always find a new place to settle – for a time at least. He found do-gooders particularly irritating. He didn't accept offers of food, money or hostel accommodation, and he didn't want to be with the junkies and alcoholics that lived under the flyovers. He kept his own company, and that was how he liked it.

As an English graduate from University College, London, Stephen was an avid reader, and whiled his time away immersing himself in literature and watching the trees. He enjoyed the occasional murder mystery, so was happy to find himself at the centre of one, as long as he could stay out of the limelight.

After, he had washed himself and changed into the joggers and sweatshirt that had been purchased for him, Stephen said to DC Richards:

"How much do I owe you for the clothes?"

"Nothing, Stephen. It's a straight swap. We took the clothes you were wearing, so you get replacement clothes. It's not charity."

"So, why do you need the hoodie and track suit bottoms I was wearing before?"

"We think the murderer was wearing them over his shirt and trousers and then dumped them in the bin, before leaving Wanstead Park in that direction." Bill pointed in the direction of Park Road.

"And that was on Monday or Tuesday, was it?"

"Yes – Monday afternoon. You didn't see him yourself, did you?"

"Yes, I did."

"You did? What did he look like?"

"He was probably in his forties. He had dark brown hair with a bit of grey. He was wearing normal trousers and a shirt as you said. I didn't see his face as he was walking away from me."

"Tell me more about what you saw."

"I was wandering around, looking at the trees – it's wonderful how the colours change this time of year. Autumn is my favourite season."

"And?"

"And I heard some rustling behind that bush over there, and then the chap appeared, carrying the track suit bottoms and hoodie. He placed them in the bin and then walked quickly out of the park."

"Then what happened?"

"He got into a car."

"Can you describe the car he was driving?"

"He wasn't driving the car. He jumped into the passenger seat. I don't know what make of car it was – I'm not interested in them. It was a silver, sporty-looking convertible. It had the hood down."

"So you could see the driver? What did he look like?"

"It wasn't a he…it was a woman."

"So, what did she look like?"

"I only saw the back of her head. She had brown, shoulder-length hair."

"And she drove off quickly?"

"No. They seemed to be arguing a bit, but I couldn't hear what they were saying. She closed the hood, and then they drove off."

"In which direction did they go?"

"They turned right into Woodlands Avenue."

"Interesting – thank you very much Stephen," commented DC Richards.

*****

Templeman received the phone call from Bill just before he was about to resume his interview of Adam Butler. Richards explained his discovery, and related in detail all that Stephen had told him. When Templeman then relayed it to DS Bebbington, she was stunned.

"So, Butler is being framed for the murder after all!" she exclaimed.

"Yes Lucy, just as I thought. This Stephen is wearing the hoodie and track suit bottoms that were used by the murderer, and the ones found in Butler's bins are identical, but planted. And am willing to bet that the driver of the convertible was Charlotte Bagley."

DS Bebbington was impressed by the way Templeman had kept an open mind about the identity of the murderer. She knew how easy it was to get fixated on one individual and then think that every bit of evidence pointed to their guilt. This is the mistake she had made. Yet, she was also annoyed by Templeman saying 'just as I thought', to patronise her. It was like a child saying 'I told you so,' in her opinion. But, it was no time to tackle him on his arrogance. Instead, she wanted to explore another idea with him:

"Do you think the murderer might be Michael Sanders then?"

"Should certainly consider that possibility. Works with Alice, the right height and body type, and if he's in love with her, then getting rid of her husband would give him the opportunity to make a move. Also know he was supposedly seeing business clients at the time of the murder. Have you checked out his alibi?"

"No! I'll take that one on the chin, Bob, but we were pressed for time yesterday and at that point all the evidence pointed to Butler."

"True."

"So, if Charlotte Bagley is involved as you suspect, the link with Michael Sanders could be through his colleague Jack Bradbury, who we know she's sleeping with."

"She might be sleeping with Sanders too, Lucy!"

"Yes! I'm not sure I'd put anything past her. So, I guess we're going to have to release Butler without charge and then investigate Sanders."

"Won't be releasing Butler yet."

"Why not?"

"Because, as long as he's still a suspect, the murderer won't be expecting us. Still got a few hours before we have to release Butler. We'll delay his interview for a little while longer."

"That will give us time to interview Sanders."

"Yes, but there's something else I want to do first."

"What's that?"

"You and I are going over to Wanstead Park. Want to see that hoodie and jogging bottoms for myself."

*****

When DCI Templeman and DS Bebbington arrived in Wanstead, they had trouble finding somewhere to park. Forensics had brought their vans, the uniformed contingent from Redbridge had arrived in a variety of different vehicles, and DCs Richards and Tyrrell had unmarked cars. The local residents were standing on doorsteps, or in clusters gossiping, enjoying the attention that their quiet corner of London was attracting. Templeman was relieved to see the press had not yet found out about the latest development in his murder enquiry.

236

Bob and Lucy walked over to the forensics tent where the lead investigator had bagged the hoodie and jogging bottoms. She was carefully examining them through the clear plastic evidence bags. Sylvia Richardson was a very meticulous and serious scientist. Templeman had known her for several years, but not once had she ever cracked a joke. Black humour was common amongst those performing her frequently gruesome role, but Sylvia always played it straight. Although she was not a particularly engaging individual on a personal level, Bob liked her, because she was excellent at her job. Templeman always respected and appreciated people who were at the top of their game.

"Good afternoon Dr Richardson," Bob said, showing her the respect he knew she deserved.

"Good afternoon DCI Templeman."

"Tell me - what have you found from the hoodie and jogging bottoms?"

"Not much so far, I'm afraid. It's going to be difficult to harvest historical DNA from these items when our itinerant gentleman has been wearing them constantly for the last five days. We'll have a try, but I suspect that Stephen's DNA will be the only thing we find."

"Mmm – did you get a size for them?"

"Yes, the jogging bottoms are for a man with approximately a 34 to 36-inch waste and a 32-inch inside leg. The hoodie has XL on it, so the person wearing it was probably reasonably tall."

"Anything else."

"Oh yes! There was one thing particularly unusual."

"What's that?" enquired Templeman, his interest piqued.

Dr Richardson picked up the hoodie in its evidence bag.

"You see this hood," she said squeezing the bag.

Templeman reached inside his jacket pocket and retrieved his magnifying glass. He gestured to Sylvia to give him the bag, which she did. He carefully felt the hood and looked at it with his magnifier. As he did so, his eyes widened and his mouth developed a smile, similar to the Cheshire cat's. DS Bebbington looked on, bemused by Templeman's Sherlockian attention to detail, and frustrated that she did not understand what was going on. Sensing her impatience, Bob turned to his colleague and said:

"Dr Richardson – please explain to DS Bebbington what you have discovered."

"The inside lining of the hood has been unsewn and inside has been inserted a significant amount of padding at the top – it could be from a thick cushion or pillow. The person has then added some extra lining which is not an exact much but the same colour. They have sewn it all back up. Also newly attached are two nylon cords attached to the top of the hood, at the front. The cords go under the chin and are fastened together using buckle clips. They make sure the padded hood stays in place. When the person was wearing the hoodie, you wouldn't have been able to see the cords from a side or back angle. Only from the front."

"Sometimes Lucy, the smallest of details makes the biggest of differences," commented Templeman.

DS Bebbington reflected on what she had seen and heard. And then she understood too.

"Thank you very much indeed Dr Richardson," said Templeman, smiling. He wanted to hug her, but knew that Sylvia was far too formal to appreciate any extemporary gestures of affection.

"Now where are Richards and Tyrrell?" he exclaimed.

Bob rushed out of the tent and found his two colleagues outside, talking to each other.

"Great work guys – I owe you several pints," he said as Richards stood grinning, appreciating the unusually effusive praise from his boss. Tyrrell knew that the breakthrough in their investigation had been due to Bill's efforts, not his own, but he would be more than happy to take up Templeman's offer of alcoholic beverages, when the appropriate moment came.

"Now, Tyrrell. You need to find out the reg, make and model of Charlotte Bagley's car. It's a silver convertible. Then check Monday's CCTV for her car going to Wanstead Park in order to pick up our killer outside Park Road. Get back to me ASAP."

"I'm on it," declared Mike.

"Richards. You told me earlier you had seen CCTV of a man with a bag going into the Blake Hall Road entrance."

"Yes, I did, Sir."

"Can you get me a photo of that?"

"I can get it straight away, Sir."

"Do that, and meet me back at the station ASAP. I know who our killer is, and we'll be arresting him soon."

THIRTY

As Templeman walked the short distance from the unmarked car to the entrance of Stratford Police Station, he felt renewed and invigorated. Lucy noticed a spring in his step as he bounded up to the entrance. He now knew that the pieces of the jigsaw were falling into place. When Bob was stressed and bogged under with work, he would try to recreate this feeling in his mind; the satisfaction and human reward of solving a difficult case. Templeman was an old-fashioned communitarian. He believed that we all had social responsibilities, and those that undermined the rules, deserved to be caught and punished. He knew that the urban community he lived and worked in was far from perfect. Yet, if he could in some small way, make it a safer place to live, that was reward enough for him.

As Bob walked through the door, he turned to Lucy and said:

"Right, let's get straight back to our interview. There are still one or two things I need to know from Mr Butler."

The delay had played on Adam's mind, as he had simultaneously wondered what was going on, and thought through various scenarios. He had imagined his court case, being found guilty, and then spending years languishing bored in a cell until an investigative journalist came to his rescue. At other moments, Adam wondered whether his interviewers would come back, tell him in it had all been a terrible mistake, apologise, and let him go. He did not rationalise that his vacillation from despair to hope and then back to despair again, was a perfectly normal phenomenon when people were subjected to extreme stress.

As a young adult, Butler had lost faith in the British system of justice when an overzealous police constable had arrested him and two friends for smoking a marijuana joint in his local park. The officer had called for backup and they had all been bundled in a van and taken to their local station. They had accepted cautions, which Butler naively thought meant nothing, until it prevented him from getting a job the following year. Having seen the police overreact to him once, he was shocked, but not altogether surprised, that they had done so again.

Butler was led back into the interview room and joined by Stuart Harvey. Once again, they sat facing DCI Templeman and DS Bebbington, with just a table between the two parties. Bob restarted the interview with:

"I must apologise for the long break, Mr Butler, but we had to be called away on an urgent matter. I can assure you, we will be concluding our interview with you today, without any further delays."

"This is most irregular," said Stuart Harvey, "it is almost twenty-four hours since you arrested my client, so if you're not going to charge him, I suggest you release him immediately."

"Thank you for reminding me of the law, Mr Harvey, which I already have quite a good grasp of. You'll also be aware that I can seek an extension in order to detain suspects for up to 96 hours. Now, Mr Butler, I'd like to turn to a matter which I'm sure you're familiar with – David Chandler's affair with Charlotte Bagley."

"Oh that! Yes, I suspected he was having an affair with Charlotte."

"How did you find out about it?"

"Gossip. A junior member of staff said they'd seen them together in Chinatown. It was off the cuff, but I thought there might be something in it. Just the way they used to interact. It didn't seem to affect us all working together effectively, so I concluded it was none of my business."

"So you didn't talk about it to anyone?"

"No, it would have been awkward. I was friends with both David and Alice Chandler, and I didn't want to do anything that would undermine their marriage. As I said, it wasn't really my business."

241

"Did you ever witness David and Charlotte together yourself – in a pub or restaurant, for instance?" asked DS Bebbington.

"No."

"So, as you were friends with Alice, as well as David, were you not concerned that he was undermining her by having an affair?" continued Lucy.

"That's a difficult question. I don't want you to think that I don't care about Alice Chandler, and I know that affairs do undermine partners. However, I was not Alice's best friend, and not responsible for her marriage, so I really did feel that this was not something for me to get involved in."

"Fair enough. But what is *your* relationship like with Charlotte Bagley. Is there any tension between you and her at work?" asked DCI Templeman

"Not really. She's always quite a live wire – funny, hard working and capable. She works well, but…"

"But?"

"But, she can be a bit too much at times. One of the reasons I believed the rumours about her and David having an affair, was that she had propositioned me once. It was after a works dinner - she'd had too much to drink. She kind of cornered me, and tried to kiss me and grab my genitals. She called me, 'Big boy.'"

Lucy coughed to hide a laugh.

"And how did you respond to this?"

"I pushed her away and told her that I wasn't interested. And that it was probably best that we both forgot about the incident."

"Okay. So, was that the only time she made advances towards you?"

"Yes. She was a bit cool with me for a few days after that, and then things just went back to normal. However, I did suspect her of doing something else."

"Please explain further."

"Well, it's difficult to talk about, because I know I'm being recorded, and I can't be one hundred percent sure it was her."

"Given your current situation, I think total transparency is probably your best course of action, Mr Butler."

"Okay. It was to do with expenses. There was a hole of a couple of thousand pounds in them, and I suspected that she had been overclaiming for quite a while, and possibly stealing from our petty cash. But, there just was not enough evidence to prove it was her, so I let it go."

As Adam Butler was speaking, Templeman felt his phone vibrate in his pocket. He discreetly looked at it, discovering a message from DC Mike Tyrrell.

The message read: 'CCTV confirms it! Bagley drove to Wanstead Park Monday 1.15pm.'

Bob typed a quick reply: 'Arrest Bagley!'

"I'm struggling to see the relevance of this line of questioning," interrupted Stuart Harvey.

"Fair point Mr Harvey," replied DCI Templeman, "We'll move on to something else. Now, Mr Butler, I'd like to take you back to the evening of Friday 15th September. You went for a drink with David Chandler that night, and then went back to his house afterwards. Can you talk me through that evening?"

"David and I met up at The King's Arms in Wanstead at about 8pm, and shortly afterwards we were joined by Alice's brother, Simon, and Michael Sanders, who works with Alice. We all had a few pints, apart from Simon who's recently given up booze. I think he was on water. Anyway, we put the world to rights, and just had a good time."

"Did you bump into anyone else you know?"

"Yes, we did actually. About 10.30pm, one of my colleagues, Marie Chevalier, walked in with a girlfriend of hers. They were even more drunk than us, and being very friendly."

"Did they join you?"

"Yes. We asked them what they wanted to drink and they both asked for double vodka and tonics. They sat down with us for about half and hour, and then staggered off just after 11pm."

"And when did you leave?"

"Well, Simon left shortly after the girls. He sort of quickly said goodbye and then drove home I guess. Michael left about fifteen minutes later, and David and I stayed for one more drink – we had malt whisky."

"What time did you leave the pub?"

"It was before midnight. David invited me back to his house. He told me he had recently purchased a 12-year-old Strathisla which he thought I would like. I'm not as much a whisky connoisseur as he was, but I knew that this one had an excellent reputation, so I was keen to give it a go."

"How did you get back to his place?"

"We hopped on a bus, which took us to Dames Road, and then we walked the couple of hundred metres to his place."

"So was Alice still up when you went into his house?"

"Oh, yes! She was in the dining room on her laptop. She said hello, smiled, and seemed happy that we were having a good evening. I made some joke about me leading her husband astray, and she said that he was quite capable of leading himself astray. I know Alice is awkward with some people, but I've always got on really well with her."

"When she said about David leading himself astray, do you think she was referring to his affair with Charlotte Bagley? Do you think she knew about it?"

"No, not at all. It was just a joke – she didn't say it in a serious or bitter way. I think she may have even laughed a bit when she said it."

At that moment, a knock was heard on the interview room door.

"Come in," shouted Templeman.

Adam Butler and Stuart Harvey were taken aback by the loudness of Bob's voice and the interruption to proceedings. DCI Templeman and DS Bebbington were pleased and relieved to see that the colleague disturbing them, was carrying an envelope.

"For the record, DC Richards is entering the room," commented Templeman.

Bill had a serious look on his face, but inside he was feeling satisfied that he had obtained a key piece of evidence, and excited that the team would shortly be able to arrest the killer. The brown A4 envelope he held, was unsealed, so Templeman simply had to lift the flap and extract the photo inside. He looked at it for a moment and then passed it to DS Bebbington. The photo was from a CCTV camera just inside Wanstead Park, pointing towards the Blake Hall Road entrance. The face of the man was clearly visible. He had brown hair with grey streaks. He was wearing dark trousers, a white shirt, and black loafers. He was carrying a small backpack. Bob recognised him straightaway, as did Lucy and Bill.

"Thank you, Richards. Please stay here for the moment," requested Templeman. Bob then turned to Adam Butler, and said:

"Mr Butler, on the day before he was murdered, someone telephoned David Chandler from an anonymous pay-as-you-go mobile phone. That telephone call was made from Snaresbrook, and we think the murderer or a conspirator made that call."

"I didn't know that, but I can assure you, it wasn't me."

245

"You were also the last person to visit the Chandlers before David was murdered – when you lunched with them on Sunday 8th October. We therefore had good reason to suspect that you were David's killer, which is why you were arrested last night. And the hoodie and jogging bottoms found in your bin seemed to confirm those suspicions."

"But I didn't kill David."

"Yes, I know you didn't kill David, but it's important that you understand why you were arrested. We didn't arrest you on a whim – that's not how we operate. However, now that we have interviewed you, and new evidence has come to light, we no longer consider you a suspect. You are free to go."

Adam Butler was non-plussed. He had already gone through the murder trial in his mind, exploring different possible scenarios. He was expecting a long fight to prove his innocence. But Templeman had suddenly done a volte-face and let him go. He was thankful it was all over, but not grateful for the misery he had endured. After a short pause, he simply uttered:

"That's a relief. I guess I'll be off then."

Adam Butler and Stuart Harvey got up and started to move towards the exit. As they did so, Bill Richards moved quickly to the door and blocked their path.

"Please leave now Mr Butler, but Mr Harvey, I'd like you to stay," insisted Templeman. DC Richards guided Adam out of the room while Stuart turned round and locked eyes with Bob. It was the look of man who was ready to joust, whose instinct was for fight, not flight. He knew what the Detective Chief Inspector was going to say, and he knew how he was going to react. Bob did not stand up, for he was in control now, and there was no need to intimidate with his height. He spoke clearly, but calmly, the necessary formula which signaled that he had snared his enemy:

"Stuart Harvey, I'm arresting you on suspicion of the murder of David Chandler. You do not have to say anything. But it may harm your defence if you mention something which you later rely on in court. Anything you do say may be given in evidence."

THIRTY-ONE

Charlotte Bagley heard the sirens below her flat, because she had opened her bedroom window to let the air in. She had enjoyed her steamy time with Jack Bradbury. Their sexual exploits had been great fun. He was young, had lots of energy and was game for anything. He had screamed at one point, when she had dug her nails into his back so hard, that she had drawn blood. She found this amusing. Yes, she feigned an apology, because she had not wanted him to stop, but she felt no remorse for hurting another human being. That had been the story of her life.

Jack had left her apartment late morning, after another round of coital exercise, leaving Charlotte tired, but relaxed. She decided to have a lazy afternoon sitting on the sofa, watching old episodes of 'Californication'' on Netflix. 'David Duchovny ain't half bad for a man of his age,' she thought to herself.

Although she had heard the sirens, it never occurred to Charlotte that they were for her. The sound of sirens was a very frequent occurrence in Stratford, so the accident of hearing them did not equate to consciously thinking about them. Just as the sound of aeroplanes stops registering with people living near airports, the noise of emergency vehicles rarely evokes a response from city dwellers.

Twenty floors below Charlotte, about to enter the main entrance of the luxury development, were DCs Mike Tyrrell and Sam Smith. They had a police van and a marked car with them. A forensics team was there as well, ready to do a careful search of Charlotte's apartment. Mike reckoned that four uniformed officers, plus Sam and himself, would probably be more than enough to arrest a five-foot-five female. The difficulty would not be dealing with Miss Bagley, but accessing the building in the first place.

"This manager is taking ages to come to the door," complained DC Smith.

"Yes. Can you imagine how irritating it would be for a tradesman under the pressure of time," replied DC Tyrrell.

Whilst they were waiting, Mike showed each member of the police team a photo of Charlotte Bagley from her Facebook profile page. He explained to his colleagues his plan, once they had all entered the building. He told one officer to position himself at the bottom of the stairs and another to watch the ground floor elevators.

"Apparently, she's a clever girl, this one. I wouldn't put it past her to get wind of our arrival, and try to flee down the stairs or a lift," he said.

Mike explained to the other uniformed officers that they would be taking the elevator up to Charlotte's apartment with him and Sam.

Seven minutes later, the manager arrived, and let them in without a word of apology for his tardiness. DC Tyrrell explained their business, and assured him that they would not be staying long, and that they would be as discreet as possible. The manager looked through the glass entrance door, and thought that parking police vehicles directly in front of the main entrance, did not demonstrate discretion.

There were four elevators, so the officers took the first that became available. Sam was amazed by how quickly the lift ascended to the twentieth floor. It took about the same time as it would an Olympic sprinter to run the distance horizontally. He was beginning to see the attractions of living in a skyscraper. It was convenient, had spectacular views and you were distanced from the hustle and bustle below.

Fortunately, the elevator took them up to a point, just twenty metres from the young woman's apartment. Mike knocked firmly on the door of her flat. Charlotte responded after a few seconds. She opened the door, wearing a pair of black leggings and a blue cotton tee-shirt with the 'evolution of man' image printed on it. She was holding a mug of tea.

249

"Hi guys," she said in a friendly voice.

"Charlotte Bagley, I'm arresting you on suspicion of the murder of David Chandler. You do not have to say anything. But it may harm your defence if you mention something which you later rely on in court. Anything you do say may be given in evidence," announced DC Tyrrell.

"Are you shitting me?" she replied. Sam suppressed a laugh.

"We're totally serious Miss Bagley."

"I suppose you want me to come down to the police station then."

"Yes, we will be escorting you there."

"Well, I'm afraid I've got ten minutes left of my episode of Californication, so you'll have to wait until that is over."

DC Smith sniggered.

"Miss Bagley. We will give you enough time to put a pair of shoes on, and then we'll be going," insisted DC Tyrrell.

"Can I put a bra on?"

"And that," agreed Mike. Sam put his hand over his mouth to stop his guffaw.

DC Tyrrell was relieved that one of the police officers with them, was a woman, because Charlotte proceeded to go into her bedroom, leaving the door open, and take her tee-shirt off in full view of everyone. Pretending not to look, all the officers were impressed by what they saw, including the female police constable.

After insisting on shutting her bedroom window and turning the television off, Charlotte was handcuffed and led out of her apartment. They entered an elevator and then experienced a semi-weightlessness as they rapidly descended to the ground floor. They led the young woman out of the building, past a group of onlookers and a press photographer, and into the police van. Charlotte was convinced that she would be back in her flat by the end of the day. Her confidence was entirely misplaced.

*****

Stuart Harvey sat down opposite DCI Templeman and DS Bebbington. He was perfectly calm on the outside, but confused on the inside. He could not believe that his plan could have possibly failed. Had he made a mistake of which he was unaware? Had Charlotte Bagley told the officers what had happened? That was just not tenable – even he never believed a word that came out of her mouth.

"So, Mr Harvey. Could you explain to us why you killed David Chandler?" asked DCI Templeman.

"I didn't. I have no idea why you think I did."

"Height, Mr Harvey – it's all to do with height."

"What do you mean?"

"How tall are you?"

"I don't know exactly. Last time it was measured, I was just under five foot ten – maybe 1.77 metres."

"Don't worry – we'll be measuring your height later. The thing is Mr Harvey – as you know, homo sapiens are very sensitive to people's height. I am a particularly tall example of the species at just over 2 metres, but your height is about 88% percent of mine. In statistical terms, that wouldn't seem a lot, but if we stood next to each other, another human being would say that I was a lot taller than you."

"I have no idea where you're going with this."

"The difference between 1.77 metres and 1.83 metres is even smaller – just 6 centimetres. Now, 1.83 metres is very slightly over six foot and that is the height we assumed our murderer was. We assumed that our killer was taller than you, so we ruled you out as a suspect. But then, this morning, at the Park Road entrance to Wanstead Park, one of my officers met a gentleman living in a tent, wearing a hoodie and some jogging bottoms. The gentleman in question had found the hoodie and jogging bottoms in a bin where you had discarded them after murdering David Chandler."

"A very interesting story DCI Templeman, but I'm afraid you are mistaken if you think I have anything to do with Mr Chandler's death."

"I beg to disagree Mr Harvey. Now, no doubt you knew that the bins at Wanstead Park are emptied at the end of every day, and that their refuse goes to landfill on a Tuesday morning. Unfortunately, you did not take into account the recycling abilities of an itinerant gentleman living in Wanstead Park. I went down there myself, and looked at the hoodie he was wearing. It contained enough extra stuffing in the hood to increase the height of the person wearing it by about five centimetres. Add to that the one-and-a-half-inch heels in the loafers you were wearing, and we soon get to more than the six centimetres needed, to make you appear the six-foot killer we were searching for."

Inwardly, Stuart Harvey was seething. He knew that disposing of the clothes had been the riskiest part of the plan, and he had placed them at the bottom of the bin, moving the other rubbish on top. He did not know, however, that Stephen regularly rummaged around in that bin to retrieve anything that was of use to him.

"Our itinerant gentleman also witnessed you leaving the park to get into Charlotte Bagley's car – a silver convertible. He said you argued with her, when you jumped into it. Were you arguing about the fact that she had the hood down, which meant she was easily recognised by CCTV on the way to pick you up?"

"I think your imagination is getting the better of you DCI Templeman."

"I think not. Here's a photo of you entering Wanstead Park from Blake Hall Road at 11.54am on the way to David Chandler's house. You're carrying a backpack which contained the hoodie, jogging bottoms, a syringe full of insulin, and some disposable gloves."

DCI Templeman passed Stuart Harvey the photo. The accused man looked at it and said simply:

"I often go for picnics in Wanstead Park at lunchtime. This proves nothing."

"Yet, we cannot find an image of you returning to your place of work in Wanstead, carrying that bag and wearing those clothes."

"I have nothing more to say to your ridiculous allegations DCI Templeman. Should you wish to question me further, you will need to do so when I am accompanied by my lawyer."

"As you wish Mr Harvey, but I do have one more very small, last question for you. Do you have a driving licence?"

"No."

"I thought not. That would explain why you did not drive to and from Wanstead Park yourself."

*****

When Charlotte Bagley found herself sat in front of DCI Templeman and DS Bebbington, she was fairly relaxed. She knew she had not physically killed David Chandler, and there was no evidence as far as she could make out that linked her to the murder. The only possible way she could be implicated in it was through Stuart Harvey, and he was far too clever to be caught. She was not intimidated by the tall detective in front of her, but she did wonder what it would be like to shag a man of his dimensions. She had never slept with anyone that tall.

DCI Templeman cautioned her, and then started the interview:

253

"Miss Bagley, today we arrested Stuart Harvey for the murder of David Chandler - a murder that you and he planned together. Now who's idea was it, to kill David? His or yours?"

Charlotte was suddenly feeling vulnerable. She knew now that she was in a corner, and the only thing she could think of in order to get out of it, was to cry. Charlotte had learnt early on in life that weeping was a way of avoiding trouble when lying failed. She was well practised at crocodile tears.

"How could anyone kill David?" she snivelled, "he was such a lovely man."

Both Bob and Lucy were unimpressed by Charlotte's fake emotion, but DS Bebbington was positively angry about a woman using tears in this way, when there were so many women in the world who had genuine reasons to weep. But staying professional, Lucy simply asked:

"Charlotte, can you tell us when you first met Stuart Harvey?"

"Stuart Harvey as in 'Harvey and Blackman'?"

"Yes."

"I met him in a pub once, when I was with my colleagues. He was with Harvey Blackman having a drink. But that was ages ago. I haven't seen him since."

"So, what were you doing picking him up from Wanstead Park on Monday lunchtime and then dropping him back near his place of work, after he had killed David Chandler?"

"I don't know what you're talking about. I loved David – I would never want anyone to hurt him."

"We have a witness who saw you arrive at the Park Road entrance to pick up Stuart Harvey. The hood of your silver convertible was down."

"That must be a case of mistaken identity," replied Charlotte.

"Miss Bagley," interjected Templeman, "when was the last time you were at David Chandler's house?"

"I've never been to his house."

"So, you had an affair with him for months and never went to his house?"

"That's right. He didn't want his wife to know, so we never went to his place. He said it would of been too risky."

"But you know where he lived?"

"Yes – Hitchen Road. I picked him up from Dames Road once. But that's the nearest I ever got to his house."

"Okay, Miss Bagley, I think that's all the questions we've got for you right now. You need more time to reflect on this situation, and maybe, tomorrow, you'll be more willing to tell us the truth," concluded Templeman.

After Charlotte Bagley had been led away, Bob turned to Lucy and said:

"Liked the way you added the bit about dropping off Stuart Harvey near his place of work. Suspect that's exactly what happened, but we'll have to prove it."

"Yes, there's still a lot of work to be done tracing both their movements. Our guys are going to be busy for some time yet."

"Indeed. But we know they did it and if we can crack Harvey, reckon he'll spill the beans on her. In fact, wouldn't be at all surprised, if it was her idea to kill Chandler in the first place. What do you think the motive was?"

"I think his motive is exactly what we said when we suspected Michael Sanders. He's in love with Alice Chandler and wants to make a move on her."

"Yep – would make sense! And *her* motive?"

"I don't think she loved Chandler. She was just playing him. And eventually he realised that. He might have rejected her, and although she didn't love him, I get the impression she's the kind of woman who wouldn't take well to rejection. And maybe he found out about her stealing. Perhaps, he was about to sack her."

"Mmm, yes – could be any or all of those. He probably got fed up with her lies."

"Oh yes, she's a pathological liar. I don't believe a word she says. Her fake emotion and her pretence that she cared about Chandler. She lied about Stuart Harvey as well."

"But there was one thing she didn't lie about."

"Not going to Chandler house?"

"Yes! Believed her when she said she'd never been to Hitchen Road. Perfectly understandable that Chandler didn't want her there. Which leaves us with a question?"

"I know," replied Lucy, determined to say it before Templeman did. "The question is: If she or Stuart Harvey have not been to Chandler's house recently, how on earth did they get the syringe and know about the tow rope in the shed?"

"Exactly."

*****

Templeman was pleased with how the day had gone as he sat in his office and reflected on the Chandler case. He leaned back in his office chair and enjoyed the memory of snaring Stuart Harvey and seeing a moment of weakness in Charlotte Bagley's face. Bob was not a vengeful person, but he was just as prone to schadenfreude as the next man. It was the baddies he liked to see suffer, not the innocent. His tranquility was disturbed by his mobile phone vibrating.

He picked it up, and saw that the colleague trying to call him, was DC Smith.

"Evening, Smith – well done on your work with Bagley."

"Thank you, Guv. She's quite a girl, that one."

"Indeed."

"But I wanted to tell you about something else, Guv."

"What's that?"

"Well, you know you asked us yesterday about the CCTV at Eagle Pond in Snaresbrook?"

"Yes. Hoping you've got something for me."

"I have, Guv. I've just had the footage through, and we've got an image of a person on a phone at 1549 hours on Sunday."

"West side of Eagle Pond?"

"Yes, Guv!"

"Who is it?"

"It's not very close-up, but it looks like that guy you arrested today - Stuart Harvey."

"Good!" replied Templeman. "I'd now like you and Richards to check CCTV for the area around Harvey and Blackman's in Wanstead, on Monday afternoon. Need an image of Stuart Harvey being dropped off by Bagley."

Templeman knew this was going to be a crucial piece of evidence, but he was also aware that there was still plenty more to do. So, when he had finished talking to DC Smith, he contacted the rest of his team.

Bob called DC Amanda Green, telling her to organise an evidence gathering visit to Harvey and Blackman's. He phoned DC Mark Holloway, asking him to do the same at Stuart Harvey's home. And finally, he called DC Tyrrell asking him to organise a visit to Barnaby Lewis, to seize Charlotte Bagley's laptop and papers - 'Tell Jim

Chapman, I urgently want to know everything about Miss Bagley's life,' said Templeman. Bob was aware that his team was going to be stretched, but he knew that they were determined to get the job done.

And Templeman also knew that *his* work was not yet done. There were still three more people he needed to talk to. One of them was Alice Chandler. But he knew these conversations could wait until the following day. It was time to leave work and go to his new home.

Templeman spent a romantic Saturday evening with Flick, drinking wine, eating an Indian takeaway and watching a film. When he told her about Adam Butler watching 'Pulp Fiction' whilst waiting for his laptop to be fixed, she told him that it was a cult classic of the 1990's. Bob told her that he had vaguely heard of it but had never seen it. She told him that he was obviously one of the least cool people on the planet. To which he replied that 'being cool' was not something to which he aspired.

He was, nevertheless, happy to cuddle up with Flick on the sofa and spend two and a half hours watching 'Pulp Fiction'. And, despite not being 'cool', he enjoyed it immensely. Bob finally understood why Adam Butler and his niece had a joint appreciation of Quentin Tarantino films.

SUNDAY

THIRTY-TWO

Bob and Flick woke up early on Sunday morning, made love, and then sat up in her king-size bed drinking filtered black coffee and chatting. Templeman was getting used to her apartment, which although small, had everything he needed. In other words, it had Flick.

"It's been quite a week, hasn't it Bob."

"Too much Flick… too much… and we're not finished yet…"

"How do you mean?"

"Been thinking."

"That's all you ever do."

"Apart from doing you… yes…" Flick giggled.

"So what have you been thinking about Bob?"

"About Sanna Malik and David Chandler."

"Yep – it's terrible… just so grim that they were taken so young and in such a way…"

"Quite so, but think I would go mad if I dwelt on that too much. No, I've been thinking that I might have been wrong."

"Wrong? What? You've arrested the wrong people?"

"No, I think I've been wrong about something else.

"What?"

"I'll explain shortly… and I need you to do an errand for me today."

Templeman leaned over and kissed Flick on the mouth. She responded by reaching inside his pajama bottoms for the part of him which was becoming all too familiar to her.

DS Lucy Bebbington only managed to spend an hour with her boys on Sunday morning. It was supposed to be her day off, but Templeman had insisted. 'One last push, and we'll be there,' he had said, as if solving a difficult case was like giving birth to a child. And in one respect it was; it was about bringing truth into the world – extracting that which was hidden in darkness and exposing it to the cold light of day.

Lucy was ambivalent about going to work. On the one hand, she would miss the time she normally spent with her family. On the other hand, she was looking forward to what emerged from the day. Working with Templeman had been exciting and revealing. Lucy knew he had to be managed, but she enjoyed the intellectual rigour he brought to the job. It meant she had to keep up with his thought processes – a challenge she relished.

DS Bebbington and DCI Templeman left Stratford Police station mid-morning. It was a sunny day and slightly warmer than usual. Bob observed that the autumn colours were emerging; the hues of browns, oranges and yellows. Yet, there was still a hint of summer in the air, causing people to continue wearing their shorts and tee-shirts. The traffic was light, so they were able to zoom up the M11 and head East to Chipping Ongar. Sundays always felt different to Lucy, even if she was working. It was a holy day, and there was something uplifting about seeing people riding their bicycles, jogging or rambling in the Essex countryside. Lucy reminded herself that this was the reason they were police officers; so that ordinary folk could go about their daily activities without too much fear of crime.

Templeman had arranged for Sally Reed to meet them at Alice Chandler's house. Sally was a police family liaison officer. She was a friendly, rotund woman in her early fifties, who had inexhaustible patience and a very astute mind. Bob knew that Alice would probably tell her to go away, although he suspected she might use a profanity to achieve that end. Yet he wanted to make sure that he had at least offered Alice the support she was going to need, even if it was ultimately a way of covering his own backside.

Templeman wanted to speak to Alice on her own, but after he had successfully ducked under the beams of the Bennett's cottage, he discovered Simon and Karen sitting at the dining room table with her. He introduced DS Bebbington and Sally Reed, knowing that Alice would come up with some sort of acerbic comment:

"You've outdone yourself Bob, today," she said, "not only are you on to your third 'sidekick' – sorry, 'colleague' of the week, but you've brought an additional pair of hands as well."

Both Lucy and Sally were shocked and offended by Alice's rudeness, as the first 'sidekick' had been brutally murdered just three days earlier. Simon and Karen just looked embarrassed. DCI Templeman was no longer bothered by Alice's directness. He had got to know her well during the course of the week, and had grown quite fond of her. But, for the sake of his offended colleagues, he thought he would remind her about social norms:

"Come on Alice – you're better than that. Please show my colleagues some respect."

"I'm not disrespecting your colleagues, Bob. I'm just taking the micky out of you."

Templeman grinned slightly and decided not to respond. It was time to move on to the serious business of the morning:

"Today, I've got some very sensitive and upsetting information to share with you Alice. It may be better if we talk to you on your own initially."

"Is this information that is likely to enter the public domain?" asked Alice.

"I'm afraid so, yes."

"Well in that case, I see no reason why we cannot share it with Simon and Karen."

"As you wish. Now, the first thing you need to be aware of is that Adam Butler is not a suspect. We do not believe he murdered your husband."

"But he was a suspect, wasn't he? And I told you he had nothing to do with it."

"Yes – to both points!"

"So do you have any idea who *did* kill David?"

"We have arrested your colleague, Stuart Harvey, for the murder of your husband. With the agreement of the CPS, we will be charging him later today."

"Stuart?"

"I know - it must come as a terrible shock for you."

"Yes, I'm shocked, but not really surprised."

"You're not surprised?"

"Well, I did shag him the Christmas before last, and afterwards, I found him a bit too intense – creepy almost. I've always thought that there was a dark side to him."

"And you never thought to share this with us before?"

"Well, he's never been to our house and you told me the killer was six foot, so I didn't think that it would be him. So, it wasn't that hooded guy after all."

"The hooded guy was Stuart pretending to be six foot by wearing loafers with a high heel and a hood stuffed at the top."

"He's a clever bastard, isn't he?"

"Yes, that's one way of putting it. But you've just told us something that may be crucial to the investigation, so we do need to question you further about it."

"The fling?"

"Yes."

"Oh, that was nothing – well, not in my mind. It was Christmas 2015. We'd all been out for our Christmas party in Wanstead. Now, I'm not normally one for physical contact, but sex is different, and I was pretty drunk. So was Stuart. We were walking along the High Street together, and as we went past our office building, he grabbed me and we started snogging. I'd always found him quite attractive, so I got really into it. Before, I knew it, we had gone into the building and ended up bonking in his office."

Lucy put her hand over her mouth to hide her grin. She was dying to say something like, 'Does that story sound familiar Bob?'

"So, was that the only time you ever had intimate relations with him?"

"Yes, but I had to be quite firm with him. I told him that it was just an archetypal, drunken Christmas party fling, and as we were both married, it was best to leave it at that."

"Did he text you or pester you in any way?" asked DS Bebbington.

"Yes, at first, but I just deleted his messages and didn't respond. Eventually, he just stopped and we went back to the way it had been before."

"Do you think he might still be obsessed with you?"

"I hope not. But seeing as you're telling me he killed David, that could be a motive, couldn't it?"

*****

Charlotte Bagley had spent a boring night in the cells. She had got used to her interesting views of central London. When she was in her £900K flat on the twentieth floor, she felt like the 'Queen of the

Castle.' She liked to look down on people and had a desire to dominate and control all around her. She had recently joined the Labour Party, not because she cared about the working classes, but because she wondered whether politics could get her into the position of power and influence she craved. She had thought about joining the Conservatives, because it more easily fitted in with her capitalist instincts, and she had a low opinion of Jeremy Corbyn. But, she reasoned that Corbyn was probably an aberration which would soon pass. No, the reason she was a member of the Labour Party, was because in her part of London, that was the only way of attaining any elected office, and thereby wielding the power she sought.

In Charlotte's mind, just as her apartment was a metaphor for superiority and success, the police cell she found herself in, was synonymous with inferiority and failure. She was therefore determined to get out of it as soon as possible.

Nevertheless, she had slept surprisingly well during her night in the cells, as she had used up a lot of energy with Jack Bradbury in her apartment, and had been exhausted. She had also convinced herself it was just a temporary stay which would end in the morning. But as midday passed without anything happening, her boredom and frustration grew, and she felt it was time to be proactive. She knew what she was going to say, and was sure that it would be enough to guarantee her release. As an officer came into the cell to give her an unappetising sandwich for lunch, she said to him:

"Please can you pass a message to DCI Templeman. Please tell him I'm ready to talk. I'm ready to tell him the truth."

*****

Jim Chapman was deep in sleep at 8.33am that morning. His rapid eye movement was accompanied by a strange dream of trying to escape a crazed gunman. He was moving across gardens and over fences, down alleyways and into woods. But his pursuer was always just about to kill him. In his dream, he could hear a loud chiming, which he assumed was from a nearby church.

But then, suddenly, he woke up to the sound of his doorbell repeatedly being pressed. He hauled himself out of bed, grabbed a fleece, and staggered towards the front door. He had already forgotten his dream by the time he answered it. He recognised the man standing before him – they worked together and had, on the occasional Friday night, been to the pub, to drink a pint or ten.

"Sorry for disturbing you so early, Jim," said DC Tyrrell, not at all feeling guilty for waking up his colleague.

"Oh! Hi Mike. It must be urgent."

"It is. Here's Charlotte Bagley's laptop. Templeman wants to know everything about her life. Well, what he really wants is something incriminating as we've arrested her for Chandler's murder. Give him a call, if you find anything."

"Will do!"

Jim didn't mind working on a Sunday. He had stayed up until 2.04am playing a new game he had discovered. He found 'Fortnite' both challenging and engrossing, but it was also proving to be highly addictive. Jim struggled with alcohol addiction, so he knew the signs. He was pleased to have something else, on which he could concentrate.

Chapman had little difficulty accessing Charlotte Bagley's personal files, OneDrive and work email account. Her 'gmail' was more complex as she had logged out of it recently, but just after midday, he managed to hack into that as well. There was surprisingly little of interest in her emails. Most of them were online orders for clothes and beauty products. It was only when Jim got to her deleted files, that he hit the jackpot. The email was sent on Wednesday 27th September, over two weeks before David Chandler was murdered, and its contents were suitably incriminating. The recipient was Stuart Harvey:

Tiger,

AB having lunch with DC – Sun 8th Oct, and working from home following times:

Mon 9 Oct, Wed 11 Oct, Mon 16 Oct, Wed 18 Oct.

Deleting DC on a Monday lunchtime easier for me as Wednesdays busier in meeting rooms.

See you Friday,

Charlie xxx

Jim was amused by Charlotte Bagley's use of the word 'deleting." He was a Doctor Who fan, and knew that cybermen always used the command 'Delete!' as a synonym for killing. He had not imagined that Charlotte Bagley shared his interest in science fiction, but after reading her email, he was starting to revise that opinion.

Chapman grabbed a Magnum ice cream from his freezer, ate it quickly in celebration, and then made the call to Templeman, who was on his way back from Chipping Ongar. The call was answered after the second ring:

"It's Jim Chapman, DCI Templeman."

"Ah, Chapman, got anything for me?" asked Bob, eagerly anticipating anything he could find that would keep Charlotte Bagley in custody.

"Yes, an email – I'll read it out for you."

After he had finished conveying the message, Templeman said simply:

"Great work Chapman – forward that to me straight away – I'm on my way to interview Miss Bagley now."

DS Bebbington and DCI Templeman were in a sombre mood during the drive back to Stratford Police Station. The meeting with Alice had started off well enough, but when they had moved on to the subject of David's affair with Charlotte Bagley, Alice had become angry and distraught. She wept openly and loudly. He wondered whether the pain of betrayal was worse than the pain of death.

Templeman realised that Alice was experiencing a double bereavement – the loss of her husband in tragic circumstances, and then the loss of his fidelity in a more predictable way. Bob had not meant to break her. He preferred the combative, probing and rude Alice to the emotionally fragile one. But, in his job, being the bearer of bad news was an all too familiar occurrence. After twenty years, it had not become any easier. Quite the opposite – he found that losing the bravado of youth had made him more sensitive to the deepest feelings and vulnerabilities of victims. In the end, Alice had readily accepted the support of the family liaison officer - Sally Reed, who was more adept at dealing with emotions than Bob.

THIRTY-THREE

Charlotte was relieved to be out of her cell and sitting opposite the giant man whom she found strangely attractive, despite his average looks. But she liked tall men; they were a challenge to a person like her, who had a desire to control others. It occurred to her that if she could get on top of someone as huge as Templeman, she really would be a dominatrix.

DS Bebbington felt contempt for Charlotte. Lucy did not normally feel loathing for the perpetrators of crime she interviewed. Many of them had dysfunctional backgrounds and tragic backstories that to a certain extent explained their recidivism. But Lucy had formed the opinion that Charlotte was pure sociopath with no feeling for others, and no compunction about harming those around her. And in DS Bebbington's mind, the fact that she was a woman, made it even worse. Lucy thought that women like Charlotte Bagley did nothing to challenge the sexist attitudes that still predominated in the world she occupied.

Templeman saw how relaxed Charlotte appeared. She was not nervous at all. He even wondered whether she was actually enjoying the situation. He also felt contempt for her, but his contempt was less visceral than DS Bebbington's. He had no illusions about Charlotte – she was a dangerous and evasive adversary, so he reasoned that his best approach was to play to her overconfidence, and then crush her hard.

"I got your message Miss Bagley. You said that you were ready to talk and wanted to tell us the truth. I'm very pleased to hear that. So, what is the truth?"

"Yes, I'm very sorry that I wasn't truthful yesterday, but it was very upsetting to hear about who had killed David. I had no idea that Stuart would be capable of something like that…"

Charlotte managed once again to affect some tears that left both detectives completely unmoved. Lucy was convinced that the Academy of Motion Pictures would nominate her for an Oscar if they were sent a recording of the interview.

"Take your time Miss Bagley, and just tell us what happened."

"Well, yesterday, I didn't want to admit to you that I had been sleeping with Stuart and it was just a huge shock when you said that he'd killed David."

"So how long have you been having an affair with Stuart?"

"Only a few weeks, but I didn't want to admit it because I also had an affair with David, and I didn't want you to think I was the sort of woman who did this sort of thing all the time."

"Having an affair is not a criminal offence, Miss Bagley. It really doesn't matter what we think about something like that. Murder, on the other hand, is a criminal offence, so you need to tell us if you had anything to do with David's death."

"No, of course, I didn't – I loved David. But I did pick up Stuart from Wanstead Park on Monday as you said, and we did have an argument, and I did drop him off in Cambridge Park near his office."

"I'm pleased that you have told me the truth about that, but maybe you can tell us why you picked him up at the park on Monday."

"He rang me about fifteen minutes earlier and suggested we meet at the Park Road entrance for a 'cuddle'. He likes to have sex outside in the fresh air – he says it makes him feel 'alive'. It was my lunch break so I agreed. It was a nice day, so I put the hood down on my car and went to the park."

"And why were you arguing?"

"Well, when I arrived, he suddenly appeared and jumped into the car, and told me to drive. I thought he had asked me to the park for a cuddle, but then I realised he had conned me and just wanted a lift. I was upset. He also told me to put the hood up. Of course, I now know why. I didn't realise he was going to use me in that way…"

Charlotte started weeping again and grabbed the tissues that were routinely kept on the interview desk. Lucy thought Charlotte was going for a Golden Globe as well.

"So did you know about Mr Harvey's plan to kill David Chandler?"

"No!"

"And did you have a plan to murder Mr Chandler, or conspire with Stuart Harvey in any way?"

"No, I told you. I loved David. I would never have wanted anyone to hurt him."

"Okay Charlotte. I understand."

"Oh good! I knew you'd understand. And I understand why you arrested me. I was having an affair with Stuart, so of course you were suspicious of me."

"What I mean Miss Bagley, is that I understand the game you're playing. I understand that you are lying to us when you said that you had nothing to do with David Chandler's murder."

Templeman held up a copy of the email that had been forwarded to him by Jim Chapman and said:

"Do you know what this is?"

"No!"

"This is an email that was discovered in the 'Trash' folder of your gmail account. It's a pity for you that you forgot to clear your Trash folder after you had deleted it from your Inbox. If you had done so, we wouldn't have found it."

Templeman passed the email to Charlotte Bagley who read it in silence.

"Whoever hacked into my gmail account must have planted this," she said.

"I think not Miss Bagley. It has a date and time on it, and we can prove its digital origins. We are now developing a compelling case against you, and you have helpfully confirmed to us today that you picked up Stuart Harvey from Wanstead Park and dropped him off near his place of work. I have no doubt more evidence will come to light. We will now share what we have with the Crown Prosecution Service and they will decide whether this meets the threshold for charging you with the murder of David Chandler. You will find out whether you will be charged shortly. In the meantime, you will remain here."

Charlotte Bagley sat emotionless in her chair. Gone were the tears and gone was the pretence of innocence. In fact, Templeman swore that he could see her smirking when she was led away.

*****

When Stuart Harvey was brought into the interview room to see DCI Templeman and DS Bebbington, he was accompanied by his lawyer – Damian Sidebottom QC. Lucy thought that Bob was acting like a headmaster, calling naughty school children into his office and then exacting some sort of punishment on them before sending them away. Of course, she knew their job was not about deciding their innocence or guilt, and certainly was not about punishment – that was for juries and judges. Yet, the process of catching people and gathering evidence did allow them to have an opinion. And Templeman was never shy about expressing his.

Damian Sidebottom was a six-foot tall, athletically-built man in his late forties. Lucy thought that if they had not arrested Stuart, Damian might have figured in their enquiries as a suspect, given his physical appearance. But, unlike the hoodie that Stuart had worn, Mr Sidebottom's Saville Row suit fitted him perfectly and made him look like someone in an elite position. Yet, he was remarkably lacking in pomposity when he spoke.

"Before we start DCI Templeman, can you tell me if you have any further evidence we need to know about," requested Mr Sidebottom.

Templeman immediately knew he would not be able to spring the incriminating email on Stuart as he had done so on Charlotte. He would not be able to produce with a flourish, the photo of him making a phone call from Eagle Pond. His plan for a dramatic coup de grâce against his adversary had been dashed.

Bob was aware that his counsel was perfectly entitled to know what evidence they had against him. He therefore proceeded to share everything with his lawyer, and was very accommodating when Damian Sidebottom asked for time to speak to Stuart Harvey in private.

When Stuart and Damien returned, Mr Sidebottom simply said:

"Please continue with your interview."

Templeman proceeded to ask a series of questions about Chandler's murder and Stuart's relationship with Charlotte, all of which Mr Harvey answered with a 'no comment.' It was frustrating that he was exercising his right to silence, but Bob and Lucy knew they had their man.

It was a relief when the Crown Prosecution Service decided the same afternoon that the threshold had been met to charge both Charlotte Bagley and Stuart Harvey with the murder of David Chandler.

"So we're almost there then," commented DS Bebbington.

"Yes, almost, but still a couple more people we need to talk to Lucy. One of them is the person who worked most closely with Charlotte Bagley - Marie Chevalier. Think she might be a very useful witness.

THIRTY-FOUR

Marie Chevalier lived in a flat in Lewisham, South London, just a few hundred metres from the Elverson Road Docklands Light Railway station. It was a straightforward, if unexciting, commute from there to Canary Wharf and Barnaby Lewis where she worked. Marie had moved to the capital from the North of France four years previously. She was brought up in Auchel, a sleepy, and rundown, ex-mining town just fifty miles from Calais. She found London a good deal more exciting than rural France and appreciated its diversity. No one worried what language you spoke and what you wore in the metropolis. Tolerance was a necessary component of living in a crowded city which never slept.

DCI Templeman and DS Bebbington rarely travelled south of the river even though they lived and worked just north of it. For Eastenders, South London was like a different country, only to be ventured into for work or if, by chance, one had a friend who had emigrated there. Other areas of the United Kingdom saw London as a single entity, but those who had lived in the capital for any length of time, became far more parochial than inhabitants of the shires realised.

Thanks to Satnav, Lucy and Bob easily found Marie's apartment block in Lewisham. It was one of the new ubiquitous developments that had sprung up since the capital had bounced back from the financial crash. With soaring property prices in the once unfashionable Lewisham, there was lots of money to be made. The majority of occupants rented, and Marie Chevalier was no exception. They had rung her earlier, so she was expecting them. Marie greeted them in a friendly and formal way:

"Good evening Inspecteur Templeman and Sergeant Bebbington," she said.

Lucy was struck by how well the thirty-year-old Marie wore her clothes. She was dressed in perfectly fitted jeans and an elegant pink top. Her shoulder-length hair was fitted with a hair band and round her neck was a simple pearl necklace. She had little make-up on, yet her skin was free of blemishes.

"Good evening Miss Chevalier," replied Templeman, "Sorry to disturb you on a Sunday, but our investigation into the murder of David Chandler has moved quickly in the last couple of days. And we need your help."

"Yes, I know. I saw you at Barnaby Lewis on Friday. You were inteurviewing my collaigue, Charlotte Bagley."

"You work closely with Charlotte don't you. How do you find her as a person and colleague?" asked DS Bebbington.

"She's 'ardworking and good at her job. I have no probleme with her work. But…urr.."

"But…what?" continued Lucy.

"But I do not like her. I do not think she is a good person."

"In what way?"

"She's always thinking of men and using her charms on them. She 'ad an affair with Darveed, and I think this is not very professionelle."

"How did you find out about her affair with David Chandler?"

"One of my employees told me. And I could see for myself – the way they looked at each other."

"Did you ever discuss her affair with anyone?"

"No, it was not my biz-ness, so I said nothing."

There was a pause in the conversation, broken by Templeman who decided that it was the right time to share with Marie the reason for their visit:

"Miss Chevalier, I've got to tell you something that you'll soon find out from the News anyway. Charlotte Bagley has been charged with the murder of David Chandler along with a man called Stuart Harvey who worked with David's wife, Alice."

"Mon dieu - that is terrible. I had no idea."

"Yes. I'm afraid she won't be back at work for the foreseeable future. But I want to ask you again about Charlotte's affair with David and take you back to the evening of Friday 15th September – last month."

"I do not remember that evening – it was over a month ago..."

"Well, let me jog your memory. On that evening, I think you visited The King's Arms with a friend of yours and had a drink with David Chandler, Adam Butler, Simon Bennett, and Michael Sanders. Do you remember that?"

"Yes, I remember now. Me and Emilie went there and I think we 'ave drunk a little bit too much."

"Did you have a private conversation with Simon Bennett on that occasion?"

"Let me think... oh yes, I remember now. I was drunk and I should not 'ave said it... I'm really sorry... I 'ave not been 'onest with you."

"What did you say to Simon?"

"I 'ad just gone to the toilette, and when I was coming back, I met Simon. He was coming out of the men's toilette. I told him I was surprised he was 'aving a drink with his brother-in-law when Darveed was 'aving an affair with Charlotte. I was drunk – it was a terrible erreur. I thought he already knew."

"And how did he respond?"

"He said nothing. He looked very upset. I could see he did not know about the affair. I knew I 'ad spoilt his evening, so I left with Emilie after that."

"Thank you, Marie. That's all we need to ask you today. We appreciate your help and realise it's going to be tough at work for you. There may also be unwanted attention from the press, but I would advise you to just say 'no comment' to them."

"I will do my best Inspecteur. That is all I can do."

*****

It was gone six o' clock in the evening when DCI Templeman and DS Bebbington left Marie's flat. Lucy had a suspicion of where they would be going next. Bob, however, was keen on making a phone call first. When he had finished talking to Flick on his mobile, he turned to Lucy and said simply:

"You know where we're going, don't you!

"Yes. Don't you think we should talk to Sally Reed first and tell her we'll need to see Simon on his own?"

"Did that earlier!"

"You've thought of everything, haven't you."

"Impossible to think of everything, Lucy, but you have to try your best to cover every base."

"So, do you think Simon will talk, Bob?"

"Have no idea. We can but hope."

"How did you know that Marie had talked to Simon on the 15th of September?"

"I didn't. Just had a hunch because of something Butler said."

"What was that?"

"Butler told us: 'Well, Simon left shortly after the girls. He sort of quickly said goodbye and then drove home.'"

277

"So, you assumed that he left because he was upset by something Marie told him"

"Exactly. Suspected it was something to do with David's affair with Charlotte Bagley. After his conversation with Marie, Simon just wanted to get out of the pub to brood on what he'd been told."

"So, you think it was Simon who gave Stuart Harvey the syringe from the cabinet, obtained the insulin from Sophie's house, and then told him about the tow rope in the shed?"

"Yes. He was so upset about David having an affair with Charlotte, that he planned the murder with Stuart."

"It's pretty extreme – killing your brother-in-law."

"Indeed, but if you're ridiculously overprotective towards your sister and already disliked her husband you might be prepared to do anything."

"But Simon used to go drinking with David. That doesn't suggest he disliked him."

"We know he used to go drinking with David in a group and when he went to his house, Simon was with his wife. But that doesn't mean that they were mates. Just that Simon wanted to please Alice. When we interviewed him, he said that he and David had a 'joint interest in Alice's health and happiness.' That's hardly a declaration of friendship about his brother-in-law. But it was the truth. Their relationship was only ever going to be functional whilst Alice's psychological and emotional needs were met. When Simon felt that David was going to cause Alice unhappiness, he engineered a way for his life to end."

"Wow, I guess that's possible, but I don't know. I mean… Simon…he just doesn't seem the type. He's a teacher…"

"…And he'd do anything for Alice. Was even prepared to be arrested because of her. He's completely obsessed with her. When their parents died, he was thirteen, she was eight. I talked to Cracker about this. She reckons he's psychologically stuck as an angry abandoned young

278

teenager holding on to the only thing that makes sense to him then – his younger sister."

"So you think that this pent up anger caused him to commit extreme acts?

"Indeed. 'They fuck you up your Mum and Dad. They may not mean to but they do…'"

"That's Philip Larkin's poem isn't it?"

"Yes. My favourite verse of that poem is the final one: "Man hands on misery to man. It deepens like a coastal shelf. Get out as early as you can, And don't have kids yourself."

"That's typically cynical from Larkin," replied Lucy, "but I suppose it does show how one thing leads to another. So you reckon Simon's parents fucked him up by dying, Bob?"

"Exactly."

"To such an extent that he was prepared to have his brother-in-law killed by Stuart Harvey?"

"Quite so."

"But what about Charlotte Bagley; it doesn't seem likely that Simon would cooperate with David's lover – that doesn't make sense."

"Agreed. I think Stuart Harvey didn't mention Bagley's involvement to Simon. Probably just said he'd sort the murder on his own."

"So both Harvey and Simon were obsessed with Alice in different ways, Bob. I wonder who's worse…"

"Impossible to say, but one thing's sure – Simon Bennett's obsession with his sister went even further than just murdering his brother-in-law."

"What do you mean?"

"He's also responsible for Sanna's murder as well."

"What? That was Jafar Malik – he confessed!"

"Jafar did it, yes, but Simon wound him up to do it."

"But they didn't know each other."

"Well actually they did. Let me explain how I made the connection."

Lucy Bebbington sat in shock. The same man had a hand in both murders? She was all ears now. DCI Templeman had a lot of convincing to do!

"Okay Bob, start from the beginning – I can't wait to hear this."

"Well, you know Lucy, it's often the small details that give you clues or a throw away comment. In the case of Simon there were two things that intrigued me. The first was when I went to speak to his Headmaster on Wednesday. He mentioned that Simon had 'helped out with the multi-faith prayer room recently'. It made me think that perhaps he had an interest in a religion other than Christianity. And then when Adam Butler told us that Simon had recently given up booze, it made me think that perhaps that religion was Islam. I therefore wondered whether he knew Jafar Malik."

"And I'm guessing you've now discovered a connection between the two men, Bob."

"Yes, I have, but before I talk about that, I just want to mention another small detail I gleaned from Detective Superintendent Michaels' investigation into Sanna's murder."

"Which is?"

"Well, before I went home yesterday, I watched the recording of Karen Michaels and Aanya Patel's interview of Jafar Malik. It contained a crucial clue. In their interview, Malik said he had 'received a sign'! Michaels and Patel assumed he meant a sign from God, but I don't think the sign was from God. It's possible of course Jafar saw Sanna on television when I was talking to the Press, but I'm not sure that was the sign he was referring to either. No, the sign he meant, was a sign from Simon Bennett. Don't know exactly what happened but I reckon Simon told him about how he'd met Sanna through the investigation,

280

that she had married a woman, and had completely abandoned the Muslim faith. He probably said something about her doing the devil's work and told him where she lived."

"But how did Simon Bennett know all that about Sanna?"

"He and his wife Karen had attended the same church as Sanna for a short while three years ago. They had even been round to Sanna's house. When DC Malik told me about it, she said Simon didn't recognise her, but I think he did. Simon's a teacher – he's an expert at connecting names to faces!"

"So he knew about Sanna, her wife and where she lived. But didn't Jafar know all that too?"

"Only after Simon had told him! Jafar hadn't had any contact with Sanna for six years, which was well before she got married, and it's possible he didn't even know that she was in a Lesbian relationship. DSU Michaels told me that Sanna's wife, Laura, had never met Jafar"

"So how did Simon Bennett know Jafar Malik?"

"Through the Al Salam Mosque in Edmonton. I asked Flick to go over there today and talk to the Imam. He confirmed that Simon Bennett had been attending the mosque regularly for the last few months and he had seen him talking to Jafar."

"So that's why you were on the phone to Flick a few minutes ago."

"Exactly."

"Okay, but what's his motive for causing Sanna's death?"

"Sanna was rude to him. When we interviewed him, there was a moment when he was talking about the past - how his grandparents had died because of the stress of their parents' tragic death. Sanna failed to acknowledge his and Alice's grief and went straight into asking him who he thought might have caused David's death."

"But that's not enough to justify murder, Bob – someone being rude!"

"No, but remember he's obsessed with his sister and thinks that Sanna is not just failing to acknowledge his grief, but also Alice's. His anger on her behalf would have been greater than any personal sleight he felt. DI Patel explained to me that complex grief causes people to do some quite extreme things. We're talking about an angry, lost, bereaved thirteen-year-old who's obsessively overprotective towards his sister and now senselessly bears a grudge against a lapsed Muslim when he, himself, is beginning to embrace that religion. And it's possible he didn't think Jafar would actually kill Sanna, but Simon wanted her punished."

"It all seems totally fucked up to me, Bob."

"It is – your parents – they fuck you up, they may not mean to but they do… and it does all deepen like a coastal shelf…"

"So are we going to arrest Simon?"

"We'll see what he says. Not enough evidence at the moment to charge him, until we get Stuart Harvey and Jafar Malik to talk. And they will talk… eventually."

"And Charlotte Bagley. Do you think she knew about Simon's involvement?"

"Possibly - we'll find out at some point."

THIRTY-FIVE

It was dark when they arrived at Chipping Ongar. And Templeman was struck by *how* dark it was. He was so used to the artificial light in and around the city, that he had forgotten that in the country, people lived totally in the dark at night; except for the occasional street lamp, or when the moon came out in a cloudless sky. Darkness was not something Templeman liked, not simply because it signified malevolence, but because he feared bumping his head. He had a genuine worry that he would develop some sort of early onset dementia because of the number of times he had bashed his head against beams, tree branches and doorways. He had even knocked himself out on one occasion. It was true he was not the most coordinated of people and he was often deep in thought, but it was usually poor lighting that caused him not to notice the height of things.

Sally Reed answered the door. She explained how Alice had calmed down and had gone off to her room to spend some time on her own. Karen had been pottering around in the kitchen, but had been persuaded to watch television in the sitting room. She assured the two officers that they would be able to speak to Simon undisturbed in the dining room.

It was a nervous looking Simon Bennett that greeted them. Lucy looked at him and felt anger. She may have had some sympathy for him if he had killed David to protect his sister, but he had also caused a colleague to lose her life. His hand in Sanna's death was unforgiveable. Bob was likewise feeling antipathy towards Alice's brother, but he was not about to let his emotions get the better of him.

"We're talking to you under caution today Simon Bennett. You do not have to say anything. But it may harm your defence if you mention something which you later rely on in court. Anything you do say may be given in evidence."

It was the second time in a week that he had been cautioned, but this time it felt different for Simon. He was now aware that Stuart Harvey and Charlotte Bagley had been arrested, and that Alice knew about David's affair. He now suspected that the Police had found out about his involvement in David's murder, but was confident that they had no clue about his connection to Sanna's.

"Mr Bennett, I am not going to waste any time here. I will get straight to the point. This afternoon, we interviewed Stuart Harvey about the murder of your brother-in-law, and he told us it had been your idea. He told us that you had wanted David Chandler dead, that you had developed the plan to make his murder look like suicide, and it was you that provided the syringe from his bathroom and the insulin, and told him about the tow rope. Why did you arrange for his murder Mr Bennett?"

Lucy was taken aback. Templeman was winging it to see whether he could get a confession out of Simon. He was sailing close to the wind.

"That's not true," replied Simon. "It was not my idea, it was Stuart's. It was him that approached me, and it was his plan to make the murder look like suicide. And it was his idea to frame Adam Butler if the Police suspected foul play. The only part of it that was my idea was to inject David with insulin, because I wanted it to be quick. I agreed with Stuart that he deserved to die because I knew Alice was better off without him, and I didn't want her to find out about his affair with that awful Bagley girl."

"You call her awful, but you were prepared to plan the murder with her."

"I didn't know she had anything to do with it. I thought it was just Stuart and me. I would have had nothing to do with that whore."

"But it hasn't quite worked out as you planned, has it? Now the sister you wanted to protect, has her life in ruins. She's lost the husband she loved, feels totally betrayed by him and is now going to lose the big brother she looked up to."

Lucy sat in silence. Bob was really going for it. He was trying to push Simon to the edge.

"I don't feel great about my sister being upset, but you know what – she's better off without David. He was never good enough for her, and he couldn't keep his dick in his pants."

"You think you're fucking God, don't you Bennett," exclaimed Lucy suddenly. "You got rid of your sister's husband and then had Sanna Malik murdered. What sort of fucking monster are you?"

Lucy instantly regretted her outburst, but losing a fellow officer and the culmination of a stressful week, proved too much for her. Bob Templeman gently laid his right hand on Lucy's left, and took over the interviewing, while Simon Bennett sat in silence.

"Yes, Mr Bennett, we've been talking to Jafar Malik too. He told us about your conversations regarding Sanna. It was you who told him about her marriage to a woman. It was you who told him about her Christian faith. It was you who told him where she lived. You were the one who wound him up to murder his sister."

"I didn't think he would stab her to death," replied Simon. "But you know what – she had no respect for Alice. I saw the way she looked at her with disdain, the way she dismissed Alice. And Sanna had no respect for her birth religion either. I've come to realise the true path is Allah. It's a pity she gave up on that path."

Bob at that moment realised that Simon was much further down the path of conversion to Islamism than he realised. He wondered whether it wasn't Simon that had influenced Jafar, but maybe the other way round: Jafar had radicalised Simon.

"Well, I'm afraid it's all over Simon," said Templeman quietly. "The game's up. You've caused too much suffering."

Simon sat in silence. Faced with the physically imposing Bob Templeman, it was difficult to see a way out, but ever since the death of his parents he had fought; fought for Alice and fought for himself. He was not about to roll over now.

Suddenly, Simon leapt up and made a beeline for the dining room door. Lucy quickly got out of her chair and put an arm out to stop him, but he pushed her aside with both hands. She fell backwards against a now standing Bob Templeman who had banged his head on a beam whilst getting up in more haste than normal. Despite the pain throbbing through his forehead, Templeman managed to stop Lucy from falling over. She regained her balance and darted out of the dining room after the fleeing Simon Bennett, who had opened the front door and was beginning a sprint away from his cottage.

He ran – like an antelope being chased by a pair of lions - down the rural road that led away from the town centre. Lucy took chase. She was an occasional runner, and with her high level of fitness, athletic frame and aided by the adrenalin coursing through her, she was able to start gaining on him. But as the darkness enveloped her, she had to grab the mobile phone out of her pocket and turn the torch on. After 400 metres, the pavement disappeared and she was forced to run down the right-hand side of the road.

Meanwhile, Bob, tried the door of the unmarked Mondeo they had arrived in, but it was locked and Lucy had the key. He quickly grabbed the whistle from his jacket pocket and blew on it hard. He wondered whether his long legs would be able to outrun Lucy's, but knew he was no match for his younger colleague. Aware of his limitations in the dark, he was forced to watch the flickering light of Lucy's phone disappearing up the road.

Simon continued running almost blind in the darkness though his eyes had begun to adjust to the dim conditions. He somehow managed to avoid the ditches on both sides of the road. He had no plan, except to establish as much distance as possible between him and his pursuers. And then, as his heart pumped fast and hard, the sweat beginning to form on his forehead and chest, the road turned sharply to the right.

He managed to negotiate the bend due to the camber and staggered on another 150 metres. He felt his right foot on the edge of a ditch and automatically looked down even though his vision was limited. As he veered back into the road, Simon spotted his feet illuminated. He looked up. The last thing he saw was the glaring lights of the van.

*****

Daryl Jones had spent the day at his girlfriend's house. He was in a good mood after a relaxed time of eating, drinking and listening to music. He had played with his girlfriend's four-year-old son in the garden. He had drunk two cans of beer at lunchtime, but that had gone through his system now. He was a self-employed landscape gardener and had a job in the morning. The rural Essex bourgeoisie paid well for his services, so he was making a good living. His van was five years old and in good condition.

Daryl was driving at 46 miles per hours as he approached Chipping Ongar on the rural road. He caught a sudden movement in front of him and assumed that he had hit a deer when his windscreen shattered. 'Fuck it,' he said, as he stopped the van and climbed out of it to inspect the damage. A breathless woman with a phone torch ran past him to the lifeless figure that lay in the ditch. He saw a large dent in the bonnet of his Ford Transit and then looked towards the woman futilely attempting CPR on what he suddenly realised was not a deer, but a man. Daryl's day was ruined.

*****

"Maybe I should resign – it was my fault," said Templeman to DS Bebbington as they drove back to Stratford Police Station later that evening.

287

"You shouldn't Bob – we need you," replied Lucy. "Yes, they'll be an investigation by the IPCC. We'll refer ourselves to them. But it will come to nothing. We won't mention that you lied to Simon. We'll just say he confessed readily and escaped our grasp. We'll say we suspected him, but we didn't know he was involved. They can't blame us for his madness."

"But we should have taken him back to the station to a safe environment where he couldn't have fled. If we had, he'd still be alive. He died under our watch Lucy."

"But if we stick together, the investigation will never know what really happened. Yes, you bent the rules Bob, but sometimes you have to take risks to get results. You can't resign – we need you, Newham needs you. Fuck it – London needs you!"

"Mmm – you're very kind Lucy, and you're right – it's not the time to quit. In any case, Flick wouldn't let me."

"No, she wouldn't, and nor would I."

It was gone eleven o'clock when Bob finally got into his Renault Dauphine. He fired up the engine and hauled the old girl out of its parking space. He felt comfortable in the old-fashioned car because in his mind, the old-fashioned ways were best.

EPILOGUE

Templeman spotted the sun emerge from the clouds at midday, creating a summer warmth that cheered him and his fellow occupant of the vehicle. Bob and Flick were poddling along the rural Essex road in his Renault Dauphine. Despite the overgrown hedgerows, Templeman had a sneak view of the fields full of wheat and maize. Bob spotted a large agricultural vehicle harvesting the rapeseed. It was a Saturday in late July 2019.

"I wish we'd taken my car, Bob. This old banger sounds as if she's going to give up the ghost anytime now."

"Don't say that Flick – she's an old lady and deserves respect. And anyway, we're going to a wedding. She'll fit in much better than your Nissan Juke-box."

"At least my wheels are safe. Bloody hell Bob, with us two in her, she can barely get up to 40."

"Speak for yourself – I've lost weight recently."

The two detectives were constantly bickering and that was how they liked it. They had yet to tie the knot themselves, but Templeman had an important role in the wedding they were attending that day. He was giving the bride away.

They could smell freshly mown grass as Bob drove round the green to the village church. There was already a handful of guests mingling around in their glad rags, with half a dozen standing outside the Royal Oak with drinks in hand. Fifty metres from the pub, the bells of the church rang to indicate the imminent matrimonial proceedings. Bob felt more than a little nervous. What if he tripped and took the bride with him? What if he banged his head on the church entrance and knocked himself out? The man who could face down dangerous criminals without a worry in the world, was getting anxious about a twenty metre walk down a church aisle.

But he was nervous, because he was giving away one of his most difficult colleagues. PC Alice Chandler had always been a determined individual, and over the past two years, had put her life back together after the terrible events of the third week of October in 2017. She had abandoned law for the police service, finding friendship and solace in the likes of Bob Templeman, Flick Featherstone, Lucy Bebbington and Sally Reed. They were her family now.

After successfully negotiating the IPCC investigation into the events of that fateful Sunday, Bob had set about atoning for Simon Bennett's death. He still partly blamed himself for the events. He and Flick had visited Alice regularly, and over time the old dynamic between him and his nemesis had returned. Alice was as rude as ever.

Alice had also found love, discovering that a second relationship could be better than the first. When her partner had proposed, she had readily accepted for he was the perfect fit for her. They complemented each other. She was combative, he was reasonable. She lacked patience whereas he was long-suffering. She was fairly short, he was fairly tall.

The bride arrived at her wedding in a 1980 red Mercedes-Benz SL convertible. The hood was down, and Alice was smiling in her strapless wedding dress with a laced bodice and full skirt. It was remarkably similar to the dress worn by Uma Thurman in Kill Bill Volume 1.

Adam Butler was at the front of the Norman church wringing his hands with nerves. He kept on looking back at the entrance to see whether there was any sign of a start to the proceedings. He noticed the last few guests head for the pews, and heard the organ quietly emit an extemporary tune. His nervousness increased as he sensed the imminent arrival of his bride.

Bob went over to Alice and offered his hand as she tried to get out of the car. She declined it.

"If you step on my dress, you can pay for the repair," she said.

Templeman sighed. He knew then why he had been so nervous.

As they got in position to go up the aisle together, Bob said:

"I know you don't like physical contact, so we can just walk down side-by-side if you like."

"No, it's fine – put your right hand on your waist and stick your elbow out. I'll reach up and grab the top of your wrist. It's not your fault you're a bloody giant."

Templeman took a deep breath and did as he was told. They awkwardly strolled up the aisle as the organist played Vivaldi's 'Gloria'. Bob was careful to take small strides and kept on looking down to avoid Alice's dress. A bead of sweat appeared on his forehead as the heat of the day and the intensity of concentration took its toll. It was a huge relief when he had finally negotiated the twenty metres of the aisle without incident.

The wedding service similarly progressed free of slip-ups. The bride did not fluff her lines, and nor did the groom. They stared deeply into each other's eyes as they exchanged vows. And the rings fitted perfectly. If a stranger had witnessed the event, they would have had no idea of the pain and tragedy which gave birth to this union.

It was indeed a bitter-sweet occasion. Flick cried for her dead husband as did Alice. They felt the agony of loss intertwined with the joy of hope. With death came resurrection, and on that day, Alice felt both. But the prevailing sentiment was the latter. Alice and Adam, whose names began with the first letter of the alphabet, felt their lives were beginning anew.

Author's Note

This is my first novel and as such, a huge learning curve. I wrote the first draft in 2021 during lockdown when I couldn't socialise with friends and family. Over the three months that it took me to write, Bob Templeman became my friend. He started off as an idea in my head and then developed a life of his own, to such an extent that by the end, I felt that I had discovered him, rather than created him. He is currently dictating to me another story of his that relates to the beginning of the Covid pandemic in March 2020. When he has given me all his memories, and if there is demand from a sufficient number of people interested in what he has to say, I will publish 'The Third Week of March.'

I have a few people to thank, who gave me the confidence to put this story out there. Firstly, my friend, John Edwards, who read the first draft and gave me much encouragement. Secondly, Matthew Hall, my proper writer friend, who has considerably more experience at forming prose than me. And the most helpful feedback I received was from another of my longstanding friends, Patricia Hall, who pointed out a critical error in the first draft of this novel that I have since corrected. Finally, thanks goes to my friend Liesl Taylor, who read the first draft and then forced me into publishing it by recommending it to our fellow book club members.

This is, of course, a work of fiction, but it is based in a part of London that I lived in for several years. Some names of institutions and roads have been made up, and where I have mentioned real places, e.g Wanstead Park or Wanstead Flats, I have done so out of an affection for them. Any errors I have made in this novel are mine and mine alone, and are not intended to be a criticism or reflection of the Metropolitan Police or anyone else.

Printed in Great Britain
by Amazon

29218271R00165